D0949601

LOCAL
GIRL
SWEPT
AWAY

LOCAL GIRL SWEPT AWAY

Ellen Wittlinger

MeritPress | fw

Published by
Merit Press
an imprint of F+W Media, Inc.
10151 Carver Road, Suite 200
Blue Ash, OH 45242. U.S.A.
www.meritpressbooks.com

ISBN 10: 1-4405-8900-3
ISBN 13: 978-1-4405-8900-3
eISBN 10: 1-4405-8901-1
eISBN 13: 978-1-4405-8901-0

Printed in the United States of America.

10 9 8 7 6 5 4 3 2 1

This is a work of fiction. Names, characters, corporations, institutions, organizations,
events, or locales in this novel are either the product of the author's imagination or, if
real, used fictitiously. The resemblance of any character to actual persons (living or dead)
is entirely coincidental.

Many of the designations used by manufacturers and sellers to distinguish their products
are claimed as trademarks. Where those designations appear in this book and F+W
Media, Inc. was aware of a trademark claim, the designations have been printed with
initial capital letters.

Cover design by Sylvia McArdle.
Cover image © Shutterstock.com/locrifa.

*This book is available at quantity discounts for bulk purchases.
For information, please call 1-800-289-0963.*

For Rose and Jane, eventually.

And for anyone who's ever called Provincetown home—
for a season or a lifetime.

Acknowledgments

Many people stand behind every author giving necessary support and encouragement. Over the years my support has often come from the Fine Arts Work Center in Provincetown, Massachusetts, which became home and family to me forty years ago and remains the place I return to when hope falters and the well seems dry. My heartfelt gratitude goes to FAWC. There would have been no books without you.

My association with Kindling Words, the writing retreat for children's book authors, goes back thirty years. Without the workshops, the white-space discussions, the bonfires in winter, and the friendships forged around the dinner table, I would be a different person and a lesser writer.

My writer-friends in two critique groups have been with me through successful times and periods of struggle. Thank you always: Pat Lowery Collins, Liza Ketchum, Nancy Werlin, Lisa Papademetriou, Jane Yolen, Patricia MacLachlan, Lesléa Newman, Ann Turner, Barbara Diamond Goldin, and Corinne Demas. And though our arrangements are less formal, I also depend heavily on the advice and knowledge of Elise Broach, Chris Tebbetts, Elizabeth Bluemle, Jeannine Atkins, Jo Knowles, and Cindy Faughnan.

Thanks, of course, to Jacquelyn Mitchard, who's been a champion for this book, and to everyone at Merit Press. And to Ginger Knowlton, agent supreme, who has been my cheerleader for so many years.

A last shout-out goes to my family, ever helpful, always loving: David, Kate, Morgan, and Mark. Thank you all.

1.

I pulled up the hood of my parka and tied it under my chin, but the rain blew sideways, right into my eyes. The four of us—Lorna out front, me bringing up the rear, the boys in between—ran down Commercial Street to the breakwater, where the road and the town and the Cape Cod peninsula were all stopped short by saltwater, Provincetown Harbor on one side, the Atlantic Ocean on the other.

Of course, it was Lorna's idea for us to go down and watch the storm come in over the ocean, even though it was almost dinnertime and our parents expected us home soon. We weren't dressed for the cold and rain, but we always did what Lorna wanted us to. We didn't even think about it anymore—it was just automatic.

She reached the breakwater before the rest of us, and I yelled into the wind, "Lorna, slow down!"

Her answer floated back to me, the same tune she always sang: "Come on, Jackie! Follow me!" I tried to hurry after the others even though the huge granite rocks were slick with rain and mud.

The breakwater, rising probably twenty feet high and half as wide, ran at least a mile out to the spit of land called Long Point and served as protection for the harbor in storms like this one. But now the waves were already crashing over it.

Lorna never walked anywhere—she raced, she galloped, she cartwheeled, she leaped. As the dark afternoon turned darker, I could just barely see her running ahead, barefoot on the slippery rocks, her blue sneakers dangling from her fingers, her white jacket blowing open in the wind. Even Finn couldn't keep up with her. He and Lucas followed behind more slowly, carefully negotiating the path, zipping their windbreakers and shoving their hands in their pockets. Thunder boomed in the distance and zigzags of lightning lit up the pillowy clouds.

It had been a cold, rainy May, and the waves that smacked into the breakwater felt like tiny razorblades when they splashed up against my legs. The roar of the wind was so loud I couldn't tell if anyone up ahead of me was talking or not. I was cold and hungry and more than ready to go home, but I didn't want to be the wimp who suggested we turn around. The sun had totally disappeared behind the clouds by then, and I couldn't tell where anyone was. Had they gone out farther? Had anybody headed back to shore? I was sure Finn wouldn't go back without Lorna—it took more than bad weather to separate the two of them.

And then there was the oddest noise behind me, or maybe off to the side—I couldn't tell exactly where it came from. A sigh or a gasp or maybe just a sharp intake of breath. But how could I hear something like that over the racket of the storm and the slapping waves? It was more like a disturbance of the air than an actual sound. I shivered, not just from the cold, and turned slowly, carefully, to look for my friends in the gloomy dark. There was Finn, just a little bit ahead of me. He was looking around too, peering into the black mist over the bay. And that was Lucas, a few rocks farther on, raising his arm to point at something. But where was Lorna?

I had to squint to see what Lucas was pointing at—something in the water, already far away. A white flash, like a pinpoint of light, was being pulled out by the tide into the blue-black harbor. What? No. Impossible.

For long seconds I refused to understand what was happening, but finally I had no choice. I screamed and clutched Finn's arm.

And then both Finn and Lucas were yelling, "Lorna! Lorna!" over and over, frantically, as if they could bring her back by demanding it.

And then Lucas jumped into the water. For a second hope rose in my chest, and I could almost breathe, but then the truth washed over me again. Lorna was, by far, the best swimmer of the four of us; if she couldn't fight the waves, Lucas, with his klutzy, splashing stroke, didn't stand a chance.

"Lucas, what are you doing?" I yelled. Could Finn see Lucas? I didn't know. I didn't know anything.

Instead of the tide pulling him out into the bay, an incoming wave knocked him back into the breakwater and he clung to the rocks, gasping. "I can't," he said. "I can't."

I pushed back my hood, trying to see better, hoping to look down and see Lorna hanging onto the rocks beside Lucas, Lorna helping him stay afloat. Maybe that white thing in the distance was only some piece of harbor trash bobbing in the cold ocean. I got down on my knees because I couldn't stand up anymore.

Finn lay on his stomach and reached his arms down so Lucas could grab hold of them as he climbed slowly back up the rocks. There was no one with him. When Lucas got near the top, he collapsed and I helped Finn haul him up, his teeth chattering, his body quaking. Then we just sat there, leaning into each other, soaked to the skin by ocean and rain and tears. The white jacket had disappeared.

I didn't realize I was holding onto Lorna's sneakers until later when the three of us sat on folding chairs in the police station, draped in blankets. A cop tried to pry them from my hands, but I yelled so loud I scared myself. I didn't know it was me screaming.

"Okay! Okay!" he said, putting his hands up like stop signs. "You can hold on to them. It's okay."

The Rosenbergs, Finn's parents, showed up first, Rudolph all business, talking to the chief of police, while Elsie gathered us, wet as we were, into her arms. She asked no questions, just cried along with us. Lucas's dads, Simon and Billy, came next, talking so fast they weren't making sense. Billy put his arms around Lucas's soaked shoulders and wouldn't let go.

Finally, my parents marched in, Dad looking tired, Mom apparently furious. She perched on the chair next to me and shook me as if she was trying desperately to wake me up.

"What's the matter with you kids?" she howled, the pupils of her eyes vibrating with fear. "How could you do this to me, Jackie? What if it was you who fell in? It would've been the end of me!"

Well, no, I thought, *it would've been the end of me*. But I didn't say that. I knew what memory had been snagged and hauled to the surface of her brain. My mother had never recovered from the death of her younger brother whose fishing boat went down in a storm ten years before, and it was probably true she wouldn't have survived the death of her only daughter too. But at the moment I didn't care about her pain. I could barely cope with the emotional stew boiling through my own body.

As our parents, horrified but relieved, bundled us into our own cars, I couldn't stop thinking about Lorna's mother. Two policewomen had been dispatched to Carla Trovato's house, the dilapidated cottage on Franklin Street, to tell her the awful news. I imagined that Carla was watching TV with a glass of wine in her hand or something stronger, already wearing her ratty old bathrobe, her bare feet propped on the grimy coffee table, waiting for Lorna to get home and make her something to eat. She'd probably think the officers at the door were there for her, that she was in some kind of trouble again, some nosy neighbor complaining about her junky yard or her loud TV. But it was so much worse than that. Her face, I thought, would turn first into that frighteningly angry scowl and then collapse into total wreckage.

Of course I didn't sleep that night. I'm sure none of us did. I sat at my bedroom window and looked out toward the harbor, even though our house was too far away for me to see the water. My father said that Coast Guard boats would troll the harbor all night, that they would find her. There was hope that she might not have been pulled out past the breakwater, might have been hurled onto the sandy spit of Long Point. But I knew what he meant. He meant there was hope her *body* would be found, not Lorna. Not my beautiful, intense, self-assured, cheeky best friend.

I stayed awake bargaining with God, even though I didn't believe that kind of thing ever worked. *If she lives,* I begged, *I won't let her take chances anymore. If she lives, I'll watch over her. I'll make sure she's more careful. I will make her follow me!* But Lorna was not found, not even her body. A special edition of the *Provincetown Banner* came out the next day, its headline set in 72-point type: LOCAL GIRL SWEPT AWAY.

2.

The whole next week, I stayed in bed. I came down with a bad cold, but that was just a good excuse. I knew I couldn't manage anything as complicated as walking or eating—all I could do was stare at the cracks in my bedroom ceiling, going over and over the events of that horrible afternoon, trying to figure out a way to change the outcome. I kept thinking there had to be a way to bring her back. There *had* to. But I couldn't come up with one, so I pulled the covers over my head and wailed.

Mom showed up at mealtimes with cups of tea and a sleeve of crackers or a bowl of soup. "It takes time," she kept saying. "You'll learn to live with it." But I didn't want to learn to live without Lorna. I didn't want to take the smallest step in that direction.

I tried to make some kind of sense of it, but the whole thing was ridiculous. An ordinary person—any of the other three of us—might slip on a wet rock and fall, but not Lorna. She was a professional traveler on this earth, graceful and fearless. Lorna didn't make mistakes. "Together the four of us can do anything," she used to say, and I never questioned the truth of it. But now, with Lorna gone, I could hear the dark echoes of her rallying cry: "The three of you need me. The three of you are useless without me." It was true.

Lorna and I had been best friends since the morning she showed up in our fourth-grade classroom. She'd been homeschooled until then, but when her dad left town, her mom gave up on that and just about everything else. That first day Lorna picked us—Finn and Lucas and me. She gave us a sly grin as if she already knew all our secrets. Her eyes sparkled like jewels and drilled right into our skulls. We fell in love with her immediately.

Finn and Lorna became a couple four years ago when we were all thirteen, so Lucas had to adore her from a distance. The golden boy and the wild girl were obviously the perfect pair, but sometimes I couldn't help wishing Finn would look at me the way he looked at her. I didn't dwell on it. I'm not stupid. Lorna was Number 1; I was clearly Number 2, and always would be. Only now Number 1 was gone and I didn't know who I was without her.

Once or twice a day I got up long enough to pull the old telephone with the long cord from the hallway into my bedroom. I tucked it under the covers, as if even the phone needed to be protected now, and called Finn. He wasn't going to school either, and we talked for hours. Well, no—we stayed on the phone for hours. We ran out of things to say pretty quickly, but we didn't hang up because neither of us could stand being alone with the overwhelming, nauseating truth of our new lives. Finn was the only one who understood what I'd lost and vice versa. We'd stay silently connected until the battery on his cell phone died and the limits of technology forced us to grieve alone.

Of course, I called Lucas too, and so did Finn, but, oddly, we were always turned away by Simon or Billy.

"Oh, sweetheart," Simon said to me, "Lucas can't talk now. He's so tired. He just needs to rest. You understand."

I tried to understand, but after the third time one of Lucas's dads ran interference, I got mad. There was no sense taking it out on them, though—Lucas must be telling them to turn us away. What the hell was wrong with him? He wouldn't talk to *us*? Finn was Lorna's boyfriend and I was her best friend. No matter how you sliced it, Lucas came in third. And now he was acting as if he was more injured, more traumatized than we were? We had the strength to call him, but he was too debilitated to get on the phone? I was so irritated by it I finally got out of bed, got dressed, and went out.

Finn's younger sister, Tess, answered the door at the Rosenbergs' and I realized it must be the weekend already if she was home in the middle of the day. The minute she saw me, Tess started crying. I put my arms around her even though it felt like lifting lead weights.

"I'm so glad you're here," she said, tears leaking down her cheeks. "Everything's all screwed up. Everybody's so sad. I can't stand it."

"I know," I said. Seeing Tess cry made me feel as if my bones were brittle. As if I'd been barbecued over a hot fire and was all crispy and crunchy. I wanted to turn around and run home to bed again, but I managed to stay put. "Is Finn here?"

She pointed toward the family room. "He hasn't gotten off the couch all week. He has to though. Mom says he has to go back to school on Monday."

"Yeah. I guess I do too." I hated to think what that would be like.

"Finn," I said, marching over to him, trying to sound tough, "you have to get up."

He was lying on his back with pillows under his head, staring at the ceiling. He rolled his eyes lazily in my direction and grunted. "Why? Because you did?"

Just looking at his blotchy face made my throat thicken. His ash blond hair, too long and already starting to bleach in the sun, fell across his forehead and over one eye. His lips, heavy with sadness, twitched at the corners. Why couldn't I just crawl onto the couch next to him and cry and cry and cry? Why couldn't he hold me and rock me, and, when there were no tears left, why couldn't he kiss me? Isn't that what would happen in a movie?

Oh, for God's sake, stop it. I shook my head to knock out the nonsense and tried to channel Lorna's energy. "That's right," I said. "I got out of bed; you can too. Let's take a walk on the beach before we forget how to use our legs."

"I don't want to," he said, flatly. End of discussion.

"I know you don't want to. I don't want to either, but we have to."

"Why?"

The question stumped me, but Tess, standing in the doorway, came to the rescue. "Because you aren't dead!" she said. "Because you have to figure out how to keep living."

I stared at her. When did little Tess get so smart?

It took him a minute, but finally, Finn sighed and sat up. He groaned like an elderly arthritis sufferer as he pushed himself to his feet, but he followed me outside as if I had a leash on him.

We stumbled a hundred yards down the beach in silence and then Finn said, "I can't stand it, Jackie. I. Can. Not. Stand. It."

"I know," I said. I had a feeling Tessie was standing at the window, watching us.

"No, I mean really," he said, angrily pushing his hair out of his eyes. "I miss her. I need her. I'll never *not* need her."

"I know. You're not the only one."

Finn looked at me then, but I wasn't sure what he saw. Our shells had been cracked open and we were oozing out all over the place. I wasn't even sure where I started or ended anymore.

"Right," he said. "I know. You were her best friend."

Something about the way he said it bugged me. *Best friend.* She *was* my best friend, of course, but the words didn't sound large enough for the way I felt about Lorna. And also, he obviously thought best friend came in a distant second to boyfriend.

"But Jackie," he went on, "I *loved* her. I always loved her. From the very beginning I was crazy in love with her."

It was as if he'd hit me with a big stick. A stick I knew he had right behind his back. A stick I was waiting for. "*I* loved her, Finn! I loved her *too*!" I was yelling and pointing to myself. "Just because I didn't want to sleep with Lorna doesn't mean I didn't love her! You don't own her, Finn! You don't own the pain of losing her!"

Then, of course, we both cried like crazy, and held on to each other to keep from falling over. And when I looked back at Finn's house, sure enough, Tess was watching.

After that, walking became our religion. The rhythm of one foot following the other calmed us. We spent hours slogging through sand and seaweed up and down the bay beach—before school, after school, every weekend—the smell of fish rising with the spring temperatures. Just the two of us—we gave up on Lucas. The mystery of his absence was irritating, but not remotely as painful as the disappearance that had changed our lives.

Sometimes we walked in silence; sometimes we talked about Lorna. Never about the accident though, only about memories.

"Remember that first day she showed up in our class?" I asked him. As if there was a chance in hell he wouldn't remember that.

"It was surprising because we almost never got any new kids," he said. "And also because we'd never seen anybody like Lorna before."

"The way she looked you right in the eyes."

"The way she whipped that long red ponytail around like a weapon."

"The way she stood up to people, even that bully, Frankie Reeves."

Finn stared into the distance. "That first day I watched her swing herself hand over hand across the monkey bars. She lifted her legs over a crossbar, let go with her hands, and swung back and forth with her eyes closed. She hung by her knees longer than I'd ever seen anybody do it, boy or girl."

I nodded. "Everybody liked her right away, but she didn't need *everybody*. She picked us."

"We were her gang. Lucas and I had never hung around with girls before that day we all walked home together. Remember that? It should have taken us fifteen minutes, but it took two hours and everybody's parents were furious. Well, I'm sure Lorna's mother wasn't—she probably didn't even know what time it was, or that her ten-year-old daughter hadn't come home from school yet."

I'd thought about that first long walk at least a dozen times since Lorna's death. Our skinny, sandy town was Lorna's playground, and she showed us how to claim it as ours too. Every curb was a high wire to balance on, every tree trunk was a ladder to its branches, every shopkeeper was a potential giver of treats, every alley was the setting for a story to act out. The beach that ran parallel to the long downtown street was not just a sunny spot to take off our shoes—it was an undiscovered planet where treasure could be found by those willing to look for it. Without even realizing it, we all started to see the world through Lorna's eyes. By the time we straggled home that day, we'd become a team, and Lorna was our undisputed leader.

"When did she start wearing that white jacket every day?" Finn asked. "She thought it made her hair look like a bonfire. Which was true."

"Last fall. I was with her the day she found it at Old Hat, where her mom works," I said. "A woman from up-Cape brought in a bunch of gorgeous old clothes from the fifties and sixties. In perfect condition. Carla snagged some dresses for herself, but Lorna fell in love with that jacket. It had black diamonds embroidered on the collar and cuffs."

"I don't pay much attention to girls' clothes, but everything Lorna wears is beautiful. It doesn't matter what it is—any old shirt or pair of jeans—she makes it look great."

I'd had years of practice ignoring the little stabs of jealousy that stung like hornets, but it still wasn't easy. "Lorna always knew what looked good on her," I said, "and that jacket fit her perfectly. Of course, Carla didn't want her to have it. She said it was a couture piece and she could get a good price for it, but you know how Lorna was when she wanted something. She just buttoned it up and walked out of the store. No way was Carla getting it back."

Finn nodded. "When Lorna sets her mind on something, you might as well not argue with her because you aren't going to win."

It broke my heart over and over, the way Finn couldn't talk about Lorna in the past tense. But at least we were both standing up now, walking around, impersonating normal people. Those first weeks Finn and I were inseparable. We'd both had an amputation, but if we leaned on each other, we could limp along. I couldn't imagine how much worse it would be going through this alone. And sometimes there were brief moments when I almost forgot about Lorna and allowed myself to feel just slightly joyful about having Finn to myself. Spending hour after hour with Finn, even this hollow, miserable shadow of Finn, was almost a dream come true. But it was a dream that arose out of a nightmare, and I felt guilty taking even a tiny bit of pleasure in it.

When we walked down the hall at the high school, people smiled at us, but almost never stopped to talk. Sometimes Tony Perry or another one of Finn's friends from the basketball team came over and silently smacked him on the back or shoulder. He didn't seem to mind, but it aggravated me. Why would you hit somebody who was already in pain? I suppose it meant, *I'm male and I don't know how to talk about anything emotional, so I'm just going to pound on you.* I understood that people didn't know what to say, but I appreciated the ones who at least made an effort. "I'm so sorry," was enough and didn't beg for a response.

I didn't have a lot of friends. Neither did Lorna or Lucas, for that matter. We didn't need them. Finn played sports, so he knew pretty much everybody. If he hadn't been exclusively with Lorna, he would have been extremely popular—he had all the attributes: looks, brains, athletic ability, even money. But popularity was a goal for suckers—Lorna taught us that. We had more. We had a gang of amigos, a winning team, an endless party, an exclusive club, a band of like-minded souls, a full circle.

But now that Lorna was gone and Lucas was AWOL (showing up at school just long enough to take tests and then racing back home so he didn't have to talk to anyone) I was lonely. Of course I had Finn, but he was hardly the comrade he used to be either, so I was grateful when Charlotte Mancini came over to us in the cafeteria one day.

"Hi, you two. Mind if I join you?"

"Hey, Char," I said. "Yeah, sit with us."

Charlotte and I had been friends when we were little kids, before Lorna came to the elementary school. After that, we drifted apart, but I'd always liked Char. She was a quiet kid when we used to hang out together, but she'd blossomed the past few years since she started getting a few parts in school plays. It was funny, but the minute Charlotte sat down, I felt a wave of comfort, almost relief, wash over me.

Finn didn't have much to say to Char, but then, he didn't have much to say to anybody these days.

"I know you both must feel pretty terrible," Charlotte said. "I wanted to say I'm sorry about what happened, and if you need anything—I don't know what it would be, but anything—I'm here for you."

"Thanks," I said, and Finn mumbled something similar under his breath.

"Do you have jobs lined up for the summer?" she asked.

"I don't yet, but Finn's working on a whale watch boat starting next week. The *Poseidon*." For some reason I felt I had to speak for Finn, as if grief had rendered him mute.

"Oh, Captain Fritzy's boat?"

Finn nodded and finally opened his mouth. "Yeah. I practically have to pay him to let me work on it, but I don't care. I want to be out on the water."

"Right. I remember you always loved boats. You used to hang around on the wharf when you were a kid and watch the fishermen unload their catch," Charlotte said. But Finn had gone back into hibernation.

"So, Jackie, you're not working at the Riptide this summer?"

I was surprised Charlotte knew where I'd waitressed last year, but then, it's a small town. "No, he hired two of his nieces, so I'll have to look around. I should have started before this, but, you know, I haven't had the energy."

"Want to work with me at my dad's place?"

"At the café? Really? I didn't know he was hiring."

"One of our regulars retired. You'd be working with me, breakfast and lunch. Tips aren't stellar, but we get busy in season."

"Absolutely! I love the Blue Moon."

"Great! I told my dad I'd ask you, but you should go by and talk to him after school. He'll pretend like he's going to make your life miserable, but he's all bark."

I felt a smile break across my face and recognized it as a first since Lorna's death. There was a lightness in my chest that felt like hope.

As Finn and I trudged down the hall after lunch, he said, "You sounded pretty excited about that job."

"Why shouldn't I be? I have to make some money this summer, and it'll be more fun to work with Charlotte than down at the Riptide."

Finn didn't say anything else, but as he headed off to his next class, I felt like I'd been scolded. Did he think I was replacing Lorna or something? That was ridiculous. Lorna was irreplaceable. But I needed a friend, I needed a little bit of normalcy in my life, and if Charlotte was offering that, I was damn well going to take it.

3.

Lorna's memorial service didn't take place until a month later, at the end of June, the day after school let out for the summer. At first it looked like there might not be one at all because Lorna's mother had gone into a drunken seclusion and was incapable of planning it. I stopped by to see her a few times, but she wouldn't even open the door. Finally, Ms. Waller, the guidance counselor from the high school, managed to force her way into the house, and she got Carla to agree to let her plan something in the school auditorium.

"We all need to find some closure," Ms. Waller told me when she called me into her office to discuss it. If that's what she said to Carla, I'm amazed she got out of there alive. "Closure" sounded to me like what happened when the lid of the casket banged shut. Only we didn't have a casket or a body or a grave. We just had a big hole in our lives.

The day of the service, I changed clothes four times. Nothing I owned sent the right message: *Everything is ruined.* I understood now why black was the traditional funeral color, not dull gray, not muddy brown. Only stark black told the world that the worst had happened, the inconceivable worst, and there was not a bit of color left in your life.

Mom went to the memorial with me, but Dad was out on his boat, unwilling to lose a whole day of fishing. We were a little late getting to the high school because of my clothing dilemma, and I was surprised to see the auditorium was almost filled. Who were all these people? Did they really know Lorna, or were they there because she was young and beautiful and she fell from a place every one of them had also carelessly walked?

Finn came up the aisle toward us wearing his usual jeans and dark T-shirt, the uniform of every teenage boy I knew. He always looked a little sharper than the other guys though, probably because Elsie bought his clothes in New York when she went to her gallery in the city. The locals mostly shopped at the mall in Hyannis, if not the Goodwill.

"We saved seats for you up front," he said, pointing. The whole Rosenberg clan was in the front row, Elsie motioning for us to join them.

"You go," Mom said, giving me a little push. "I'll stay here in the back."

"No! Mom, come with me!" I begged. I wanted her by my side for this, but I wasn't surprised when she backed away. Not only did she hate funerals, but she pretty much despised any public gathering of more than two or three people. It was kind of amazing she came at all.

"There's plenty of room up front, Mrs. Silva," Finn said.

"Oh, I know. Thank you, Finn. But I don't like to traipse up the aisle in front of everybody. I'm fine back here." She plopped into a seat in the very last row, and I could tell by the set of her jaw she wouldn't change her mind. If she had her way, Teresa Silva would be completely invisible.

As I followed Finn up the aisle, I spotted Charlotte in the crowd, sitting with a girl from our Spanish class. Finn's friends from the basketball team were all there too.

"Wait." I pulled on Finn's arm. "There's Lucas with Simon and Billy. They should be up front with us. We should all be together."

Finn scowled in Lucas's direction. "Good luck with that. He won't even talk to us."

"Not true. I talked to him this week."

"For more than thirty seconds? Did he want to hang out with you?"

"He had a dentist's appointment that day—"

"There's an original excuse."

"Look, I don't know what's going on with him either, but I'm asking him to come up front with us," I said.

"Well, hurry up. The service is starting." Finn loped up the aisle without me.

Lucas was sandwiched between his fathers who seemed to inflate around him like protective packaging as I approached.

Simon was on the aisle and I leaned over him to speak directly to Lucas. "You should all come up front. Finn saved seats so we could be together." Simon, Lucas, and Billy exchanged nervous glances, as if I were speaking a language they didn't quite understand.

Mr. Coleman, the high school music teacher, started pounding out a somber piece on the out-of-tune piano just as someone with a loud voice came stomping down the aisle behind me.

"Oh, leave me alone, will ya? I don't need you holding my hand!"

Carla Trovato, wearing what looked like old black pajamas, her faded rusty hair pulled back into a lumpy bump on the back of her head, sideswiped me, then bounced off down the aisle, followed closely by Ms. Waller, who was attempting to grab her arm.

"There are still some seats in the front row," Ms. Waller said.

"Where do you *think* I'm going? I'm her mother, for Chrissakes."

Ms. Waller stopped in her tracks for a second as if she'd been smacked, then rallied and trotted after Carla. I was so absorbed in watching this little drama I almost forgot what I was doing until Simon tapped me on the hand. "Sweetheart, I think we'll stay where we are. It's getting crowded up there."

I tried to pin Lucas with my eyes, to see if this was his choice or Simon's, but he wouldn't look at me, so I gave up and went to sit by Finn.

"Wouldn't come, would he?" Finn asked, frowning. "Told ya."

"I give up," I said.

I was so aggravated by Lucas's behavior I couldn't pay attention to the Unitarian minister, not that he was saying anything of interest. He didn't know Lorna, and he was giving what I assumed was his standard speech for young people "taken before their time." All I could think about was that Lucas didn't want to be with us, didn't even want to talk to us. Something was very wrong and I couldn't bear not knowing what it was.

We sang a few hymns, everybody but Carla, who was fussing with something in her purse and didn't even stand up. I closed my eyes and tried to remember Lorna's face. I still could, of course, but I wondered how long it would be before I'd forget some of the details. I swore I'd never forget her luminous eyes.

"My eyes have no color at all," I could hear her say. "Yours are chocolate brown and Finn's are blue as water, but mine are see-through eyes."

"That's not true," I'd argued. "They're hazel."

"Hazel is a name, not a color," she'd come back. "In eyes it just means a muddy mixture. I have alien eyes." She'd narrowed them into slits. "I can see right through you."

I was sure she could.

The minister asked if anyone in the audience wanted to say anything, to give a remembrance. At first no one came up. Most of the high school kids looked down at their laps as if they were afraid someone might call on them. Finally, Ms. Waller took the microphone herself to start things off. She said Lorna was a leader whom other students looked up to. "She had a bright future ahead of her," the guidance counselor said with a quivery lip. Which made me remember how hard Ms. Waller had campaigned to get Lorna to consider college. But Lorna hadn't even wanted to talk about it. She always said, "College is a waste of four years. I want to start living my life *now*!"

The principal got up and stumbled through a few sentences about what an asset Lorna had been to the school, which everyone knew was a total lie. Lorna would burst out of her chair at two forty-five every afternoon, thrilled that the school day was over. You couldn't pay her to stick around after class for a meeting or a rehearsal or a practice of any kind, ever. She wanted to get out, do as she pleased, make her own rules.

A few more people stood up, but I couldn't bear to listen anymore. None of them really knew Lorna, not the way I did. But I was my mother's daughter. I couldn't stand up in front of all those people and admit how much I'd lost. I twisted in my chair to look across the aisle at Carla whose crossed leg bounced up and down in time to a soundtrack no one else could hear. She smirked and shook her head when an elementary school teacher described Lorna as "kind and sweet." Of course, Lorna would have hated that description herself, but couldn't Carla at least *pretend* she liked her daughter, even at her memorial service?

Finally Ms. Waller took the mike back. "If no one else has a remembrance, there are refreshments out in the foyer provided by our generous PTA parents."

People started to shuffle in their seats and stand up, but suddenly Finn jumped to his feet. "Wait! I want to say something."

Ms. Waller brought the microphone over to him and rubbed his arm as she handed it to him. Finn cleared his throat and began, his voice low and growly. "First of all, Lorna *was* beautiful, and she *was* strong-willed and a leader and all of those things people said about her. But she was more than that too. For me she was . . . everything. She changed my life. She *was* my life. And now I don't know how to . . . live . . . without . . ." Which was all he could say. He cleared his throat again, handed the mike back to Ms. Waller, and sat down.

I was glad Finn had had the courage to say what I was thinking, but hearing his words was not comforting. It reminded me that things would not really get better, that we would miss her forever. Why, I wondered, not for the first time, was she so special to us? Could I explain it if I had to? Why did she seem more beautiful to us than anyone else? There were other girls with lovely hair and perfect skin—Gillian Bates, for example—and Tiff Medieros could be a crazy daredevil sometimes. There were even other girls who were graceful and funny, like Carrie Costa. But no one combined all those attributes in quite such a stunning way. And no one else hid such depths behind her deep-set eyes or saw so clearly our own depths. No one else made us love her the way Lorna had.

Ms. Waller was weeping as she brought the service to a close. Finn had triggered tears all through the auditorium even though he was unusually dry-eyed himself. After a minute or two people mopped their faces, wandered out into the hallway, and stood in clumps around card tables full of punch and coffee and cookies. I couldn't imagine swallowing anything around the golf ball that was stuck in my throat.

Finn and I stood together and a bunch of kids circled around us. I looked for Lucas, but wasn't surprised not to find him. People were saying kind things to us, but for some reason it all irritated me. Everyone was very respectful of our grief, but they were enjoying the drama a little too much. I felt like some low-level celebrity that everybody wanted to stand next to so my pitiful bit of fame—best friend of the dead girl—might rub off on them.

A boy named Joe shook his head and said, "I can't believe she isn't coming back." How many times had Finn and I said the same thing this past month? Others in the circle nodded, as if he'd voiced a new and profound idea and not just a repetition of the constant refrain that played in my head.

Then, without meaning to, I repeated my other obsessive thought, the thing I couldn't get past. "How could Lorna have slipped? She could run across the whole breakwater and start back before the rest of us even reached the far end. It doesn't make sense."

My mother, standing nearby, overheard me and sparked to life. "Tragedies never make sense, Jackie!" She sounded completely exasperated. "You kids, you don't think terrible things can happen, but they can. If you don't respect the power of the water, it'll take you down. Have you forgotten that the ocean stole your uncle from us? Nature is unpredictable. It has no mercy!"

There was no point arguing with her, at least not now, but she was wrong. Yes, the weather had been wild that night, and yes, we took a stupid chance walking out on the breakwater in such a storm. And if any of the other three of us had been swept off the rocks, I could blame the untamed natural world. But we weren't. It was nature's child, the breakwater ballerina who was carried off, and there had to be something more to it than chance.

A buzzing noise behind me seemed to be growing into a rumble. I turned around to see Ms. Waller standing in front of the coffee urn, trying, without much luck, to calm Carla down.

"You know that's not true, Mrs. Trovato. You're just upset. Why don't you have a cup of coffee?"

"What do you know about it?" Carla said, her voice slurred. She shoved aside the Styrofoam cup Ms. Waller held out to her and coffee slopped over the side.

Ms. Waller tried again. "It was a terrible accident—"

"It was not an accident!" Carla screamed. Everybody in the hallway turned to look at her. "She did it on purpose. To hurt me! Everything Lorna did was to punish me! Don't you know that?"

Mrs. Waller looked stunned and her smile wobbled.

"You people are idiots," Carla said, sneering at those closest to her. She grabbed the coffee cup from Ms. Waller's hand and threw it on the floor, splashing coffee on all the surrounding shoes and ankles. Everybody squealed and jumped back. While they grabbed for napkins to wipe off the hot liquid, Carla made for the double doors and escaped.

4.

"What do you mean he's *gone*?" Finn said. "Gone where?"

I leaned against the doorjamb at his house, breathless, having run the last six blocks. "I just saw Simon . . . at the grocery store, and he said they put Lucas . . . on a bus to New Hampshire . . . yesterday afternoon . . . right after the memorial service."

"What?" Finn came outside, slamming the door behind him. Without thinking, we started walking our usual path down to the bay beach. "He left town without even telling us he was going? Not a phone call? Not an e-mail? What the hell is wrong with him?"

I shook my head. "I don't know. All I could get out of Simon is that he's going to be a counselor at some summer camp in New Hampshire."

"Are you kidding me? How can Lucas be a camp counselor? He can barely swim, he's never ridden a horse, and he's scared of bugs!"

"I don't know. Maybe he'll play the guitar at campfires or something."

"This is insane." Finn plowed through the sand at a fast clip and I had to scurry to keep up. We passed the skeleton of a washed-up goosefish being picked over by half a dozen screeching gulls. I'd seen these garish corpses all my life, but their big-mouth death grins gave me the creeps every time.

"I've never heard Lucas say one word about wanting to work at a summer camp." Finn was so angry, he was snorting. "He's running away from us. He's been avoiding us all month and now he's left town altogether. There has to be a reason! But what is it?"

I shrugged. "There must be something we don't know."

"What could he possibly know that we don't? He's been acting like this ever since . . . does he think it's our fault or something?" He stopped beneath a deserted pier and I finally caught up to him.

"I think Simon and Billy know more than they're telling us," I said. "But they're not going to rat out their own kid."

Finn leaned up against one of the old pilings and let his eyes close for a second. "God, Jackie, sometimes I feel like I just can't take one more thing. Do you feel that way? Losing Lorna was so *huge* and so *awful* that I'm barely holding on as it is. Any other little problem—in school or with my parents or this thing with Lucas or whatever—it's too much. I can't take one more thing!"

"I know." I put my hand on his bare arm and watched his face dissolve into hopelessness.

Will this ever end for us? I wondered. The two of us had been slogging down the beach as if it were quicksand, day after day, our hearts cracked wide open. I felt like I was seeing everything through a gauzy veil now. Nothing was bright anymore, and there were no sharp edges. One shape bled into the next, and I stumbled on stairs and bumped into people on the street as if I were wearing glasses that belonged to somebody else. Not one thing was easy.

And Finn was obviously in terrible shape. He'd lost weight the past month, and there were dark circles under his eyes now. I stood there staring at him as he opened his eyes and let them fall on me. He looked so destroyed, it killed me.

I didn't plan what happened next—I'd never have had the nerve to do it if I'd thought about it at all. It was the way Finn looked at me with, well, longing. Not that I thought he was longing for *me*, of course not. But I was there, and I was suffering too, and it just seemed for a moment as if I might be able to fix things, make him, make us both, feel a little bit human again. But really, I wasn't thinking at all, because if I had been I'd never have reached up and put my lips against his.

For a second or two, the fog seemed to lift. I started to believe my kiss could penetrate Finn's grief, push it back, replace it with gentle hope. His hands reached for my shoulders and mine stretched up behind his head, clasping his neck. But then, as I pressed closer to him, I realized that his arms were not actually wrapping around my shoulders, not at all. In fact, they were pushing at me, pushing me away.

I jumped back, horrified at what I'd done.

Finn was glaring at me as if I'd betrayed us all. "Jackie! What the hell are you doing?"

"Oh, my God! I'm sorry! I don't know . . . I just thought . . ." It was a bad dream and I was not waking up from it.

Finn held his arms straight out in front of him, as if defending himself against any further attacks. "Is everybody going crazy? What did you think—?"

"No, I wasn't thinking. You just looked so sad, Finn, and I . . . I don't know. I'm so sorry!"

"Of course I'm sad! Isn't *sad* who we are now? Did you really think that was going to help anything?"

"No! I—" I couldn't even look at him. "Please, can we just pretend it never happened? I *am* crazy. I don't know what I'm doing."

I turned my back to him and we didn't speak at all for a minute or two. I could hear him breathing hard, huffing like a bull in the ring. Oh, my God, I was an idiot. I'd loved Finn for so long. I'd imagined kissing him hundreds of times, but I'd kept my secret locked up tight. How could I have let it get loose? I'd ruined everything. Everything! Finn's anger ballooned behind me, and I felt suffocated, as if a plastic bag were tied over my head.

"Okay," he said finally, his voice tight. "I guess neither of us knows what we're doing these days. I get that. But, Jackie—"

I turned and answered his question before he could ask it. "It'll never happen again. I promise you."

He nodded, but he didn't look convinced.

"Finn, I promise. Please don't be mad at me. I need you."

"I know. I need you too, Jackie. Just not like that." Which was obvious, but still felt like a punch in the gut.

"I should get back," Finn said. "I'm on the boat for the afternoon whale watch."

I followed him down the beach, keeping a decent distance between us. The goosefish smiled at me with its hideous teeth as I passed. Trying to find a normal tone of voice, I said, "Has the boat had big crowds?"

"Not bad."

I shuffled along behind him, hating my idiot self. "And you've been seeing whales?"

"Some. Two finbacks yesterday and a minke that swam right under the boat."

"Cool." There was a long silence during which I replayed my lunge at Finn and was mortified all over again. Would I ever be able to erase that scene from my consciousness? Would Finn?

Keep talking. Act normal. "I wonder if Lucas will have e-mail at that camp," I said.

Finn turned and gave me a scornful look. "Why? You're not going to write to him, are you?"

His anger was right there, just barely below the surface. He wasn't just mad at Lucas anymore—he was mad at me now too. Maybe he was even mad at Lorna.

I was beginning to come to terms with the idea that we'd never be "the four of us" again. With Lucas gone we weren't even three. And now maybe I'd ruined the possibility of even two of us remaining friends. The thought of being without all of them, of being alone, was terrifying. Who was I on my own?

I weighed my words carefully, so they couldn't be misconstrued. "I thought I would," I said. "We can't just ignore him."

"I can," Finn said. He picked up a rock from the beach and hurled it far out into the water. "Whatever his stupid secret is, I don't want to know it."

5.

"It's cool that your dad trusts us to close up the café this afternoon," I said. The two of us were in the kitchen of the Blue Moon, me refilling sugar dispensers, Charlotte washing coffee pots.

"Believe me, he doesn't trust us," she said. "He just didn't have a choice. My grandma had a doctor's appointment up-Cape and she can't see well enough to drive herself."

I swiped an arm across my sweaty forehead. It was early July and the kitchen was steamy. "He doesn't even trust you? You're his kid. You grew up in the Blue Moon."

"If he could, Dad would run this whole place by himself. Fry every egg, pour every cup of coffee, figure up every check. Unfortunately, he's only one person. Oh, Jackie, you spilled sugar on the floor—sweep that up right away."

"I will after I finish filling these," I said.

Charlotte grimaced. "You should really stop and do it now so you don't slip in it. I know it sounds crazy, but I've had restaurant safety drummed into my head since I was two years old. Dad would have a fit if he saw that on the floor."

"Okay." I put down the sack of sugar and dutifully got the broom. Charlotte had a few idiosyncrasies, but I was willing to put up with them in return for the friendship that had blossomed between us the past few weeks as we worked together at the café. Finn was apparently no longer comfortable around me—we hadn't walked on the beach together since the day of the humiliating kiss—and Charlotte was filling a little bit of the void left by the loss of all my other friends. I was more than grateful that the friendship we interrupted years before seemed to have picked up where it left off in the fourth grade.

The two of us enjoyed each other even though the fun we had was neither hilarious nor wild. It didn't make people stare or smile or shake their heads in disapproval. It was never breathtaking. But it calmed me, and I couldn't think of anything I needed more at the moment.

I finished filling the sugar containers and moved on to the small tabletop maple syrup bottles, topping them off from a big jug. "Remember that time when we were kids and we played 'restaurant' in your kitchen?" I asked Char. "We mixed all kinds of disgusting stuff together and tried to get your mother to eat it."

Charlotte grunted. "She played along until she saw the huge mess we'd made."

"There was ketchup on the walls, the floor, the countertop . . ."

"You were squirting it at me!"

"You started it by throwing that grapefruit," I said, laughing.

Char turned from the sink, smiling, but her face closed in on itself when she saw what I was doing. "Those bottles are awfully close to the edge of the table, Jackie."

I shoved them back a little. "We used to have fun together. How come we . . ." A thought crossed my mind all of a sudden, and I wondered if it could be possible. "It wasn't because of Lorna, was it? I mean, I know she and I got to be friends right away, but I wasn't . . . I didn't hurt your feelings, did I?"

I guess I was looking at Charlotte and didn't notice that the jug I was holding had nudged one of the bottles to the very edge of the table. When it hit the tile floor, it exploded with a sickening crash. Glass shards swam in rivers of syrup that raced off in all directions.

"Jackie!" Charlotte threw her sponge into the deep sink, her face livid, her voice bubbling with anger. "What's wrong with you? You're so careless! My dad would *kill* you!"

I was as surprised by Charlotte's response as I was by the accident itself. Murder seemed like an overreaction to my crime. "I'm sorry! I'll clean it up." But the syrup was already seeping into my sneakers and when I tried to move, I left gooey footprints.

"Don't move!" Charlotte ordered. She grabbed a rag and dragged over a garbage can.

"I'll do it," I said, but I wasn't sure what to do first. "I should probably take off my shoes."

Charlotte picked the large pieces of glass out of the syrup and threw them in the trash, then sighed. "Wait a minute. I'll get you a towel to stand on so you don't cut your feet."

A few minutes later I was standing barefoot on a towel in front of the sink, washing maple syrup out of the ruts of my sneaker soles while Charlotte mopped up the floor in silence. "I'm sorry," I said again. "I guess I wasn't paying attention."

"I guess you weren't."

"God, Char, it was an accident. Why are you so mad?"

"Are you kidding? If my dad was here he'd still be screaming at you."

"Okay, but you're not your dad."

Charlotte stopped mopping and met my eyes. "Sometimes you don't think, Jackie! Of *course* you hurt my feelings. What did you think? I felt totally rejected. The day you met Lorna was the day you stopped talking to me!"

I could feel myself shrink from five feet, eight inches to the size of a grasshopper or maybe an ant, something you might step on and hardly notice. I stood there, stranded on my towel island while Charlotte struggled with her sticky feelings.

"Really?" I said. "I stopped talking to you? I don't remember—"

"Well, I do. Believe me."

There was pain in Charlotte's eyes and I had to look away. "So, if you hate me, why did you help me get this job?"

Charlotte went back to mopping. "Don't be so dramatic. Of course I don't hate you. I mean, I kind of did at the time, but then I saw the way it was. I knew you couldn't help it. The same thing happened to Finn and Lucas. Everybody else became invisible to you once Lorna took you over."

That was how I remembered it too—we'd all been *taken over*. Lorna's super-sized personality had reeled us in as easily as fishermen haul in bluefish when the schools are running on the outer beaches practically begging to be caught. But why hadn't we widened our circle to include Charlotte?

"I'm so sorry I ignored you like that. I don't remember . . ."

Charlotte shook her head. "Don't worry about it. It was Lorna who did the choosing, and I wasn't chosen. When I look back, it makes total sense. Lorna demanded worship, and I didn't adore her the way the rest of you did."

I was surprised to hear this. I guess I thought everybody adored Lorna.

"I admit I was jealous that she could just waltz in and grab my friend away," Char went on. "I probably shouldn't even be saying this now. It's awful what happened to her, and to you and Finn and Lucas too. But back then I was ten years old and all I knew was that you liked her better than you liked me. I was mad, but, you know, I got over it." She looked at me with an embarrassed smile. "Well, more or less."

I was furious with my fourth-grade self. "God, Char," I said. "I guess I was a dumb kid. I'm sorry I was such a jerk."

Charlotte stuck the mop into the bucket. "I forgive you. Just don't ever do it again."

"If I ever act that stupid again, you have permission to smack me."

"I'll keep that in mind."

I watched her wedge the mop into a tight corner. "So, obviously, you never liked Lorna much," I said.

Charlotte shrugged. "Actually I felt kind of sorry for her. She seemed so needy. She was the queen bee, but she needed the three of you buzzing around her all the time, telling her how great she was. It was like she was starving and you had to constantly feed her."

I fell back against the sink, stunned. "*Needy?* That's how she seemed to you? *We* needed *her.* She was the one who made everything happen. She made us who we are!"

Charlotte was quiet for a minute and then said, "She made you who she wanted you to be. It was like she owned you. All of you." She nodded toward the maple syrup jug. "Do you think you can refill the last few bottles without spilling anything while I finish the floor?"

"Sure."

I didn't know what to say about Char's odd notion that Lorna "owned" us, so I concentrated on putting my shoes back on and completing the syrup assignment. Of course, Lorna had been our undisputed leader, but that wasn't a *bad* thing. Sometimes I thought I'd barely been alive before I met her. Charlotte had been jealous of Lorna—she'd admitted that—which blinded her to Lorna's better qualities. And I was at least partially responsible for that. If I'd been mature enough to see that Char felt deserted when I started hanging out with Lorna and the boys, surely I would have made sure she was included in the group. Wouldn't I? Charlotte had cast Lorna as the villain, but it was really my fault.

"You *should* be mad at me," I said, screwing the cap on the final bottle.

Char butted me out of the way so she could pour the bucket of dirty water into the sink. "I'm not mad at you, Jackie. God, it was years ago. I guess I just needed to vent a little." She stored the mop and bucket in the back room. "You can head home. I'll lock up."

But things felt unfinished and I didn't want to leave yet. "There's some iced tea left in the fridge. Should we have a glass before we go?"

"Okay. Sure."

I poured us each a glass, plopping in lots of ice cubes. We perched on stools and took long drinks. When I glanced over, I noticed Char had a sly smile on her face.

"What?"

"Okay, I'm going to admit something that will make you feel better," she said. "I was kind of glad when Lorna and Finn became a couple because I knew you had a thing for him. How mean is that? See, I was a jerk too—you just didn't know it."

I could feel the blood drain from my face. "I never told you I liked Finn."

Char laughed. "Please. It was obvious. I sat across the aisle from you in freshman algebra. You used to stare at him like he was a pork chop and you were a stray dog."

"Thanks. I thought you weren't mad at me?" I was glad Char felt comfortable enough to tease me, but this particular joke reminded me of my recent disastrous mistake with Finn. "Stray dog" was a little too close to the truth; I was hungry and lonely and I slobbered all over him.

"It's no big deal. Everybody's had a crush on the Finnster at some point," she said. "Cute, rich, and he doesn't even strut around like a rooster."

"Does that mean you had a crush on him too?" I asked.

"I admit it." Charlotte downed most of her iced tea. "I got over it though. I prefer to crush on people who at least know I'm alive. I'm not a fool."

Right. Not a fool, like, for instance, *me*. I tried to shunt the conversation onto another track. "You dated Kevin Spinelli last year, didn't you?"

"For about five minutes. Drama Club kids trade partners constantly, but so far—for me at least—nobody's stuck. What about you?"

I shook my head. "Nope. Well, I dated Lucas for a while sophomore year."

"Right. I remember that."

"We only did it because Lorna wanted us to. She'd been with Finn for ages already and she thought it would be perfect if Lucas and I were a couple too. It was kind of ridiculous. Lucas had a huge crush on Lorna, and I . . ." *Stop talking about this!*

"You were still into Finn," Charlotte said matter-of-factly.

Remembering that time made me cringe. Lucas and I had tried so hard to make it work. It seemed like it ought to. The First Place boy and girl were such a perfect match. Didn't it make sense that the Runners-up belonged together too? Lorna kept telling us we were a great couple, but I knew Lucas wasn't feeling it either. And still, we held hands and bumped hips and pretended the kisses meant something. And Lucas pined for Lorna while I longed to be with Finn.

I tried to make a joke of it. "We'd only kiss each other when Lorna was around, to convince her we liked each other. Isn't that romantic? I mean, we *did* like each other, so it wasn't horrible or anything. Just stupid."

"How long did you keep that up?"

"A month or two. Amazingly, it didn't wreck our friendship."

Charlotte got up and rinsed her tea glass and put it in the sink. "Don't get mad, but I was just thinking, now that Lorna's gone . . . I know you still like Finn. Maybe the two of you . . . you know."

An ice chip slipped down my throat and I choked on it, then shook my head wildly. "No," I sputtered. "No, no, no."

"Why not? Stranger things have happened."

"Not to me," I said. "Can't happen."

"Why? Because Lorna wouldn't like it? Is she *still* running your—"

"You don't get it, Char. Finn's not interested."

"How do you know?" Charlotte insisted.

"I *know*. Believe me." I turned my back on her and carefully lined up the syrup bottles as if they were a marching band, but Char's accusation stuck in my head. No, Lorna *wouldn't* like it. I couldn't even imagine how angry she'd be if she knew I'd kissed Finn. He was *hers*.

6.

When I left the Blue Moon, I headed over to the Jasper Street Art Center where I often worked for a few hours in the late afternoon helping Elsie with office work. I needed to save as much money for college as I could over the summer, even though whether I was going to college at all was still a subject for debate in the Silva household. Neither of my parents had been to college and only one of my three older brothers had had any interest in going. And even Michael only made it as far as Cape Cod Community College. I had higher aspirations. I wanted to get off-Cape and go to a real art school.

JSAC was irresistible to me and I would have helped Elsie even if she wasn't paying me for it. I loved wandering through the closed gallery and sniffing around the pungent studios where so many young artists had started their careers. I loved being a part of the place, belonging to it, at least a little bit.

Finn's and Tess's parents, Elsie McGavrock and Rudolph Rosenberg, had moved from New York City to Provincetown twenty years ago to open the Art Center on the grounds of a sprawling old inn they'd purchased with the proceeds from Rudolph's Pulitzer Prize–winning novel. Elsie, an abstract painter, had spent the last two decades as director of the Jasper Street Gallery and the fellowship program.

"Oh good, you're here." Elsie's eyes lit up as I walked into her office. "I've got lots for you to do today. The website needs to be updated with next month's gallery shows and readings. And there are envelopes to stuff and mail out to the incoming Fellows. They should have gone out last week."

"No problem. I can take them to the post office on my way home."

Elsie stood and gave me an aromatic hug. "Thank you, sweetie. You're a peach. I'm unraveling this afternoon. Oh, before I forget, I brought you goodies!" She hauled a bag from beneath her desk and handed it to me. "I found some information online about filling out the FAFSA form, which I'll be happy to help you with. And, because you've started making collages now, I'm loaning you my Joseph Cornell book, and then just for fun, I got you a copy of that new Rothko book you were looking at here last week."

"You did?" I pawed excitedly through the bag. "You didn't have to do that." Elsie was my fairy godmother. She always knew just what I needed.

"Of course I didn't *have* to, but I love feeding your spirit, and you're so appreciative of it, unlike my two adorable children who couldn't care less about art. Oh, and I also talked to my friend at RISD and he gave me some advice for you, which we'll talk about before you fill out the application."

The Rhode Island School of Design was my dream school. Elsie had studied there and just listening to her talk about "Riz-Dee" made my brain explode—it sounded like paradise to me. Since the first time I followed Finn into his house—was I ten? eleven?— and saw all the paintings on the walls, the thick art books on the coffee table, all I could think about was making art. Elsie said I reminded her of herself when she was a kid, and she encouraged me with rolls of paper, half-used tubes of paint, and hand-me-down sticks of charcoal and pastels. Then, last year, she gave me the best gift of all, her old SLR digital camera.

But the most helpful thing Elsie gave me was her time. When I was a kid she spent hours looking through art books with me, explaining materials and techniques. Later, she guided me through Leonardo da Vinci and Rembrandt, explaining the methods of the Old Masters, then brought me into the nineteenth century with Van Gogh. I could feel my mind expand as she explained how Van Gogh used color as a way to capture emotion. I soaked up every word that came out of Elsie's mouth. She was living proof of her own belief that art was as much about passion as technical mastery.

Now she ran a hand through her thick, honey-colored hair, which was just beginning to gray at the temples. She seemed more distracted than usual. "What was I doing when you came in? There are so many details to wrap up this week, I swear I'm losing it."

"Why don't you go work in your studio while I do this stuff? I'll answer the phone and if it's important I'll come get you." As much as I liked having Elsie around, I could tell she was longing to escape her mundane duties and paint.

She perked up. "I really shouldn't—there's so much to do here. But I haven't been in the studio all week."

"Which is why you're having a meltdown."

"You know me too well, Jackie. Maybe I *will* go paint for an hour or so. Do you mind holding down the fort? You can try out the new photo program I just installed—you'll love it."

"Go. Get out. Paint," I said, laughing.

Elsie sprinted out the door, heading for the small studio she kept for herself at JSAC.

As I settled myself at the computer, I wondered, not for the first time, whether the work Elsie found for me to do those afternoons was really all that necessary. Elsie was determined to help me find a way to go to art school, even though Teresa and Marco didn't have the money or the inclination to send me, and I sometimes suspected that this job had been at least partly manufactured to keep me near the inspiration of the gallery while adding a few extra dollars to my savings account.

The website updates didn't take long. I had my camera with me, as usual, so I could have tried out Elsie's new photo editing program, but I usually preferred to print my pictures exactly as I took them, without any digital manipulation. I'd settled into envelope stuffing when I heard footsteps approaching from the Common Room down the hall. *Could it be Finn?* He was often pressed into service here too, for basic handyman jobs. My heart started to trot.

It wasn't Finn, but I wasn't disappointed to see who it was.

Cooper Thorne always entered a room as if stepping onto a stage, his extravagant smile backed up by bone-deep confidence. Eight years ago Cooper had been the youngest writer ever admitted for a JSAC residency, and now he was the assistant director of the place. A few months ago his first novel had been published to very good reviews, and he had a perpetual cat-with-the-feathers-still-in-its-mouth look on his face. Who could blame him?

"Hey, Jackie! This is getting to be a regular gig for you."

"I know. Elsie gets busy this time of the year." I held off making eye contact with him as long as possible. A full-on eyeball blast from Cooper had been known to tie up my tongue like a calf at a rodeo. "She's in her studio if you need her."

"Not at all. I'm just looking for a friendly face at the end of a long day, and I'm more than happy to see yours."

I glanced up at him and, sure enough, whatever I was about to say melted in my mouth like cotton candy. I needed a drink of water.

Cooper Thorne had green eyes that sparkled with flecks of gold, like turquoise stones, and a shock of dark hair he was constantly flinging back with a toss of his head. The combination made it seem as if he was flirting with everyone he spoke to. Or maybe he really *was* flirting with everyone, but only in the sweetest way. For all his success, he never seemed arrogant. And then, of course, there was the incredible wattage of his smile, which could electrify an entire building.

Over the years I'd crossed paths with Cooper many times, at gallery shows or at the Rosenbergs' house, but until this summer, he'd never paid much attention to me. I'd noticed him, of course, but only as that good-looking guy who worked for Elsie. The last few weeks, though, something had changed. I'd been running into him a lot at the Center and he was always very nice to me. It was probably just my overactive imagination, but whenever I was around Cooper now, it almost seemed as if something was bubbling up between us—friendship or . . . something. I tried not to look at it too closely.

"You almost done with those?" he asked, pointing to the pile of envelopes.

"This is the last one."

"Good. It's five-thirty. Let's go sit down and have a beer." I looked up in surprise and he laughed. "Oops. I keep forgetting how young you are. *I'll* have a beer. You can have a Coke."

As I sealed the final envelope, I heard him feeding quarters into the soda machine in the hallway, the can clunking down the chute.

"They don't have beer in there, do they?" I asked as he handed me the cold can.

Cooper put a finger to his lips and whispered. "I keep a few bottles in the mini-fridge in my office. Don't tell Elsie."

Right. Elsie adored Cooper. She probably wouldn't care if he was doing Jell-O shots in his office.

Cooper popped the cap off his bottle and I followed him to the Common Room, empty in the late afternoon. Of course he was only paying attention to me because nobody else was around—he was just killing time. Still, when he fixed me with those startling eyes, I was happy to forget how old *he* was too.

He flopped onto the sagging couch and propped his bare feet on the ancient coffee table in front of him. Even in shorts and a T-shirt, Cooper managed to look well-dressed. I tried not to stare at his long, tan legs, which were covered in soft sun-bleached hair.

"You must be tired," he said. "Elsie said you work a full shift at the Blue Moon before you come in here."

"Yeah, it's kind of a long day, but I like both jobs." I sat down carefully, as if the couch were a seesaw and putting too much weight on my side might send Cooper flying into the air. If only I had more experience with guys so I didn't always feel so uncomfortable. How were you supposed to tell if somebody was just being friendly or if his attention meant something more?

"I admire you, Jackie," Cooper said. It was the last thing I expected to hear him say.

My mouth was dry, and I drank some of my Coke before replying. "You do? Why?"

"The way you soldier on. You've had a lot to deal with the past few months, but you haven't crumbled."

"Crumbled?"

He laid a hand very gently on my arm. "It must have been terrible for you to be there, to watch your friend drown."

Oh. There were whole moments now when I didn't think about Lorna. The terrible thing about forgetting, though, was that when you were reminded, the punch was almost as bad as the first time you felt it and it was hard to breathe. I took a long drink of my soda, trying to recover.

"It was really dark," I said, finally. "We couldn't actually see too much."

He shook his head. "God. It's so unbelievable. She was there one minute and gone the next."

I nodded, a little disappointed that, even though Cooper said he admired *me*, the conversation was turning out to be about

Lorna. I tried, these days, to keep a pillow tucked around my heart, so the misery could lie down and rest, and maybe even be smothered by the soft comfort. But all it took was someone saying her name and immediately the white jacket rose to the surface of my memory again, and the pain woke up screaming.

"I guess it's no wonder Finn's always in such a miserable mood. I feel so bad for you both. Although, I think you're a more resilient person than he is. Finn's stuck in a very dark place."

I wasn't sure how to take that. Did Cooper think I wasn't as affected by Lorna's death as Finn was? Did everybody think that? That I was a second-string mourner? It seemed very drama-queeny to insist I was just as miserable as Finn, and maybe that wasn't even what Cooper meant. He acted as if he were complimenting me.

"Don't misunderstand me," he said, removing his warm hand, which I instantly missed. "I know you're upset about what happened too, but I think it's admirable that you're getting on with it. Life sucks sometimes, but if you let yourself sink down into the misery, sometimes you can't find your way out of it. Nothing ever seems good again. But I don't think you're like that. I think you're a positive, optimistic person, and eventually you'll be fine."

"You think so?" I hated the whine in my voice, like a five-year-old begging for a pat on the head.

"I do."

"I hope you're right. I want to be happy again," I said. And then the most appalling thing happened. Just as Cooper was praising my ability to bounce back, *tears* started beating down my cheeks.

"Oh, my God, I made you cry," he said, taking his feet off the table and leaning forward. "Now I feel terrible."

I tried to soak up the moisture with my hands, but I would have needed a sponge to staunch the flow.

I could see that Cooper was looking around for something to give me to wipe myself up with, but there was nothing obvious in the room. And then, suddenly, he whipped off his T-shirt, wadded it up, and held it to my face, dabbing at my tears.

"You'll be happy again, Jackie," he said. "I know you will. I'll help you."

I was so surprised by both offers, his clothing and his help, that I stopped crying immediately, but I kept the T-shirt up to my face anyway so he couldn't see my shock. What did he mean he'd help me? Just that he was willing to absorb a few tears, or more than that?

I was embarrassed that he was sitting next to me without a shirt on, and I was excited that he was sitting next to me without a shirt on. I kept my face hidden in his T-shirt for the longest time. It smelled of lilac, as if it had gone through the wash with Elsie's clothes.

7.

On my days off I got up early, loaded my camera, drawing pad, and pencils into my backpack, and headed away from town, sometimes to the marshes near the breakwater, sometimes to the beach at Herring Cove, but most often, like today, I headed to the dunes across Route 6. I liked the dunes best because the people I was likely to come across out there weren't tourists, but artists, writers, and other old hippie types spending their summer living off the grid in one of the weathered, mouse-infested dune shacks that dotted the National Seashore land.

I went to the dunes to see what I'd seen so many times before—sand, beach grass, cloud formations—but to see them differently every time, to watch them change. I loved spending long hours lying on my back in the dunes, watching the clouds mass and pull apart, first hiding the sun, then lifting the curtain on a high-noon performance, casting shadows that changed the landscape minute to minute.

Being out here always made me think of Lorna, partly because everything made me think of Lorna, but mostly (and oddly) the dunes reminded me of her because they were the one place I often came without her. I loved drawing and taking pictures out here, but Lorna didn't enjoy watching me do it. She didn't really like *watching* anything. Lorna liked being out front—she wanted to *be* watched.

In truth I didn't really want her around anyway when I was working on art projects. Lorna thought being an artist was a pretty useless goal. When I daydreamed out loud about becoming a famous painter someday, Lorna scoffed. "*Famous?* The only people who'll know who you are are people who go into art galleries. My *life* is going to be art," she said. "*Me*, not something I draw or take a picture of." That seemed perfectly possible to me.

Lorna knew I liked being alone sometimes, but she couldn't understand it. She hated being alone. More than once she'd made a joke about what a loner I was, and I could tell she was a little angry about it.

Once when we were little kids, the boys and I hid from her. We'd been running around in a wooded field off Harry Kemp Way and somehow she got separated from us and we hid. Maybe we knew it would freak her out—I can't remember. We could see her from where we were hiding though, and at first it seemed funny that she was so distraught.

"Where *are* you?" she yelled, turning in wild circles. "I hate you for doing this to me!"

We snickered under our breaths.

But then she fell to her knees and cried as if her heart was broken. "Don't leave me! Don't leave me *alone*," she wailed, and suddenly the game wasn't so hilarious anymore.

When we came out of hiding, she wouldn't speak to us. Her tears had dried in dirty streaks down her face. She stomped off, furious, and we followed her home, begging her to forgive us, to speak to us again. But she didn't, not for the rest of that day. And though we often teased each other, we never tried to trick Lorna again.

Maybe that was what Charlotte meant when she said Lorna was "needy." She depended on us because, well, we didn't let her down the way her parents did. Char's idea of Lorna as someone to be pitied as much as admired had lodged in my head and I couldn't get it out. Obviously, the three of us had needed Lorna at least as much as she'd needed us—no doubt about it. But I could see that our need for her and hers for us was not as out of balance as it might have seemed.

As I hiked through the dunes I thought of Lorna asking, "Why do you take the same picture over and over?" I'd tried to explain, but she was an impatient listener. The thing was, every time I clicked the shutter I became more aware of the subtle variations in my surroundings, the small secrets that rose to the surface and were sucked back under. I loved the way a photograph could stop time, put a frame around it. It captured a moment and held it forever, even if the world kept changing. Lorna was like that now, too, mounted, matted, framed, alive only in photographs.

The last time I'd been on the dunes, it was so hot I emptied my water bottle before noon and had to hike to the ocean to cool off. But today it was overcast and rainy, the clouds so dramatic I couldn't make myself leave until I was so wet my shoes belched water every step of the walk home.

"For God's sake, you're dripping wet!" Mom greeted me the minute I came through the door.

I don't think I've ever come into this kitchen without seeing my mother at work, chopping up vegetables or cleaning fish. This afternoon she was tossing handfuls of potatoes into a big black pot that sat on top of our ancient stove. She waved me back into the doorway.

"Take those shoes off before you come in here. Don't you have enough sense to get in out of the rain?"

"I'm in, aren't I?" I toed off my soaked sneakers.

"Go upstairs and change clothes, and then come back down here. I want to talk to you."

Damn. As the youngest of four, I was used to flying under my parents' radar, but since my older brothers had all (finally) moved out of the house last year, Mom had begun paying more attention to me, which drove me slightly crazy. I slipped into dry clothes, toweled off my hair, and padded back downstairs barefoot.

"You hungry?" Mom asked. Which must be the most-often asked question in this house. When my brothers were around, the answer was always yes.

"Not really. I took an apple with me."

"An apple's not a meal. Make a sandwich," she ordered. She opened the refrigerator door and got out two packages wrapped in white butcher paper, enough salami and American cheese to feed all three of my relocated brothers.

"I'm not hungry, Mom. I had an—"

"I don't want to hear about your *apple*. There are fresh rolls in the breadbox. No daughter of mine is going to starve herself."

There was no use arguing about it. I got out the bag of rolls. For years Mom had been getting up before dawn six mornings a week to knead dough into round loaves for the Portuguese Bakery. Our breadbox was always stuffed with baked goods. I cut a roll in half and topped it with a thin slice of cheese.

Teresa handed me a plate. "Where were you this morning? Dunes again?"

I nibbled at my sandwich and nodded.

"I don't know what's so great about sitting out there in the middle of that big sandbox hour after hour."

"God, Mom, people come from all over the world to see the place we live—it's beautiful! Have you even been to the beach in the last decade?"

"I've got too much to do to sit around on my butt and get skin cancer." She took a bag of carrots from the fridge. They looked a little dried up to me, but I didn't say anything.

"Do you even own a swimsuit?"

She wrinkled her nose. "Why would I need a swimsuit? I can't swim."

"Really?" How had I not known this? "You grew up in Provincetown and you never learned to swim?"

"We're surrounded by a dangerous ocean, Jackie, not some fancy swimming pool. There's nothing beautiful about that ocean to me."

This was a conversation I'd spent my life trying to avoid—the lethal effects of the killer ocean. I perched on the lip of the chair and scarfed down my roll, which was, in fact, delicious.

Mom frowned. "I guess you were taking pictures out there again. Doesn't that get boring?"

"No."

"It's the same everywhere you look."

"No, it's not, Mom."

"*Pictures*," she said scornfully as she whacked up the large, knotty carrots. "That's all you ever think about."

It was an old argument and I didn't take the bait. "Why did you want to talk to me?" I asked. Might as well get it over with.

Mom pointed her knife at me. "This college idea of yours. Your father and I have been talking. You have to start being more realistic about your future."

Oh damn, it was *that* talk. I clenched my jaw.

"College is one thing," she continued. "If you wanted to go to Cape Cod Community like Michael, get an apartment in Hyannis with some other girls for a few years, that would be okay. You're smart—you could get a business degree or a teaching certificate. You could get a loan—we'd figure it out. But art school? It's a silly idea for people like us, Jackie."

Us? I wanted to scream. "And what kind of people are we, Mom?"

"Simple people," she said immediately. "We don't have grand ideas like the kind Elsie McGavrock puts into your head. Going off to Boston or New York or someplace like that. Do you know how much it costs to go to a fancy art school, Jackie? To live in a city? A lot more than you can make working at the Blue Moon in the summer, I'll tell you that. And we don't have the money to help you pay for it."

I stared at the tabletop, rolling stray breadcrumbs together into a pasty ball. "I know. There are scholarships," I said, but so quietly I could hardly hear myself. The whole question of college was so big it overwhelmed me. Getting into the school. Getting the money to go. And then actually packing up and moving there. I hated to admit it, but that was what scared me most: leaving Provincetown, the place I knew so well the streets and alleys were practically extensions of my own body. I didn't just live in this town—it lived in me.

"Even if we did have the money," Mom said, "it's like throwing it away! Art school? What good is being an artist? Who makes a living at that?"

"Some people do." But I knew I didn't have a solid argument against her worries. I debated the issue with myself all the time. Even if I worked while I was in college, I'd be lucky to cover the cost of housing and food. I couldn't possibly earn enough to pay tuition. And even if I got a scholarship, what would happen afterward? How *would* I make a living? I knew being an artist wasn't a practical decision, but if everyone was practical there wouldn't *be* any artists. Maybe if I'd never seen those books of Picasso and Matisse, never held a charcoal pencil, never looked through a camera lens, I could be happy working in a real-estate office or teaching elementary school. But now I knew what I'd be missing. Without the chance to make art, to learn and get better at it, my life would feel so small.

"Who makes a living at it?" Mom wanted to know. "Finn's parents? Sure, they've got money, but it's just because his father won that big prize. Most people who write books or paint pictures don't live in a big house like they do. Most of them are lucky to have some little room over a garage. They wait tables until they're too old to stand up straight. Is that the life you want? I hope not."

She took a package of thawed codfish chunks from the refrigerator and located her fish knife. "It's like you've been bewitched by that Rosenberg family," she said. "Those people think they're Provincetown royalty or something."

"No, they don't. Elsie's invited you over lots of times, and you always come up with some excuse not to go. You're the snob."

But she wasn't listening to me. She was whacking up the fish with such force I was a little afraid she was going to slice off a finger and throw it in the pot with the seafood. "They're not even *from* here!" she continued. "What right do they have to give you advice? Just because they've got money doesn't mean they can run everybody's life!"

"Mom, Elsie isn't running my life. She got me interested in art, is all. She knows I love it and she wants to help me figure out how to keep doing it."

"Well, she needs to mind her own business. She's not doing you a favor making you want things you can't have. We're not rich people, Jackie. We have to make the best of the life we were given."

"That's what I'm trying to do! Elsie's helping me apply for grants and scholarships. There are ways to—"

"She's giving you false hopes! And then what? When all your big dreams fall apart, you'll be back here, crying on my shoulder. And I've got enough problems as it is."

I liked to think I was anesthetized to my mother's bitterness after years of listening to her complain. Still, it stung to be characterized as just another one of her many problems. But it also made me more determined. If I didn't get into art school, or if I couldn't come up with the money, I'd figure out the next step then. But I didn't intend to spend the rest of my life sitting around this fish-stinking kitchen listening to Teresa Silva repeat her list of resentments.

"I know you think I'm hard on you, but I'm just trying to protect you from disappointment," she said, sounding the tiniest bit apologetic. "I'm not saying you can't apply to that Tiz-Dee or whatever it is, if you've got your heart set on it."

"Riz-Dee. Rhode Island School of Design."

"Whatever. You'll see it's way too expensive. You should apply to some regular places too. Cape Cod Community, or, if you're determined to go off-Cape for some reason, UMass Boston or one of the state schools. That's the kind of place people like us go."

People like us. What did that even mean? That you were born a certain way and could never escape it? That if your parents scraped by all their lives, you were never going to have an extra shoelace either? That you shouldn't even *try* to make your life better?

My mother's default emotion was hopelessness, but it hadn't always been that way. When my older brothers were kids, Marco and Teresa actually laughed once in a while. The boys would roughhouse with each other until something got broken. "*You drive me nuts!*" Mom would yell at them, but there was pride in her voice as well as irritation. Dad would laugh off their bad behavior, saying, "I was a wild animal too at their ages."

And then, just as I got old enough to join in the romping, everything changed. Uncle Peter's fishing boat sank one miserably hot July day in a sudden squall, all hands lost at sea. For the next year Mom begged Dad to quit fishing.

"I can't do nothin' else, Teresa," he'd say, sorrowfully. "What should I do in this town? Open a hot dog stand? Sell jewelry to the tourists? Fishing is all I know how to do."

Finally she gave up trying to convince him and resigned herself to being mad at the world. My brothers graduated high school and two out of three joined Dad on his boat, the *Sally Marie*, named after my grandmother. Mom was worried sick every minute they were gone, and Dad, who was more susceptible to guilt than his children, took to stopping at the Old Colony Tap to knock back a cheap whiskey or two before coming home for dinner.

I was the good kid, the one who didn't worry my mother, who did what she was supposed to. But I was tired of being quiet and invisible. I couldn't spend the rest of my life standing in front of a kitchen stove just so my mother knew where I was every minute.

Mom had her back to me, stirring the simmering brew.

"How come Michael didn't want to work on the *Sally Marie* too?" I asked, steering the conversation away from my own future. "Did he always want to go to college?"

Mom gave a brief, triumphant smile. "I talked him into it. I couldn't stand having *all* my men out on the water." She shook her head. "I don't know what Marky and Bobby are gonna do, though. They got girlfriends—pretty soon they'll get married, have a few kids. The *Sally Marie* can't support another generation. I can't see the future for them."

She looked so forlorn, I leaned my head against her shoulder. "Mom," I said, "you can't see the future for any of us. Nobody can."

8.

The summer months passed quickly, long days of work, darkened by grief, but also sweetened by budding friendships with Charlotte and Cooper. The last week of August the Jasper Street studios had to be cleaned out for the new fellowship recipients who'd take up residence soon. From the office window I saw Finn and Tess, armed with mop, broom, bucket, and garbage bags, head into Studio 9. Over the summer other artists rented the spaces, and I knew from years past that the mess they left behind infuriated Finn.

I'd been keeping my distance from Finn all summer, but I decided I'd go talk to the two of them after I finished updating the website. Having Tessie around would make it less uncomfortable, and I didn't want to have to avoid Finn forever.

Elsie looked up too when her children walked past the building. She glanced at me and a sigh escaped her. "He'll be okay, won't he?" she asked.

"Who?" I knew she meant Finn, but I didn't want her to guess that I was thinking about him too.

"Finn. Sometimes I'm afraid he'll never get over Lorna. But he will, won't he?"

I didn't know what to say. I wanted to reassure Elsie, but I was pretty sure Finn never would get over Lorna and I didn't want to lie. Finally I said, "It hasn't been that long."

She nodded. "I know. You're right. And I don't mean to make light of the effect of it on you too, Jackie. I know you must miss her terribly."

My fingers went slack on the keyboard. "I can't believe it's been three months already."

Elsie narrowed her eyes. "What was it about Lorna that made you all so loyal to her? I know she was an exciting person, but she could be difficult sometimes too, couldn't she? A little bossy?"

I was taken aback by Elsie's criticism. She seldom had anything negative to say about anybody. "Lorna liked being in charge, if that's what you mean. But none of us minded that. We did what she wanted us to, but that was because it was more fun than anything we came up with."

"Until it wasn't." Elsie's eyes locked on mine. "I'm sorry. I know you loved her, but as Finn's mother, I worried about the way she led the three of you around. I hoped that Finn . . . well, it doesn't matter now."

"Lorna was the best thing that ever happened to us!" I couldn't believe Elsie didn't understand this.

A frown puckered her brow. "It seems to me you and Finn and Lucas were the best things that ever happened to Lorna. You supported her when her parents didn't. Or couldn't. Without the three of you, she would have been a sad little girl."

I thought about the way Lorna, at ten or twelve, would pull her long fiery hair in front of her eyes, closing the curtains so we couldn't see the emotions trampling her face. "She *was* sad sometimes. It made me want to protect her, which was ridiculous because she was a lot stronger than me."

"Oh, Jackie, I doubt that. You have an inner strength Lorna never did. I'm sure that's what she saw in all of you."

I didn't want to argue with Elsie, but if I was strong, I was pretty sure I had Lorna to thank for that too—she was my role model.

Elsie pawed through the file cabinet, a little distracted now. "I like your new friend Charlotte. Hanging out with her must be helping you get over Lorna, isn't it?"

Why did she want us all to "get over" Lorna? It wasn't going to happen. "Charlotte's great, but no one can replace Lorna."

"Of course not. I'm sorry. I put it badly," Elsie said. "I just meant it's healthy that you have a new friend. That's what I worry about with Finn—that he's stuck in the past. He can't move forward."

She was right about that, but I didn't confirm her fears.

"I'm finished here," I said. "I'll go say hi to Finn and Tess before I leave."

"Oh, do that." Elsie brightened up. "They should be done soon too. Finn can give you a ride home."

Don't get your hopes up, I thought as I walked across the parking lot toward the row of studios. Half a dozen bulging trash bags were stacked outside the open door of Studio 9. I heard Finn complaining before I saw him.

"Why can't these friggin' geniuses clean up their own messes? They can't even take a minute of their precious time to throw out the moldy food in the back of the refrigerator. I'm surprised they can manage to flush the toilets for themselves."

I stood outside the window for a second and watched as Tess filled a bucket at the sink in the corner, her arms long and graceful. She didn't look like a child anymore, another reminder that time didn't stop, whether you wanted it to or not.

"Most of them aren't that bad," Tess said. "There was this really sweet guy, Neil, here this summer. A sculptor. We had a long talk one day about how you can tell who's trustworthy and who isn't. He says you can tell by a person's voice."

Finn put down the dustpan and gave her a suspicious look. "Really? What's 'a person's voice' supposed to sound like?"

"You know. Honest."

He groaned. "And what does old Neil think honesty sounds like? A throaty whisper? An Italian tenor? Does it have a reggae beat?"

Tess sighed. "Why do I try to tell you anything?"

I knocked on the open door. "Hi guys. Don't let me interrupt your argument."

"Hey, Jackie. Come in. You can be on my side." Tess grinned as she lifted the bucket from the sink, slopping water onto the painted wood floor.

Finn glanced at me, then looked away. "Did you hear this? Some artist guy was bullshitting Tess about how honest he is and she bought it. She's so naïve." He turned to his sister again. "Did you tell old Neil you were thirteen years old?"

"You're disgusting, Finn. He wasn't coming on to me. Besides, I'm almost fourteen."

Finn flattened another pizza box and stacked it on the mattress with half a dozen others. "Thirteen and a half. And, by the way, when did you start wearing so much makeup?"

"Oh, my God, Finn, shut up! You sound like Mom! I hardly wear any makeup compared to my friends."

"Ask Jackie. It makes you look older than you are. Guys'll take advantage of you. Tell her."

I put up my hands and stepped back. It wasn't the first time I'd heard these two squabble, and I knew better than to get in the middle of it. Not that they ever drew blood. In fact, I'd always envied their relationship—they teased and argued, but they stuck up for each other too. As opposed to my three brothers who traveled as a pack, continually punching each other like prizefighters, but never taking much notice of me.

"You think I'm stupid, but I'm not." Tess squirted Lysol into the bucket and swished the mop around in the water. "You need to get a life, Finn, and stop bugging me about mine."

Finn grabbed a broom and attacked the floor beneath the bed.

"Are you giving that to Jackie?" Tess pointed to a box full of art supplies—pieces of canvas, sheets of newsprint, and half-used tubes of paint.

"Oh, yeah. Those are the discards from this year's spoiled brats."

Finn always saved any left-behind art supplies for me, even though he was conflicted about it. I rifled through the box excitedly.

"There's some great stuff in here. Thanks."

He grunted. "You know I hate aiding and abetting you in this art business." I was actually happy to hear him grumble at me. It was the most normal conversation we'd had in months.

"God, Finn, you're such an old grouch!" Tess said. "Mom loves your new collages, Jackie, the ones that are layered on top of cloud photographs. I do too."

"Thanks, Tess."

Finn sighed. "I'm not saying I don't like the pictures. I'm just not sure Mom should encourage you so much."

Tess plopped the mop back into the bucket. "Why the hell not?"

"Yeah, Finn," I said. "Why the hell not?" I'd heard his objections before, but I was glad to have a safe subject to talk about, even if we disagreed.

"Don't get mad. It's not about how good you are. It's about you thinking this is going to be your life's work. Like taking photographs is a real *job*."

"It *is* a real job for some people," I said.

He shook his head. "You don't get it. Art's a big game, and a lot of people lose. Making art that somebody wants to pay for is an unrealistic goal for . . . well, you know."

I did know, but I'd never heard him put it so bluntly before and it hurt my feelings. "You mean it's unrealistic for somebody like me? A *poor* person. You sound just like my mother. She thinks only rich people should go to art school."

"I don't know why *anybody* wants to go to art school," Finn said. "Is it living in Provincetown that makes people think they need to write sonnets or dab oil on canvas? Not everybody needs to express themselves creatively."

"Maybe not," Tess said, as her mop swabbed the floorboards and her brother's sneakers simultaneously. "But Jackie does, don't you?"

I nodded and tried to swallow the anger that pushed up into my throat.

Finn went into the small bathroom and returned in a minute, dragging a badly mildewed shower curtain behind him. He rolled it up and stuck it in a trash bag.

"Look, Jackie, I'm not saying you won't make it. Maybe you will. Maybe you'll turn into one of these conceited jerks we get here who think it's beneath them to speak to anyone without a book contract or a New York gallery. But I hope not."

"Jackie would never do that," Tess said.

"They all do." Finn pointed an elbow toward the open doorway. "Speak of the devil," Finn said, his lip curling up on one side. "There's the Crown Prince of Affected Assholes."

Elsie and Cooper were standing in the parking lot, talking. I hadn't seen Cooper all week, and my stomach fluttered a little at the sight of him. I'd missed him, missed his soft voice and comforting presence. But I didn't contradict Finn. He'd always been a little jealous of Cooper, maybe because his parents liked him so much. Anyway, I didn't want Finn, or anyone else, to suspect I had a little crush on the guy. It could only be embarrassing.

Tess looked out the door. "Who? Not Cooper?"

Finn glared at his sister. "Of *course*, Cooper!"

"You're crazy, Finn. He's, like, my favorite person. He's nice to everybody."

Finn groaned. "Oh, my God, you must be related to Mom. You're both genetically blind to douchebags."

Tess rolled her eyes. "I don't think so. I can see *you* without any problem. Why don't you stop bitching and take the trash out. I want to finish this floor and *go home*."

Finn hoisted a bag onto his shoulder and grabbed another with the other hand.

"I'll help you," I said, grabbing two more bags.

He gave me a quick grin. "See what I mean? You don't have the jerkitude necessary to be an artist."

I figured that was as close as I'd get to an apology. Cooper smiled a warm greeting as I lugged the bags to the Dumpster, and for a moment I didn't care what Finn thought.

Finn and I were washing our hands in the custodian's room when Tess came in to empty her bucket and rinse out the mop.

"How come you don't have a boyfriend, Jackie?" she asked, out of the blue.

Tess had always been adorably outspoken, but it wasn't usually at my expense. I felt my cheeks color. "I don't know."

Finn was careful not to look at me. "You're so nosy, Tess. Maybe Jackie doesn't want a boyfriend. Did you ever think of that?"

"Bull. Everybody wants a boyfriend. Unless they want a girlfriend." Tess took off her wet sneakers and slipped into flip-flops. "You should be Jackie's boyfriend, Finn," she said lightly.

"Tessie!" I couldn't believe she'd said that.

"Ignore her," Finn said, flatly. "She thinks she's being outrageous, but she's just annoying."

"No, I'm not!" Tess pouted.

Finn dried his hands on his jeans and bolted out the door.

"It just makes sense," Tess said to me. "You guys have known each other forever and you're both tall and nice-looking. And you know Mom loves you, Jackie, and so do I."

"Tessie, you can't pick out partners for other people. It doesn't work that way."

"But you've always liked Finn, haven't you? I watched you two walk on the beach once. You looked right together."

I was starting to feel sick. Why did everybody but Finn think he and I would make a great couple? "Tessie, I like Finn, but that's not the point. Besides, he's still in love with Lorna."

"Well, he can't be in love with her *forever*," Tess said, with the certainty of a thirteen-year-old.

Finn pulled his gently used Prius up to the door and honked the horn. "Come on, Tess. I want to get home. Jackie, your art stuff is in the backseat so I might as well drop you off too."

He sounded resigned to his duty.

"I can walk. I always walk—"

"Get in, Jackie. Don't be silly."

The command surprised me, but I figured he was embarrassed by Tess's remarks too. I climbed silently into the backseat.

Tess got in the front and slammed the door. She was quiet for a minute as Finn turned the car toward the West End. Then she turned and glared at her brother.

"Lorna's not coming back. You know that, right?"

9.

I liked to leave my house early so I could meander to the Blue Moon, taking pictures along the way. This morning I walked down Cottage Street past the clapboard house where Lucas used to live, and felt the familiar ache of longing for my disappeared childhood. I wanted to feel it, wanted to roll around in nostalgia a little bit.

All four of us used to live in the West End within a few blocks of each other until Lucas's dads saved up enough money to open the bed-and-breakfast inn on the other end of town. Finn still lived in his family's enormous place on the bay beach, with views all the way up the arm of the Cape to Wellfleet, and Lorna's mother still owned her ramshackle house on nearby Franklin Street. At least I assumed she did—I hadn't seen her in months. I felt like my ten-year-old self was following me down the streets where we used to run, a pack of loud, skinny, barefoot monkeys, pushing and shoving each other, laughing at just about everything. Now I was a kind of tourist, looking for the remains of my life, taking photographs of what we'd left behind.

I went to the breakwater first. I'd probably taken more pictures of the breakwater than of any other spot in town—at all times of the day, in every kind of weather. Since the accident, I didn't walk out on it anymore—I hadn't all summer—but I still liked seeing it through the lens, framing it in the viewfinder.

Walking back into town along the beach, I slowed down at Dugan's Cottages, a row of shabby shacks that rented during the summer to last-minute vacationers willing to tolerate a little mold to have the beach outside their door. Unheated and without insulation, they were boarded up from the end of August through late May. The spot was prime real estate, and developers had tried to buy it for years, but Mrs. Dugan wouldn't sell. She said she wanted to keep one little piece of Provincetown the way it had been for half a century.

When we were kids, Dugan's Cottages were our off-season hideout, especially Cabin 5, which backed up to a patch of pine trees and could be approached without anyone seeing us. The way the cottage was tucked back into the trees, it was invisible from the street, and in the winter that stretch of beach was always deserted. All it took was a screwdriver to pry the boards off a grimy window. The four of us spent hours in that cottage, pretending to be thieves or pilgrims or pirates, runaways hiding out.

When we were little, we sometimes played "house" too, the way kids do. As I remembered it, Lorna never wanted to be the mother, whether because it was too boring a role or because her model for it was such a bad one, I didn't know. But I liked playing the part of the perfect mama who kissed knees, settled arguments, and tucked her children into bed. I was often a single mother, because Finn never wanted to be the father, and neither he nor Lorna was willing to play the child very often. Lucas could sometimes be coerced into one of those roles, but the other two preferred more dramatic parts.

Finn liked to pretend he was the captain of a ship that had wrecked on our shore, someone who'd had many adventures he'd happily recount to those of us more shore-bound. But Lorna usually wanted to be a mysterious person of some kind. Someone whose life we had to guess at. I think she didn't always know herself who she was supposed to be, but she liked to hear our guesses: circus performer, famous actress, amnesia sufferer found wandering on the dunes. That last one was her favorite role, a woman with a cleanly erased past who might have been anything, but now had to start all over.

As we got older the cabin became our clubhouse where we shared secrets we told no one else. Some were about petty arguments with family or classmates, some about stand-offs with teachers, but sometimes the topic was more important and we took our roles as confidants seriously. When Lucas's dads were fighting a lot and he was afraid they might split up, we huddled around him on the creaky sofa and listened intently to the fears that never materialized. When Lorna's mother was arrested for shoplifting a bunch of expensive cheeses from the Stop & Shop, we let Lorna pace and curse and throw things until she settled down. Every one of us offered her rooms in our houses should Carla go to jail. That didn't happen, even though Lorna kind of wished it would (and so did we).

Finn and Lorna may have used the cabin for other purposes too, the last few years. They'd been sleeping together since they were fifteen, and the cabin would have provided the privacy that neither of their houses did. But that was a subject they didn't talk about with me or Lucas. Why wouldn't they sleep together at Dugan's? From September through May Cabin 5 was our own secluded refuge and no adult ever knew.

I hadn't walked past the cabin all summer. In season it was usually rented, and I hated seeing other people in our place. But I noticed that Mrs. Dugan, never a procrastinator, had already gotten someone to board up the windows, even though it wasn't quite Labor Day. I walked the perimeter of the place, taking shots of the rusty hinges and weathered shingles. I wondered if it was still furnished with the same ancient, uncomfortable furniture—the couch springs broken, the mattress on the bed moldy, the pots and pans in the tiny kitchen pitted and burned? Even as kids we knew it was kind of a crummy place to spend a vacation, but it was a palace to us, our headquarters, our home.

Daydreaming, I lost track of time. Before I knew it, it was almost seven and I had to run to the café. Most of the shops weren't open yet. Tourists slept late and the locals, out early, didn't need lighthouse key rings or sweaters for their dogs. By ten o'clock Commercial Street would be thronged with the usual assortment of characters: vacationing parents blocking the sidewalk with their double strollers, young men in short shorts, high heels, and silvery makeup handing out flyers for the drag shows, hand-holding women in matching Cape Cod sweatshirts, and a smattering of year-rounders trying to keep up a normal pace as they headed to the pharmacy to pick up prescriptions.

I loved all of it: the quiet, dawn beach and the pushy throngs on the sidewalk. The smell of fish on the wind and the scent of incense from the head shop. I loved the flapping boat flags strung across Commercial Street, faded after a season of sunlight, and the rainbow banners flying in front of stores selling everything from antique mirrors to lobster salt-and-pepper shakers. I breathed it in like pure oxygen, wondering if I would ever be able to live anywhere else.

"My last day for the season," I said as I started another pot of coffee through the machine.

"I know," Char said. "Dad'll give you some weekend shifts this fall if you want them. He likes you."

I laughed. "I guess you didn't tell him about the syrup fiasco then?"

"What he doesn't know can't come back to bite us in the ass," she whispered.

"If he needs help later in the fall, I'd love to pick up some shifts, but I want to get my portfolio together the next few weeks, not to mention all the other application stuff. Early decision deadline for RISD is November first. Money won't matter if I don't get in."

I picked up the full coffeepot and made the rounds of the room. The man at the table in the window, a regular customer who usually stayed long enough to read the *New York Times* front to back, asked for his fifth refill of the morning.

Charlotte carefully sliced bagels, her bandaged finger proving it's the most dangerous job in the café. When I came back behind the counter she said, "I can't believe summer's over already. And we're seniors in high school. That's just weird."

"I know."

"Has Lucas come back yet?"

"Not that I know of."

"He's coming back though, isn't he?"

I shrugged. "Don't ask me. He doesn't answer my e-mails."

"I always kind of liked Lucas. I mean, he's a little goofy, but . . ." Charlotte's voice trailed off and her eyeballs bulged as she looked over my shoulder. The bell on the door announced an entrance, but the look on Charlotte's face was reporting a ghost. Who the hell had just come in?

"Um, maybe you shouldn't turn around," Char said.

But what else could I do? I couldn't run into the kitchen and hide—I *worked* there.

So I took a deep breath and turned slowly to face the customer. For just a moment I thought it *was* a ghost. But then I recognized Carla, her hair dyed the exact bold coppery-red that Lorna's had been naturally, parted in the middle and hanging straight down the sides of her face. Her cheeks glowed with sparkly blush and her mouth was thick with dark red lipstick. Her bony legs looked translucent beneath short white shorts, and a skimpy tank top, which I was sure had once belonged to her daughter, drooped at her neck. She looked like Lorna, but Lorna old, haggard, scary, and probably out of her mind.

"Well, look who works here!" Carla sang out. "I wondered what the hell happened to you!"

"I, I came by the house," I stuttered. "I knocked on the door, but nobody—"

"Yeah, I was hiding out for a while. But then they told me they were gonna fire my ass from the store if I didn't start coming in, and I only had about two nickels left in the bank, so I got my shit together. Onward!" She punched her right arm into the air, and then, a little unsteady on her platform sandals, gripped the countertop. "Nobody keeps Carla Trovato down!"

I wondered if she was drunk. It wouldn't be the first time she was wasted at ten in the morning. On the other hand, her regular personality was so bizarre, you couldn't always tell.

Charlotte disappeared into the kitchen, but I was sure she was listening to every word.

"So you're still managing Old Hat then?" I asked Carla.

A low growl curled out of her mouth. "For what it's worth. Nobody wants that old vintage crap anymore."

"I don't think that's true. The store always seems busy."

Carla's lip turned up at the corner and I could feel her scorn coming before it hit me. "Whatayou know about it, wiseass? You think you're so smart!"

Her disgust ripped a hole in my memory. Lorna's mother had always been like this—irritable and mean. You tried to feel sorry for her—husband gone, only child drowned—but it was hard. She didn't allow sympathy.

I had the same sick feeling in my stomach that I remembered having at ten when I first hung out at Lorna's house. I'd tried to act nonchalant when her mother swore at her, but the poison between them infected me too. My parents cursed sometimes, when they were arguing or when their kids were driving them crazy, but their voices were never full of contempt like Carla's. I didn't know how Lorna could stand up under the ugliness. After a few visits to the Trovato house, I always asked Lorna to come to my place instead. She never argued.

"Some of these idiots around here, they come into the store just to stare at me—I know they do." Carla's voice got louder as she ranted. "They don't want to buy anything. They just look at me with their big, leaky cow eyes. They want me to start bawling in front of them or something. They want me to give 'em a show." She grunted. "Fat chance!"

"Well, I'm glad to hear you're doing okay," I said, turning aside to ring up some other customers who were waiting by the cash register.

"You think I'm doing *okay*?" Carla laughed loud enough to get the attention of the paper-reading man in the window who frowned at the disturbance. The couple at the cash register exchanged a meaningful glance as they pocketed their change and left. "God, I forgot how naïve you are, Jackie. You're so clueless. Even Lorna used to say that."

She did not. I wiped any lingering trace of kindness from my face. "Can I get you something, Carla? Coffee?"

Carla looked down at the red plastic watch flopping around her skinny wrist. "Damn it, I'm late again. Just give me a coffee to go. Large. Black."

My hand trembled as I poured the coffee into the paper cup. The liquid was very hot and under normal circumstances I would have given the customer a second cup to help absorb the heat, but there was nothing normal about these circumstances. *Spill it all over yourself,* I thought. *I don't care.*

Carla slapped a lid on the cup, oblivious to the coffee's temperature, and tossed two dollar bills on the counter.

"Come by the store," she said as she headed for the door. "I'll give you a discount."

As soon as she was out of sight, I fell back onto a stool. Charlotte was immediately beside me.

"Oh, my God. That was Lorna's mother, wasn't it? She's awful!"

I nodded. "Good thing it's my last day here for the season. Now that she knows where to find me she might stop by to insult me every morning."

"Was she always like this?"

"Since I've known her. Like this and worse."

An ugly scene I'd witnessed years before flashed back to me, one I'd revisited often over the years. It must have been the summer we were twelve. I had a hand-me-down banana bike that had belonged to one or more of my brothers, and Lorna would perch on the seat behind me to ride out to the beach at Herring Cove. I still looked like a stick figure at that age and wore an old, worn-thin, racer-back tank suit, but Lorna was already filling out and she'd gotten a string bikini somewhere, maybe Goodwill, that fit her perfectly.

She attracted a lot of attention in that suit. Grown men would turn around and look at her, which gave me the creeps, but I think she kind of liked it. Finn and Lucas didn't go to the beach with us much that summer, and looking back on it, I think they were probably uncomfortable around Lorna in that suit. Until then we'd just been four pals, and even though I had secret feelings for Finn, and I'm sure both Finn and Lucas had their dreams about Lorna, on the surface we were best friends in a perfectly sexless way. Until Lorna wore that bikini and made it impossible.

So it was just the two of us at Herring Cove that day. We'd already been in the water to cool off and were just about to lie down on our towels when we heard her tearing up the sand toward us. Carla, drunk and mad. I don't know where she came from. She must have been riding around with one of her drinking buddies and spotted us. She flew at Lorna, grabbing one of her arms and yanking it so hard I felt the pain in my own shoulder.

"You stupid little slut!" she screamed. "What the hell are you doing prancing around out here half naked?"

Lorna tried to pull away from her. People all around were staring at us and I knew she was embarrassed, but Carla was unstoppable once she got going.

"You're just asking for it, aren't cha?" Carla yelled. "Advertising yourself like a cheap whore! You might as well just take the whole thing off!" She grabbed one of the strings at the side of Lorna's bikini bottom and yanked the bow open.

"Mom!" Lorna jumped away from her and managed to get the string tied again, but I could see her hands shaking.

A middle-aged man who'd been sitting nearby with his whole family got up and came over to Carla and started telling her to leave the girl alone or he'd call the police. He had his cell phone out and everything. The beach was crowded and it felt like about a hundred people were staring at us. We were a cheap show for the tourists.

While Carla cussed out the man with the cell phone, Lorna took off running down the beach. I figured she'd wait for me at the changing rooms, so I gathered up our towels and lotion and rode my bike there.

I found her pacing around the outdoor drinking fountain. The look in her eyes was so murderous I thought if she'd had a gun or a knife she'd probably go back and finish Carla off. I kind of wanted to myself. Instead we rode to my house and didn't say a word about it. Not then and not ever.

"I can't even imagine having a mother that whacked out," Charlotte said. "When she first walked in, with that weird outfit and everything, I thought for a minute . . . I mean, she looked so much like . . ."

"I know."

Charlotte shook her head. "It makes more sense when you see her mother."

I was stumped. "What makes more sense?"

She flushed and turned aside, noisily rearranging dirty dishes in the plastic bin. "Well, I just mean, if you believe what some people are saying. Which I don't, necessarily."

I stood up, putting myself in Charlotte's line of vision. "What are some people saying?"

"You know. That Lorna . . . that maybe . . . it wasn't an accident."

I stumbled backward. "Who says that? *Who*?"

"I don't know. Some people. I shouldn't have said anything."

"Well, those people should shut the hell up! They didn't even *know* Lorna!"

"But her mother said it too, didn't she? After the memorial service?"

"Charlotte, are you really saying you believe that woman who was just in here? Who is obviously out of her mind?"

The man in the window didn't appreciate the continuing noise. He folded his unfinished newspaper under his arm and gave us a disgusted look as he headed out the door.

"I'm not saying I believe it, just that I understand why people do," she said. "Personally, I think she just fell. She wasn't the suicidal type, was she?"

"Lorna absolutely did not kill herself. I *know* that, Charlotte. I don't know what happened, but I know it wasn't that." How could I not know what happened? I was *there*!

Charlotte nodded. "Okay. I'm sorry I said anything."

I grabbed the plastic bin from her hands and took it back to the dishwasher, but I couldn't put aside the disturbing conversation so easily. I came back out with a tray of clean coffee cups and banged it onto the counter. "I feel like I have to prove it now. I hate that people are talking about her like that."

"It's a small town," she said. "They'll forget about it as soon as they have something else to talk about."

A young couple pushing a stroller came bumping through the door, arguing. Charlotte grabbed two menus and led them to a corner table.

No, I thought, people wouldn't forget about it. They'd remember the story they'd made up themselves starring Lorna as the girl who killed herself by jumping off the breakwater in the middle of a raging storm. She'd become part of the mythology of Provincetown, like the severed hand found in the dunes years ago, or the fishing boat that disappeared without a trace two miles outside the harbor. They'd turn her into a mermaid or something, and blame shipwrecks on her.

If only I could figure out the truth. But already I could feel Lorna slipping away from me, lost not only to the waves, but also to gossip and rumor.

10.

My stomach tightened when I came around the corner and saw the JSAC gallery all lit up. It was opening night for the new season and Carolyn Winter, the artist whose show was hanging, had come up from New York for the occasion. Her canvases had been bought by the Museum of Modern Art in New York City, the Boston Museum of Fine Arts—by museums all over the world. It wasn't unusual for well-known artists to visit Jasper Street, but Carolyn Winter was Elsie's old friend and she'd promised to introduce me tonight, which made me nervous. What were you supposed to say to famous people?

The crowd spilled out the door onto the street, women in bright-colored clothes and men with scruffy beards in animated conversation. JSAC was the most exciting place in town, I thought, to everyone but Finn. Of course, he'd be here anyway. Rather than pay for a bartender, Elsie usually roped Finn into standing behind a table of cheap wine with a dark scowl on his face that stopped everybody but the total lushes from asking for a second free drink.

"Sweetheart!" Elsie called as I walked into the small, boxy gallery. Her turquoise dress swirled around her hips as she turned away from the knot of people she was talking to and put her arm around my waist.

"Big crowd, huh?"

She nodded. "Carolyn has a following."

I stared at the walls, a little overcome by seeing the work of someone I admired at such close range. I'd purposely stayed away from the gallery the past few days while the canvases were being hung so that the spectacle of twenty-five Carolyn Winter paintings all hanging here together would overwhelm me. But what I always forgot was that openings were parties, which was frustrating to somebody like me who just wanted to stand quietly and look at the work. People walked in front of you, dropping cracker crumbs, spilling wine, and yakking endlessly. I'd have to come back later in the week to experience the paintings the way I wanted to.

Elsie unwound a fuchsia silk scarf from her neck and tied it around mine, which lessened the navy blue cloak-of-invisibility look I had going. "This color looks great on you," she said. She took my hand and led me into the main room where a lanky woman in a black dress and an enormous silver necklace was holding court. As always, the circle opened to admit Elsie.

"Carolyn, this is Jackie Silva, the girl I told you about."

"Of course." Carolyn Winter extended a clammy hand in my direction.

"I'm honored to meet you," I said in a hushed tone. "Elsie showed me your book and the pieces she owns and I just love your work!" The other people standing in the circle smiled at me condescendingly, as if I were twelve. What *should* I have said?

"I'm happy to know the next generation finds something of interest in my work," Carolyn Winter said, staring over my shoulder at someone behind me. I knew Finn would be incredibly annoyed by her, but Carolyn Winter was famous for good reason, and I was willing to put up with a little arrogance from someone whose work I admired so much.

From out of nowhere, Cooper appeared. He smiled at me, which I imagined turned my face a lovely oven-baked red. "Jackie's an artist, too," he said to Carolyn Winter. "A good one. And she's still in high school."

"*Is* she?" Carolyn Winter's icy composure melted a little as she turned to Cooper. "And you should know about youthful talent. You were quite the prodigy yourself, weren't you? An *enfant terrible*."

Cooper laughed easily and said, "I'm not really all that terrible."

"But you've published now, haven't you? And rather successfully, I hear."

I could tell Cooper was pleased the guest of honor recognized him. It didn't surprise me, though—he was the kind of person you didn't forget.

"Jackie makes the most *wonderful* photo-collages," Elsie said, a valiant effort to bring the conversation back to me.

But it was too late. Carolyn Winter was being drawn off to another circle of admirers and didn't hear. I wasn't surprised. She must meet young artists all the time—why would she be interested in me?

"She's busy now. I'll show her the pieces I have at the house later this evening," Elsie said, then flew off in another direction.

But Cooper's eyes were still fastened on me, and as the rest of the group followed the artist, he came closer. "Don't stare at the star. Artists are skittish animals. You'll scare her away."

"I wasn't staring."

"Sure you were. Your eyes got huge and smoky. Beautiful, really."

I looked down at my ragged fingernails, ashamed that Cooper recognized the longing on my face.

"Don't let people like that impress you too much," he said. "She's just having her fifteen minutes of fame."

"I don't think so," I said. "She's the real thing."

He shrugged. "Maybe. Maybe not. Just because her paintings sell for ridiculous prices now doesn't mean she'll last long. The art world is fickle."

Standing next to Cooper with Elsie's expensive scarf wrapping my neck, I felt a little bolder than usual and dared to be a little bit flirtatious. "Is the publishing world fickle too? Do you think you'll last?" I looked up at Cooper and, over his shoulder, saw Finn glaring at me from his station at the wine and cheese table. God, couldn't I have fun for *one minute* without being caught out by him? Did I have to be sunken in gloom constantly, just because he was? I felt my cheeks flush hot, but not with embarrassment.

Cooper laughed and put a hand on my arm. "I don't know. I'm trying to enjoy my fifteen minutes without looking too far ahead."

I made sure that Finn could see me grinning up at Cooper. The hell with him. "I haven't read your book yet, but I want to. I was so busy with work this summer and now there's all this college stuff to do, but—"

"There's no rush," he said, kindly. "You're young. I'm sure your own life is much more interesting than anything I could make up."

That certainly wasn't true, but I didn't say so.

"It's stuffy in here," Cooper said. "Let's go outside a minute and catch a breeze."

"Sure," I said, as if it were no big deal to me one way or the other.

He put a hand on my elbow, which seemed like such an adult thing to do, and led me past the meager wine selection and skimpy platter of Triscuits and Brie to the open door. I could feel Finn's disapproval grab at me as we passed, and I was amazed at how easy it was to ignore him.

We headed away from the crowd, toward the back of the long studio building where the gallery lights didn't quite reach. Cooper let go of my arm and leaned against a post, at ease and smiling.

"I'm glad you're here," he said. "I get so tired of the artificiality at these things. I like that you don't pretend to be someone you aren't. You're just *you*, Jacqueline. No pretenses."

"Nobody calls me Jacqueline," I said, pretending I hadn't heard the rest of his lovely sentence.

"No? I think I will. You deserve a more sophisticated name than Jackie."

I tipped my head to the side. "You know, I'm named after Jackie Kennedy Onassis. She was pretty darn sophisticated." Was I actually *flirting* with Cooper? When did I learn to do that?

He cocked his head to match mine. "She's got nothin' on you, Jacqueline Silva."

And then I realized how simple it would be to lean into him and wait for him to kiss me. Surely he would. It just seemed like what ought to happen next. Or maybe I could even kiss him—although I was pretty scared by the terrible outcome the last time I tried that maneuver. But this was different. Cooper wasn't an unhappy teenager mourning his girlfriend. He was a full-grown man who obviously liked me. He'd kiss me, wouldn't he? What was the big deal? Cooper Thorne must have kissed a lot of girls in his life—kissing one more wouldn't be a life-or-death decision for him.

The problem was that, somehow, I'd gotten to be seventeen years old without ever having kissed anyone but Lucas Baskin-Snow—I couldn't count my humiliating attempt with Finn—and that experience had not taught me much about technique. What if I was a lousy kisser?

Cooper put his hands on my arms and rubbed them gently shoulder to elbow until an electrical current hummed through my body.

"You chilly out here?" he said.

"I'm good," I said.

"You *are* good." His voice was quiet and seemed to penetrate my skin.

I took one careful step toward him and was just about to tilt forward into his magnetic field when I heard someone coming up in back of me.

"Jackie? Are you out here?" Finn called into the darkness, swinging a flashlight back and forth. His tone of voice implied that he was my babysitter and I was being a very naughty girl.

"I'm right here," I said, backing away from Cooper. "What do you want?"

Finn shone the flashlight into my eyes and I put up my hand against it. "Do you really need that thing?"

"It's dark out. I wondered where you went." Finn lowered the light and stared, not at me but at Cooper.

"We came out to get a little air," Cooper said, evenly. "It's stuffy when the gallery's full. In more ways than one."

Finn shifted his gaze to me. "You should come in. Simon and Billy are here. They've got news."

That got my attention. "Is Lucas coming back?"

"Yeah. Come on. They'll tell you."

"Go talk to your friends," Cooper said, giving my arm a gentle squeeze. "I'll see you later."

"Okay." I hated turning away from him, but I had no choice. Finn's timing was terrible, or maybe it was perfect.

11.

"I can't believe you were out here with *him*," Finn said as he lit the path back into the gallery. "Do you know how old he is?"

"Of course I know how old he is."

"He's *thirty*!"

"I know, Finn!" Although in truth I'd been thinking twenty-eight, twenty-nine, which seemed a lot younger than thirty. "Why is this your business?"

He got quiet. "It's not. Except, we're friends and I don't like that guy."

"Oh, we're friends? I wasn't sure."

He ignored my sarcasm. "Why does everybody think Cooper's the greatest thing since soy lattes? I thought you had more sense."

"You know, Finn, you're the only person I know who *doesn't* like Cooper. How did you get to be so much smarter than everybody else?"

He grumbled at that, but he shut up.

Billy Snow, in striped shorts and flip-flops, grabbed me the minute I came through the door and hugged me hard enough to crack a rib. "Here's my girl! Don't you look great with that scarf! Here, let me tie it for you—I watched this YouTube video that shows you twenty different ways to tie a scarf." He flipped the thing over and under in a very complicated series of steps, as if his reputation depended on getting it tied perfectly. Something had obviously changed since he and Simon gave me the cold shoulder at Lorna's memorial service a few months ago.

Simon's Oxford shirt was tucked neatly into his ironed jeans. As usual the two of them seem to have dressed for completely different occasions. "Stop fussing at her," Simon told Billy as he leaned down and kissed my cheek. "We've missed you, hon."

"It's been a while," I said, tactfully. I knew exactly how long it had been, and I'd missed them too, almost as much as I missed Lucas. Simon and Billy had always liked having the four of us gather at their house so they'd have a front-row seat for our conversations. Billy provided gourmet snacks in return for being allowed to hang out and act like a teenager himself. Simon, I think, had some idea that we were going to divulge important secrets that he'd be the first parent to hear. But since Lucas left they'd apparently been hiding out at their B&B, the Foxtrot Inn, keeping a secret of their own.

"Tell her what you told me," Finn said.

Simon smiled hugely. "Lucas is coming home. He'll be here Sunday afternoon."

"Really? Why's he been gone so long? How come he never—"

Simon interrupted my questions. "I know you guys'll want to see him right away, so come over after dinner on Sunday. I'll make a cheesecake for dessert."

"And espresso. We've got a new machine," Billy added.

I looked at Finn, who didn't seem all that eager. "Well, I guess I can come," I said.

Finn shrugged. "Okay."

I figured he was pissed off that Simon and Billy expected us to drop everything and dash right over to see Lucas the first possible minute he was back, when Lucas hadn't even bothered to e-mail us the entire summer. It *was* annoying. But we had to go. We needed answers.

"We missed him this summer," I said.

Simon looked a little embarrassed, and I thought he might actually apologize to me, but then Billy started hitting him on the back and pointing toward the other room. "Look! Candace is here! How did she sneak in without us seeing her?"

Billy left in pursuit of his friend, and Simon rested a hand on my shoulder, briefly. "So, we'll see you two Sunday then? Around seven." He smiled and went off after Billy.

"That was kind of weird," I said.

"*Kind of?* How about extremely weird?" Finn shook his head. "We're supposed to go over there and eat dessert and pretend like Lucas didn't just disappear on us? I'll go, but Lucas better have something to say this time. I have to go guard the booze, but hang around and I'll give you a ride home after, okay?"

I nodded and Finn returned to his station. The crowd was starting to thin out, which gave me a chance to actually see the pictures on the wall. It also allowed me to glimpse Carolyn Winter standing in a far corner with Cooper, dipping her pinky finger into his glass of wine and then daintily licking it clean. God, did *she* know how old Cooper was? Did she know how old *she* was? I walked into the other room so I didn't have to watch my idol tarnish any further.

Before long the gallery emptied out and Finn started cleaning up the mess. The cheese platter had been decimated—colored toothpicks lay scattered on the plate like tiny Pick-Up Sticks—and somebody had squashed a bunch of purple grapes into the wood floor.

Rudolph stood in front of the pastry plate from the Portuguese Bakery, stuffing a custard tart in his mouth. He was wearing an expensive gray jacket that puckered a little at his waist. When Rudolph saw Finn he pointed to the smushed grapes. "Somebody could slip on that," he said, his mouth still full.

"Unless somebody cleaned it up," Finn said. He looked his father in the eye as he grabbed a roll of paper towels, ripped off a sheet, and bent down.

Rudy laughed good-naturedly. "You're the one who longs for a life of menial labor, Son, not me."

"You think fishing is menial labor?"

"I think it's damned hard work the likes of which you've never done in your life."

"Neither have you."

"Nor do I aspire to."

Finn rolled a trashcan over to the table and deposited soggy napkins and picked-over crackers into it. While I waited, I kept busy dumping the dregs out of wine bottles and gathering up the stained tablecloth. Rudolph scooped up the remaining tray of pastries.

"Jackie, have you had one of these?" he asked. "They're excellent! Try one." He held the platter under my nose.

"I'm really not—" I didn't want one, but somehow Rudy got a tart into my hand anyway. He was a hard man to say no to.

"She doesn't want it, Dad," Finn said. "Tell him you don't want it, Jackie."

"It's okay," I said, taking a nibble. "Thanks . . . Rudolph." Finn's dad liked everybody to call him by his first name, but I was never quite comfortable doing it. When I told Finn I felt odd calling a literary lion Rudolph, he said I should just think of him as Rudolph the Literary Reindeer.

Rudolph beamed at me. "Good, isn't it?"

Finn rolled his eyes. "Her mother probably *made* it."

For a moment Rudolph was confused, but then a light went on. "Oh, I forgot your mother works at the Portuguese Bakery. Lucky you!"

"Aren't you guys taking Carolyn Winter out for dinner?" Finn said.

"That's the ritual," Rudy said, glancing across the room. "Looks like she's glommed onto Coop."

Finn stacked the empty wine bottles into a box. "There's a perfect match."

"Oh, he'll deflect her gracefully," Rudy said. "He's used to women falling all over him."

The last bite of pastry turned to wet cardboard in my mouth.

Finn shook his head. "I don't get it. What's the big deal about that guy?"

I felt like he was really asking me, but I stayed silent.

Rudy raked his hand through his long gray hair. "Women like a winner, Son. He's a good-looking guy *and* he got a decent review in the *New York Times*. Not that I think that necessarily places him among the immortals."

"You mean, like you and Charles Dickens?" Finn said.

Rudolph ignored the jab. I concentrated on wiping custard off my sticky fingers.

"You and Jackie should go out too," Rudy said, jovially. "The night is young and you start back to school next week."

I was careful not to look at Finn. Why was everyone in the Rosenberg family trying to push us together? After our beach mishap, I found it excruciating, and I was sure Finn did too. "I told my mom I'd be home early," I lied.

"Well, let Finn drive you home at least."

"I *intend* to drive her home, Dad. Could you butt out, please?" Finn banged closed the legs of the folding table and leaned it against the wall. "I don't need you to arrange my life for me."

"Well, I'm not sure that's true," Rudy said, chuckling.

"Let's go, Jackie," Finn ordered, without looking at me.

"Wait!" I was trying to untie the complicated knot in Elsie's scarf.

From across the room she saw what I was doing and called over. "Keep it, Jackie. It looks better with your complexion than mine."

By the time I jogged out to Finn's car, he was sitting behind the wheel, glaring at the odometer. "Why do my parents have to have their fingerprints on everything? *Go out with Jackie. Apply to the college I went to.* Like I can't think for myself. They even do it to you—*Wear this scarf. Meet this famous person. Eat the stupid tart.* Why can't they back the hell off once in a while?"

"They make you crazy because they're your parents, Finn, but they're really generous people. Your mom's always giving me things. And look how much time and money they've put into the Center. They've helped so many artists and writers. You can't blame them for wanting to help their own son too."

"I don't *want* their help." Finn started the car, but kept grumbling. "Anyway, they're only running an art center. It's not like they're saving the rainforests or something."

"Supporting the arts is not trivial, Finn. I know art isn't important to you, but for some people it's . . . well, it's a way to pull yourself up out of the muck of everyday life."

Finn was quiet as we drove down Bradford Street. Finally he said, "I think I like the muck of everyday life."

He made me smile. "Well, you can afford to like it. You didn't grow up with a matching set of depressed parents who think being broke is hereditary, like bad eyesight or weak ankles. To me, art is a luxury I always thought was out of my reach."

He nodded. "I guess I get that. Sorry if I'm being an asshole." He calmed down and slowed the car as we turned the corner.

"It's okay," I said. "An asshole wouldn't apologize. I take it Rudy's still pushing Dartmouth?"

"Of course he is, but I'm sure as hell not going to his alma mater."

"It's a good school, Finn."

"I don't care. If I go to college, I'm going someplace they've never heard of Rudolph Rosenberg."

"And where would that be?"

"I don't know. Russia? Antarctica? Mars? I don't even want to go to college. Does everybody have to go to college?"

I narrowed my eyes at him, though he couldn't see me. "No, you can be a waiter like my brother, Michael. Or a fisherman, like everybody else in my family."

"What's wrong with that? I'd like to be a fisherman."

My eyes bugged out of my head. "I heard you say that to Rudy, but I assumed you were kidding."

"Well, I wasn't. You know I've always loved boats."

"Finn, fishing isn't just riding around on boats—it's the hardest work there is! Look at my father—he's spent his life fishing and what does he have to show for it? Back spasms, no health insurance, and not enough money to retire. And he's one of the lucky ones. Most small fishermen have already gone out of business."

"Your dad's got his own boat," Finn said, "and he's out in the sun every day working alongside two of his kids."

"Yeah. Ask Marky and Bobby what a great legacy that is."

"So he's not rich. I don't need to be rich."

"There's a big difference between 'not rich' and 'can't afford to fill the gas tank of your twenty-year-old truck.' Don't you think my dad would've liked to be able to send his kids to college, Finn? For a smart guy you can be really stupid."

He stopped the car in front of my house and we sat in silence.

"Maybe I am stupid," he said finally, "but I don't want to leave here. I don't want to live in a college dorm with a bunch of idiots whose idea of a good time is funneling booze into their stomachs until they throw up. I feel like I'm already too old for it."

That I understood. "You're not stupid. I didn't mean that. But, Finn, not all college kids are drunken morons. You have to find the right school and do it *your* way. Do you really want to stay in Provincetown forever and hang around the Old Colony Tap drinking beer with my brothers? How is that better?"

"Maybe it's not better. But it's here."

Of course. "Here. Where Lorna is?"

He didn't answer, but I knew I was right.

12.

Finn called around five o'clock on Sunday. "You want a ride over to Lucas's later?"

"I'd rather walk," I said. "It's a nice day."

"I could walk with you."

"Why don't I just meet you there?" Then I hung up before he could argue with me. I'd decided to spend as little time with Finn as possible from now on. It was too confusing. I kept getting mad at him, then feeling sorry for him, then wanting to help him, then before I knew it I was having heart palpitations all over again. It had to stop.

Walking toward the inn, I could see Finn sitting in his car out front. He climbed out when I came alongside, but we didn't say anything to each other as we approached the house. I guess we were both kind of nervous about having whatever the big secret was revealed to us. Billy threw the door open before we got to it and hugged me as if he hadn't seen me in years.

"Come on in. It's great to have the house full of kids again!" He led us into the parlor, which looked just as I remembered it: thick red drapery pooling on the dark wood floors, fat leather armchairs gathered around a marble fireplace, an enormous vase of sunflowers on the coffee table.

And there was Lucas pacing nervously in the middle of the room, his curly hair now long and sun-streaked, pulled back into a bushy ponytail. He was tanner than I'd ever seen him and more filled out too. Arms that used to hang from his shoulders like coat sleeves from a hanger were now taut with muscles. He held out a hand to Finn.

Despite his misgivings about coming, Finn smiled sincerely and said, "Good to see you, man," and pulled Lucas into a brief hug.

"You too," Lucas said, almost shyly. "Both of you." I went forward for my hug and was surprised to feel the tension in Lucas's arms as they gripped my back.

"As promised!" Simon came in from the kitchen carrying a tray. "This is my Great-Aunt Betsy's cheesecake recipe, so please don't tell me any of you have given up dairy."

"Unless you want to see a grown man cry." Billy chugged out past him to get the espresso started. Lucas's dads seemed even more chirpy and vivacious than usual, as if they were a little bit uncomfortable around Lucas now. Maybe this beefed-up guy was not the kid they remembered either.

We were all kind of awkward and a little too giggly while Billy passed around the dessert and coffee, but finally Finn asked the questions we came to have answered. "Where did you go? Why didn't you come back 'til now?" And I realized I was holding my breath.

Lucas busied himself forking through his cheesecake as if there was a treasure hidden in it. "My aunt got me a job at a summer camp up in New Hampshire. I wasn't sure I'd like being a camp counselor, but actually it was great. I took the kids hiking and we camped out in the mountains a few times. I even taught archery, if you can believe it."

"Huh." It seemed like Finn wasn't sure he *did* believe it.

Billy banged Lucas on the back. "Who says two gay men can't raise an athletic son?"

"Nobody in this room, Dad." Lucas rolled his eyes, but continued. "When camp ended, some of the counselors were going hiking in the White Mountains for a few weeks, and they asked me to go along. I know, it's weird, right? I never thought of myself doing stuff like that. Tromping through the woods, sleeping in a mummy bag, the guy with the Timberland boots and the enormous backpack. Turns out I liked it. Who knew?" His smile was crooked.

"We're glad you came home, Lucas," I said. "We missed you."

Lucas sipped from his tiny coffee cup, then swirled the remains in a circle. "At first I wasn't sure I would come back," he said quietly.

Finn's face clouded over and his dessert plate clanged onto the coffee table. "What are you talking about? This is your home. I still don't understand why the hell you left here to begin with. It wasn't for some last-minute camp counselor job."

Simon jumped up and started stacking plates. "Billy and I will go clean up the kitchen so you can talk privately. You don't need a couple geezers listening in on everything."

Lucas used to have to beg Simon and Billy to give us a little privacy. Now their speedy exit from the room, grabbing up napkins and teaspoons, seemed planned.

"We need to talk, and they already know what I'm going to say," Lucas explained.

A jolt of fear zigzagged up my spine. I knew Lucas's desertion had to have something to do with Lorna's death. Could he have something to tell us we didn't already know? Was this the missing piece that would answer my questions? My stomach churned the strong coffee and cheesecake into a toxic concoction.

"Does this have to do with why you left town so quickly?" I asked. "Without even talking to us?"

Lucas closed his eyes and took a deep breath, as if searching for something inside himself. "I'm sorry I wimped out on you, but I couldn't deal with it. I had to get away someplace I wasn't reminded of it all the time."

But he wasn't getting off the hook that easily. I sat forward, readying my body for whatever was coming. "It was hard for all of us, Lucas, but Finn and I helped each other. Why didn't you want to be with us? How you could just leave like that without even telling us you were going?"

Finn scooted to the edge of his chair, waiting to hear the answer.

Lucas pinched the bridge of his nose. "I thought if I went away I wouldn't keep seeing that white jacket bobbing in the ocean every time I closed my eyes."

White jacket. How could two such innocuous words cause such excruciating pain? Those three syllables cut like a whip.

"It didn't work, though," he went on. "You can't force yourself to forget something like that. But while I was in the mountains, my head cleared a little bit. I started feeling kind of . . . angry, I guess, that I didn't really know what the hell happened that night. I still couldn't make any sense of it. And I knew I had to come back and talk to you two."

The ache in the room was like a living thing. It was as if the three of us being together again completed a circuit that brought the pain back in all its electric splendor. It crawled out of the dark corners of my brain where I'd stuffed it away in order to walk, eat, speak, act like a more or less normal person. I glanced at Finn and I could tell that his scars had burst open too. He gasped through parted lips as if a plastic bag were wrapped around his face and he couldn't get enough air.

"Why didn't you at least call us, Lucas?" My voice was sharper than I'd intended it to be. "Or e-mail. You were just *gone.* First Lorna and then you!"

"I know. I'm sorry. I was so screwed up about the whole thing."

"So was I! So was Finn! You think you were more screwed up than *we* were?" A few tears threatened to fall, but I willed them away. I had no idea I was so mad at Lucas.

"No, of course not, but there were things . . . you didn't know. Things that were driving me crazy."

Finn was alert now. "*What* things we didn't know?"

"I thought . . ." Lucas paused, and then spit out his sentence. "I thought Lorna's death was my fault."

Finn gave a short, dismissive laugh and jumped up from his chair.

I could feel my lips pull back from my teeth as if I were growling. "Why would it be *your* fault?" I barked at him. "You mean, because you couldn't save her? None of us could!" Even though I'd never discussed it with Finn, I *knew* that this was a part of the story he couldn't bear—the fact that Lucas had leaped into that cold black water in a ridiculous attempt to save Lorna, while he, her boyfriend and a much stronger swimmer, continued to stand there on the breakwater, helplessly calling out her name.

"That's not what I mean," Lucas said. His head dropped low between his shoulders, his voice barely audible.

"I think it's strange that you're claiming Lorna's death as *your* fault," I said, my voice getting louder and louder. "Why on earth would that be true? Or do you think we're *all* somehow responsible? Are you blaming us?"

"No! Jackie, just listen to me for a minute. Something happened that I didn't tell you about."

Finn walked behind Lucas's chair and leaned over him. "Tell us now, Lucas. Right now."

Lucas looked him in the eyes and his face turned gray. "Lorna was pregnant."

I jumped and let out a startled laugh. "No, she wasn't! Where did you get a crazy idea like that?"

"From her," he said. "She told me . . . it was mine."

Finn's mouth hung open. "Man, how much weed did you smoke out there in the woods?"

But Lucas stammered on. "We were only together once. I knew it was a lousy thing for me to do, but I had such a crush on Lorna—more than a crush—which she knew, and when she came on to me that night—"

Finn had turned away from Lucas, but now he wheeled back around. "She *came on* to you? What are you talking about? Are you saying you *slept* with her?"

Lucas kept his eyes on his shoes. "I knew she was playing with me. I mean, I knew she wasn't throwing you over for me—I'm not that dumb—so I figured sleeping with her wouldn't be such a big deal. I mean, it wouldn't affect your relationship with her or anything."

My eyes could not have opened any wider. "Lucas, she was Finn's girlfriend!"

"I *know* that!" Lucas stood up and plodded over to the fireplace, his shoulders slumped. "I'm not proud of it, Jackie, but you know how I felt about Lorna. I never thought for a minute that I—and all of a sudden she wanted me to sleep with her! It was like a miracle!"

Finn stumbled backward, looking for something to lean on. He stepped on the puddle of velvety drapes, slid, and caught himself on a bookcase.

"Cheating on your best friend is a miracle?" I yelled. "That's a new one."

Miserably, Lucas shook his head. "*Lorna* was the miracle. Try to see it from my point of view. I thought you'd understand this, Jackie."

"Why? Because I need a miracle too?" The question came out like a spitball. And then the memory of Finn fending off my impulsive kiss bloomed in my brain. Okay, yes, I'd wanted a miracle too, but I never would have gone after it if Lorna were still alive.

Finn rumbled into the silence between Lucas and me. "If this bullshit is true, which I doubt it is, why are you suddenly confessing to us now?"

"Because I want you to know the whole story. A couple of days after we, you know, were together, Lorna came to me with a pregnancy test. It was positive. She said it had to be mine because you'd been in Florida for two weeks. I didn't know anything about that stuff—how long anything took—and I just figured she knew what she was talking about."

"Everything you say gets crazier and crazier!" Finn's voice was only a notch below a shriek.

"If Lorna had been pregnant," I said, "she would've told me before she told anybody else. I was her best friend."

Lucas banged his hand on the mantelpiece. "Why would I make this up? That's why I thought it was all my fault! For months after she died, I was totally freaked out, until finally I got up the nerve to do a little research and it turns out those tests aren't accurate that fast. It takes a couple weeks, not just days. So, it couldn't have been me. At least I don't think it could."

"So, she wasn't actually pregnant," I said, looking at Finn. "Unless . . ."

"We always used a condom. Every time. Besides, if Lorna had been pregnant by me, she obviously would have *told me*." Finn headed for the door. "I don't know what you're trying to prove, Lucas, but—"

"Look, Finn, I don't understand it either," Lucas said, "but why else would she want to kill herself?"

Finn spun around so fast he knocked the vase of flowers off the table. Water and golden petals sprayed everywhere. "*Kill* herself?"

I stood up then too. "Lucas, that's ridiculous. I know people are saying that, but—"

"Who's saying that?" Finn interrupted.

"Lorna would *never* have killed herself, for any reason." I stepped over the flower debris to get to Finn, but Lucas grabbed my arm. "Jackie, think about it—it never made sense that she fell off the breakwater. *Lorna?* She danced over those rocks."

"I'm gonna dance over *you*, asshole!" Finn yelled as he came for Lucas. He grabbed him by the shirt and they stood eye to eye, but Lucas didn't try to defend himself, didn't blink, didn't so much as put up a hand to deflect a punch. It almost seemed like he wanted Finn to hit him.

After a few seconds, Finn let him go, stomped to the door, and flung it open. "Tell Simon and Billy thanks for the dessert. But it'll take more than cheesecake to get this taste out of my mouth."

"I'm sorry," Lucas whispered to me, but I didn't answer. What was there to say?

I looked back at Lucas before following Finn outside. I climbed into the front seat of the Prius without asking and buckled myself in because I was pretty sure Finn wouldn't purposely hit anything if I was in the car with him. When he pulled over in front of my house he turned off the engine and slumped forward, his head resting on the steering wheel. I couldn't think of a thing to say. Finally he turned his head to look at me.

"Lucas is right about one thing," he said quietly. "Lorna could never have fallen off those rocks."

I nodded. "I know."

13.

Charlotte was shoving books into her locker while I mumbled Lucas's revelations into her ear. "That's insane," she said. "Why would Lorna sleep with Lucas? Then again, why would he make it up?"

"I don't know. None of it makes sense."

"Lucas thinks she'd kill herself over a pregnancy? It's not 1950, and this is Lorna we're talking about. Wouldn't she just get an abortion or something?"

Charlotte's voice was getting louder and people were beginning to look at us, so I steered her toward the door, speaking as quietly as possible. "I don't know, but even Finn agreed that Lucas was right about one thing. Lorna couldn't have fallen off the breakwater."

Charlotte made a slightly disgusted face. "Really? She was so perfect? She couldn't have an accident? Even in a storm?"

I shook my head. "It's what I thought from the very beginning, but nobody said it out loud, so I didn't either. Because, if she didn't fall, there was no explanation."

"Except that she did it on purpose."

"Which is also impossible."

"Well, unless we're living in the *Twilight Zone*, those are the only two options. She fell or she jumped. Unless somebody *pushed* her."

I stopped walking. "Are you kidding? You think Finn pushed her? Or Lucas? Or *me*?"

"Of course not, but something happened to her because she ended up in the water. And when you look at all the options, falling is the most likely. Isn't it?"

I sighed. "I guess. I'm so tired of thinking about it. Am I going to spend my whole life trying to figure this out?"

"Seems like it. Here's a new topic: Did I tell you Lucas is in my Spanish class?"

"He is? Did you talk to him?"

"No, but I will. He looks different. He looks good."

"Yeah."

"But, you know, sad. Lonely."

"Well, that's *his* problem. He screwed over his friends."

"Jackie, if Lorna slept with him, it wasn't only his fault. In fact—"

"I can't believe that happened. I would have known."

We'd reached Bradford Street and I turned left toward JSAC. But Charlotte got in a final word before she headed for the West End. "Maybe Lorna had a few secrets she didn't share with you, Jackie. Just sayin'."

ॐ

Elsie was in her office when I got to the Center. I figured Finn wouldn't have told her anything about the night before and I didn't intend to either.

"Hey, Jackie." Elsie was unpacking boxes of lavender T-shirts that said "Jasper Street Art Center" in small red letters across the front. "These just arrived. What size are you? Medium?" She tossed me a shirt.

"Thanks." I held it up to my chest. "These are gorgeous."

"Aren't they? Cooper helped me pick the colors."

Cooper. He didn't seem to be around at the moment, which was good. I had enough confusing stuff to think about.

"Can I use your computer to work on some photos?" I asked Elsie.

"Sure. Use the new program. I have to go pick up Tess at Emma's house in a few minutes, so I won't be in your way."

I downloaded the pictures I'd shot the afternoon before and brought one of them up in Elsie's new program. Just to try it out, I intensified the contrast and played with the color saturation a little. I hadn't realized a small piece of driftwood was in the corner of the shot—I cropped it out. The photograph was more interesting now, but it didn't present the actual truth anymore, and I wasn't sure how I felt about that. Did truth matter more than beauty—or did enhancing the image bring out a new kind of truth? After all, every time I framed a shot, I chose what reality to show and what to leave outside the borders. Wasn't that how art worked? You made choices and found your own truth.

Elsie leaned over my shoulder to take a look. "That one's amazing! Look at those clouds—print that out."

"I'm thinking I might take four or five of the cloud photos and line them up in a row all together to make one long picture, and then collage on top of it."

"I love that idea," Elsie said. She hopped up to sit on the desk. "By the way, before I forget, I want to apologize for Friday night. I was so annoyed with Carolyn for acting like she couldn't be bothered to talk to you."

"It's okay. She's a superstar. I didn't expect her to have a big conversation with me."

Elsie twirled a turquoise ring around her finger. "Well, it's her loss. Becoming self-centered can be an occupational hazard for artists."

"Finn would agree with you," I said, "but it's not true for everybody. You aren't self-centered."

"I'm not good enough to have a big ego," she said, sliding off the desk. I'd never heard Elsie put herself down like that before, and I was at a loss what to say. But she wasn't waiting for a response.

"Off to pick up Tess," she said. "If you see Cooper, tell him—Oh, wait. There he is. Coop! Come and see the T-shirts!"

I raised my hand in a brief wave as he came into the room. After all that flirting on Friday night, I didn't know how to act around Cooper anymore. I'd almost kissed him, hadn't I? Or did I just imagine that? He smiled at me, same as always, and I decided he'd probably already forgotten about it, his world obviously not rocked by standing outside in the dark with a teenager for fifteen minutes.

He and Elsie discussed where to sell the T-shirts until she looked at her watch and groaned. "Late again." She grabbed her purse and took off out the door.

Elsie's exit sucked all the normalcy out of the room, at least for me. I couldn't think of one thing to say. As my photographs chugged out of the printer, Cooper shuffled through them.

"Very nice," he said. "I can see why Elsie picked you."

"What do you mean, 'picked me'?"

He grinned. "You're her protégé. Don't you know that, Jacqueline?"

Jacqueline. The name bounced around in my brain like a hard-hit tennis ball. "I don't think—"

"Absolutely you are! Believe me, I know a protégé when I see one. I used to be Rudy's, you know." He jumped up on the desk, the spot Elsie had recently vacated, but somehow he seemed closer than she had.

"You aren't anymore?" I asked.

He shrugged. "It's not the same now. Rudy prefers to mentor the inexperienced and unpublished. Once you step into his limelight it puts him off a little. Also—" Cooper leaned over as if he were about to tell me a secret, even though there was no one else in the office. "I did a bad thing," he said, grimacing.

I scooted my chair back a few inches. He was so attractive up close, I could barely look at him. Even if I avoided his eyes, there was no body part that didn't make me nervous—his hands, his hair, the taut, tan skin of his arms. "What did you do?"

"Yesterday I was interviewed on NPR about my book."

"Really? That's amazing!"

"Yeah, well, maybe not. I said how grateful I was to my college English professors and my graduate school friends, blah, blah, blah, and somehow I forgot to say anything about Rudolph or the Center."

"Oh. Is that bad?"

"'Inexcusable' will probably be Rudy's word. I was so nervous and excited, it didn't even occur to me until later. It airs next week, and I'm steeling myself for Rudy's anger. I mean, of course I should have said something, but really, doesn't the guy get enough adulation? There's always somebody blathering about him in the *New Yorker* or the *New York Times*. It's not like his stature is in any danger of being eroded because I forgot to mention his name. Still, I'll have to grovel and apologize. That's how it works—the more famous you are, the more you need to have your ego massaged."

I gave a vague nod, not sure how much I agreed. Sure, Rudolph had a sense of himself—who wouldn't in his position? But he never seemed self-centered or snobby around people who had fewer achievements than he did. Not like, for example, Carolyn Winter. But then again, I imagined that two novelists might be competitive with each other in ways I didn't notice.

Cooper touched my arm lightly and I practically leaped out of my skin. "Speaking of the famous Rosenbergs, what's the deal with you and Finn?"

"The deal?"

"Yeah, are you a couple now or what?"

"Me and Finn? Why would you think that?"

"The way he came looking for you when we left the gallery together the other night. I know he had some excuse, but it seemed to me like he was coming to claim his property."

I wondered if Cooper could tell how thrilled I was that he'd finally mentioned Friday night, even though he had a completely incorrect take on it. "No, it wasn't an excuse. Believe me, Finn and I are just friends, and barely even that some days."

Cooper's glittering eyes sought out mine and locked them down. I felt like he could see right into my brain. "Jacqueline, don't let Finn fool you. Maybe he doesn't admit it, but he definitely thinks you're his. He might not be ready to stake his claim, but he doesn't want anybody else to do it either."

I was so stunned by Cooper's totally wrong idea, I didn't know how to respond. He hopped off the desk and put a hand on my shoulder where it burned through the cloth of my shirt. I was tattooed by his fingers. He stuck out his other hand.

"We're friends, aren't we?"

"Of course," I said. I took his warm hand into mine and felt my fingers melt.

"Good." He leaned forward and kissed me on the cheek. The kiss accidentally grazed the corner of my mouth and I instinctively turned toward it. The slight brush of his lips against mine left me feeling bee-stung. Swollen.

He pulled away and grabbed a T-shirt off the stack. As he turned to go back to his own office, he pointed to me. "Jacqueline, I will see you later. That's a promise."

14.

Five eight-by-ten photographs of clouds were spread out end to end on the floor of my bedroom. I'd already rearranged their order half a dozen times and still wasn't sure I had it right. The colors were muted—greenish water below gray-blue sky with just a tinge of sundown scarlet showing through the mackerel clouds.

Scraps of other photographs lay around me too. I'd been carefully cutting out images I thought I might use: birds, fish, lanterns, nautical flags, neon signs, store window displays, lobsters, rowboats. I strung the flags across the sky and then looked through some of the words I'd snipped from newspaper headlines—*winners, coast, lost, bridge, blaze, mystery, guilty, break, crisis*. I put *crisis* in the middle of the red streak of light and stood back to look at it.

"Jackie!" Dad yelled up the stairs. "Somebody here to see you."

I went to the top of the stairs. "Who?" Charlotte usually called first.

Lucas stood there next to my father. "Hey," he said.

I'd been wondering what his next move would be, whether he'd want to talk more, or if, now that he'd delivered his message, he'd just disappear again, strap on his new boots and hike out of town. At least he wasn't running away this time.

"Come on up," I said.

As Lucas climbed, Dad bellowed from below, "You keep that door open, you hear me?"

I almost laughed. *As if.* Dad wasn't home much in the daytime, and he didn't spend a lot of time keeping up with his children's social lives. For all I knew, he thought I was still dating Lucas. Man, did that even happen in this lifetime?

Lucas ducked his head as he entered the room, as if he thought he'd gotten too tall for the space. "Your dad hasn't changed much," he said.

I kept my hands on my hips. "I guess you think you have?"

He sighed. "I know you're trying to be snotty, but I *have* actually changed. I'm not the same person I was when I left. You don't even know me anymore."

I backed up and sat on my bed, thinking he was right about that. Lorna's death had made us all different people.

"I think I met the new guy last night," I said. "He was *charming*."

Lucas stepped over the photographs on the floor and, though he hadn't been invited to, he perched on the creaky rocking chair in the corner. "Not gonna give me a break, huh?"

"I don't know what to say to you, Lucas. You disappeared for three months and then came back to tell us you slept with Lorna, she might have been pregnant, and you think she killed herself. Are you a big jerk or a big liar or a big idiot? Or all three?"

"Idiot I'll cop to, and maybe jerk too, but I'm no liar. Jackie, we've been friends for seven years. Can't you give me the benefit of the doubt? You always believed everything Lorna told you, even the crazy stuff."

"Lorna never lied to me."

"*I've* never lied to you," Lucas said. "And that's not even true about Lorna. She lied to us all the time."

"No she didn't!"

"She pretended afterward that she was joking, but she liked to see what she could get away with. Like that story about her father and the bear."

Well, okay, he wasn't wrong. Lorna had enjoyed fooling people. She liked to make up long, involved stories that were, technically, not true. Like the time she told us a tree had fallen on her father and severed his leg, which had then been picked up and carried off into the woods by a bear. She could be so convincing, you *wanted* to believe her. Then, when she knew she had you, she'd burst out laughing and admit she'd made it up.

"Those were more jokes than lies," I said.

"I'm not sure she knew the difference." He leaned back in the rocker and I noticed that his eyes were bloodshot, as if he hadn't been sleeping much. Well, who had?

I grabbed a pillow and hugged it to my chest. "Lucas, I'm not trying to be mean—"

"Sure you are. You and Finn have chosen sides and, as usual, Lorna wins."

"Lorna wins? What are you talking about? She's dead!"

"And therefore can't be disputed."

I sighed. "Okay, convince me. Why would Lorna sleep with you? Why?"

The corners of his mouth drooped, but he didn't look away from me. "I don't know, Jackie. To make Finn jealous? To make me deliriously happy? Just for the hell of it? I didn't know then and I don't know now. But I'm telling you, she wanted to. It was *her idea.*"

"Walk me through it. Not the raunchy part, just the lead-up. How did it happen?"

His eyes glazed over. "She came by my house one night at the end of April break. Finn was on vacation. I don't know where you were. She said she was lonely and would I come over and take a walk with her. I figured there was nobody else around and maybe she was having some trouble with her mom or something and needed to get out of the house."

That much of the story sounded plausible.

"Once we started walking, she seemed a little bit manic, but, you know, that wasn't so unusual. All of a sudden she grabbed my hand. I acted like I didn't think it was weird, but I was totally shocked. The cottages were still closed up, but she pulled me down the path and—"

"Dugan's Cottages?"

"Yeah."

I let the pillow drop to the floor. "Wait. You're telling me you had sex with Lorna in *Cabin 5*? On that dirty mattress we used to use as a trampoline?"

"Why are you making it sound disgusting? You know how crazy I always was about Lorna, and she totally wanted it. I know you think I'm lying about that, but I'm not. Christ, Jackie, I was a virgin, you know that. She *seduced* me."

"Oh, you poor thing!"

But, in fact, Lucas's use of the word "seduced" had begun to convince me he was telling the truth. Suddenly I could almost see what had happened. Lorna at her most flirtatious, charming Lucas, then pulling away, laughing, taunting, tempting him. I'd seen her do it to Finn lots of times—he'd be practically panting before she gave in and went off alone with him. I used to watch her and wonder when she first realized she had that power. Lucas would have been confused by having that energy turned on him, and Lorna would have been completely in charge of the situation. I remembered how hard it used to be for me to resist Lorna when she really wanted something. And, of course, Lucas didn't want to resist. This was his *miracle*.

Lucas's shoulders sagged and he turned away from me, letting his eyes settle on the bookcase next to him. The shelves were crammed with paperback novels, everything from Judy Blume to Sebastian Junger, but on top there was a simple memorial: a picture of Lorna and a pair of worn-out blue sneakers.

"Her shoes." Lucas picked them up and wrapped the worn laces around his fingers. His voice thickened. "You kept them."

"Of course I kept them." Seeing the effect that Lorna's wrecked shoes were having on Lucas choked me up too. I cleared my throat. "I couldn't just throw them in the trash."

He settled the sneakers carefully in his lap as if they were baby animals, then picked up the photograph and studied it. "Did you take this?"

I nodded. It was the only picture I had of Lorna by herself, without Finn by her side or all four of us crowded in together. She'd never liked having her picture taken, which frustrated me because I longed to take a photograph that would capture what I loved about her—her fearlessness, her spirit, her grace. In this photo she stared, unsmiling, at the camera, her hair flying in the wind, her front foot off the ground. She seemed to be annoyed that her forward motion was being slowed by the camera, by me.

Watching Lucas with the picture and the shoes, it occurred to me that while Finn and I were leaning, sometimes awkwardly, on each other, Lucas had had to do his mourning alone, holding on to terrible secrets. Why hadn't I thought of that before?

Mesmerized by the photo, Lucas hardly seemed to realize there were tears running down his cheeks. "There's something we don't know about that night, Jackie. It drives me crazy. How can we not know? I have to know!"

"Me too." And just that quickly, I remembered why I'd always liked Lucas—he couldn't hide his feelings any better than I could. The two of us had always been a pair of exposed nerves, ever alert for joy, but taking every misunderstanding and angry word to heart. Our emotions flashed across our faces and dribbled from our eyes. Before I thought about it too much, I stood up and wordlessly held out my arms.

Lucas was across the room in seconds. "I'm sorry I left," he said. His voice was muffled against my shoulder, but I could still hear the sob in it.

"I wish you hadn't."

"I know, but, Jackie, everything was ruined, and I thought it was my fault." He still held the blue shoes in one hand and I could feel them knocking into my back.

"It wasn't anybody's fault. It was just the most horrible thing that ever happened to us."

We held on to each other and cried, and it was all just as fresh as those first days when Finn and I couldn't stop our tears. The days when Lucas must have cried alone.

We slowly pulled apart, and Lucas ducked his head. "Thanks for forgiving me."

I grabbed a bunch of tissues from the box by my bed and handed some to him too. "Turns out it wasn't that hard."

"You're not mad at me anymore?"

"Apparently not. Even though you're stepping all over my photographs."

Lucas looked down at his feet, horrified, then jumped back. The soles of his fat boots had left a studded outline on several of the pictures. "Oh, Jesus. I forgot they were there!"

"Your feet?" I got down on my knees to examine the damage, but already I liked what I saw. The boot trail went across the water and up into the cloudy sky.

"No! I mean . . ."

"Don't worry. You did me a favor. The giant footprints give the whole thing a new perspective. Yeah, I can definitely work with this. In fact, here, step on this one too."

He did and we laughed, but then got quiet again. He sat down on the floor next to me.

"Do you really think Lorna might have killed herself?" I asked him.

Lucas stared at the blue shoes. "I think Lorna might have done *anything*. But I don't think she ever expected to die."

15.

On September 10 I woke up before dawn, just as I had on the tenth of every month since May, no alarm clock needed. In the bathroom mirror my eyes looked red and puffy, as if I'd spent the night before doing something more exciting than re-reading every line of *Macbeth* three times. I hung my camera around my neck and went downstairs.

Mom was already up and washing out the oatmeal pot. My dad was probably long gone. A fisherman's day can last twenty-four hours, so he liked to leave the dock early.

"Aren't you late for work?" I asked Mom.

"Day off," she said. "How come you're up so early?"

"Going out for a little while. I'll be back in time to get ready for school."

She looked me right in the eyes, then walked away. "It's starting to rain. Wear something waterproof."

I'd already layered a sweater over a long-sleeved T-shirt, but I went to the closet for my slicker.

From the pantry Mom said, "Four months today, isn't it?"

More than most people, Teresa Silva understood the importance of anniversaries. Every November 27, the date of my uncle's shipwreck, she allowed herself to spend the day in bed, an indulgence she didn't give in to the other 364 days.

"Yeah."

"Going down there, aren't you?" She frowned as she took the top off an old Thermos bottle and sniffed it.

I nodded.

"Take some coffee along. You'll get cold. The wind is sharp."

I watched her fill the Thermos three-quarters full with coffee and then dump in a generous amount of milk before screwing the top back on. When she handed me the bottle her eyes were foggy behind her glasses.

"Thanks, Mom."

"People used to say you could hear the voices of drowned folks right before a rainstorm, but I never did. It's just a superstition," she said, as if she wasn't a firm believer in dozens of old wives' tales.

"I'm not expecting to hear her," I said. I was, however, hoping to *feel* Lorna. To somehow be with her again.

"Don't want you to be disappointed." Mom went back into the pantry, but came right out again as if she'd forgotten why she went in. "Are you walking out on it? The breakwater?"

"I'm not sure. Maybe."

"Be careful. Tide's going out."

Which is all she had to say in order for one of her groundless superstitions to wedge itself into my brain. *An ebbing tide lures the careless to a watery grave.*

Clouds were thick on the horizon as I approached the breakwater. It looked as if we might get a good soaking before long. The sharp wind didn't carry Lorna's voice, but it did make my ears sting, and I was glad to find an old watch cap in the pocket of my slicker. When a thin ray of sun sliced through the gray morning and fell on the rock trail in front of me, I took a picture.

But looking through the viewfinder I noticed something I hadn't seen with my eyes. There seemed to be someone sitting out on the rocks, maybe a quarter of a mile away. Who'd be out there this early? I framed the figure against the weak, rising sun, and then I knew. Of course.

I had to steel myself to get past those first few boulders, keeping to the center, not looking over the edge to where the surf crashed against the rocks. *You used to cross the breakwater all the time,* I reminded myself, but still fear choked me and made me stop in my tracks a dozen times. I put down the Thermos and my camera, so I wouldn't drop them if I stumbled, and forced myself to take one step after the other.

The farther I walked, the bigger the spaces became between one rock and the next. Sometimes I had to leap the divide, hoping my foot wouldn't land on a slippery spot or a chunk of seaweed thrown up by the tide. And then I *did* slip, not much, not badly, but I stayed down on my hands and knees for a few minutes to gather the courage to continue. Those last few yards the sound of the waves pounded in my ears so loudly I couldn't hear my own footsteps.

Finn couldn't hear them either. He sat cross-legged looking out at the horizon, his hair whipping in the wind, and when I touched his back lightly, his scream cut through the humid air. He fell forward, away from my hand.

"It's me!" I shouted, pretty sure I knew who he thought it was. "It's only me!"

Finn stared at me for a few seconds, stared right through me. Then he took a deep breath and let his eyes close. "Jackie, my God, you scared the crap out of me!"

"I'm sorry. I didn't realize . . . I'm sorry."

"It's okay," he said, but he didn't sound like he meant it.

"Can I . . . do you mind if I sit here with you?"

He hesitated a moment, then patted the rock next to him. "Sure. Have a seat."

Carefully, I lowered myself onto the flat stone. "I didn't know you came out here much." I had to yell into the wind.

"I don't. I never come out here."

What else was there to say? I looked up at the clouds, moving in fast. Just an ordinary, dreary day. But not for us. For Finn and me rain will never be ordinary, clouds will never be insignificant, the ocean will never be predictable, the tenth day of every month will always remind us of what we've lost.

Finally I said, "How long have you been out here?"

He shrugged, then shivered. "Before the sun came up. An hour or so, I guess."

"You must be cold. You don't have a hat or gloves."

"I'm fine."

I reached over and touched his fingers. "Your hands are freezing."

"I don't care," he said, wedging them into his armpits. "It won't kill me."

I was silent for a moment, then said, "What do you remember about that night?"

Finn groaned and let his head sink down onto his crossed arms. "Come on, Jackie. Haven't we gone over this enough? I remember the same things you do."

"I know, but I mean the details. Like how she was acting, where we were all standing, how long it took us to—"

"Jackie, please. I don't need this today."

"Well, maybe I do!" I was surprised by the anger in my voice, but I didn't back down. If we didn't figure it out, who would? "Why did she want to come down here that afternoon? She knew the weather was going to be bad. She didn't even have a decent coat on."

Finn shook his head. "I don't know. She talked about it all day, how this big storm was supposed to come in around six o'clock, and we should all come down here and watch."

"Well, why did we—"

"Because. We always did everything she wanted us to. You know that."

"We should have said, 'We're not going. It's a crazy idea.' Why didn't we?"

Finn turned an exhausted, wind-burned face to me. "Why are you doing this, Jackie? What's the use? I'm so tired of going over it. I was just starting to think I'd finally managed to stuff all the memories of that night into a little . . . a little *bag*, like an extra kidney that fit deep inside me." He cupped his hand to show me the size. "It was tied up tight so nothing could spill out. I knew it was there, but I didn't have to *touch* it all the time. I could go minutes, hours, sometimes most of a day, without thinking about the worst moments of my life."

The corners of his mouth turned down into a scowl. "And then Lucas came back with all his secrets or lies or whatever they are, and that little bag ripped right down the middle and everything leaked out all over. She's here again. Right *here*." He put his hand on his chest, the place where Lorna was still in residence, and tears spilled from his eyes.

"Oh, Finn." I couldn't stop myself. I put my arms around him and drew him tightly against my shoulder, and he allowed it. He cried so hard it was more like howling, and the wind carried it out to sea. At some point I crawled right into his lap, my legs on either side of him, my arms around his shoulders, getting as close to him as possible so I could feel his ruptured heart banging into my own, so there was almost no division between the two of us. And then I cried too, only this time it was for Finn, not Lorna, because maybe he would always be like this, broken, ruined.

We stayed like that a long time—five minutes? Ten? I had no idea. Finally Finn calmed down. He sat up and pushed away from me, gradually, until I couldn't feel his ragged breath on my neck anymore. I ran my fingers along his cheekbones, mopping up tears, before I crawled out of his lap.

"You still love her," I said, leaning into his side.

"Don't you?"

"I do. But, sometimes I think . . . she didn't love us the way we loved her."

Finn shrugged, wiping his face with his sweater. "Probably true. It was harder for her. Which made me want to keep trying, you know, to reach that part of her."

I understood completely.

"She was so beautiful," he continued, "but not in some shallow, hair-commercial way. She just . . . glowed! The lights were always on inside her. You couldn't contain her."

"I know," I said.

"When she laughed, you couldn't stay mad at her. Her laugh was like . . . bells or scales on the piano, or, I don't know, like rain when you really need it."

I could hear that laugh. I could feel it run up my spine.

We were both quiet for a minute and then Finn said, "Thanks, Jackie."

"What for?"

"Listening. Talking."

And there it was again, that tender, needy look on Finn's face that seemed to be an invitation. His eyes snagged mine and held on. What did he want? Was I supposed to understand what that look meant? I wrenched my eyes away, not willing to make a fool of myself a second time. We were friends, Finn and me. He'd made it clear we could never be more than that. I was reading the signals wrong, or maybe I was making them up altogether.

I leaned lightly on his shoulder as I got to my feet. "I'm glad you were here," I said.

And without looking back, I started my careful walk to shore. The rocks weren't as frightening to me now, maybe because I could see land ahead of me, or maybe because I felt Finn watching my every step.

16.

As always at the beginning of a new school year, all thirty-six seniors were required to attend the afternoon assembly in the auditorium, like it or not. I walked in with Charlotte and saw Finn sitting with his friend Tony Perry. There were open seats next to them, but sitting so close seemed risky, especially after the confusing emotions I'd felt this morning on the breakwater, so I led Char into the row just ahead of them. I wondered if my eyes looked as droopy and sad as Finn's did. We exchanged brief smiles before Charlotte and I settled into our uncomfortable seats.

Almost immediately I saw Lucas coming down the aisle. He was headed in my direction until he saw who was sitting behind me—then he veered off and sat across the aisle. Ugh. Wouldn't anything ever be *normal* again? Couldn't we figure out a new normal?

Ms. Waller stood on tiptoe in front of the microphone, going on and on about how important this year was going to be for us. She knew we all had a lot on our plates, but that was no excuse to goof off. Those who planned to go to college needed to schedule appointments with her to make sure they were on track. There were forms to fill out, tests to take, and endless deadlines to remember.

"Have you gone in to talk to her yet?" Charlotte asked.

"Last week," I said. "Elsie's helping me figure out the FAFSA forms today after school."

"Oh good, then you can help me," Char said.

Tony leaned forward. "I thought our parents had to fill those things out?"

I swiveled in my seat. "They do, but my parents keep putting it off. I decided I better figure it out myself and just tell them where to plug in the numbers."

"Why is this so complicated?" he asked. "Getting into college is like a part-time job."

"You're going to college?" Finn sounded surprised.

Tony nodded. "I hope so. My dad thinks I can get a basketball scholarship. You know, not to anyplace big, but I don't care as long as they pay for it."

"Where would you go?"

"My dad's got a list. Small, private schools mostly. I guess they like to get people from other parts of the country, so we're thinking maybe somewhere in the Midwest."

"I didn't know you wanted to go to college," Finn said. I turned back around, but I was still listening.

"Why not?" Tony said. "If I get the chance to, I'm going. If I stick around here I'll just end up being a carpenter like my dad."

"What's wrong with that?" Finn grumbled.

"The Cape's already full of unemployed carpenters. Besides, I want to go someplace I don't know every single person in town. Don't you?"

"No. I like it here. I want to be a fisherman," Finn said.

I have to admit I was pleased when Tony exploded with laughter. "Are you kidding me? Nobody can make a living fishing anymore, even families that have done it for generations. I guess you don't really need to make a living though, huh?"

It took Finn a few seconds to respond. "What does that mean?"

"It means you're rich, bro. Didja forget?"

"I'm not planning to live off my parents, Tony. Geez."

Tony clicked his teeth. "Well, I wouldn't plan on the fishing career either, man. Seriously, dude. How can a guy like you not go to college?"

Huh. *A guy like you*. It hadn't occurred to me that Finn got pigeonholed like that too.

He didn't have to answer the question because Mr. MacCracken, who taught history, came over to tell them to be quiet. I was glad to hear somebody else getting on Finn's case about this dumb fishing idea. Becoming a fisherman was his excuse for staying in P'town where he could be reminded of Lorna every minute of every day.

When the assembly was over, Finn and Tony took their time extricating their long legs from the auditorium chairs. I scooted into the aisle quickly and waited for Lucas to walk past. I could tell he was planning to ignore us, so I grabbed him when he came near. By that time Finn was standing in the aisle too, scowling.

"Hey, man," Tony said to Lucas. "I heard you were back. How's it going?"

"Good, good," Lucas said, careful not to make eye contact with Finn.

"Doesn't he look great?" I said, my voice more cheerful than necessary. "He's been hiking in the woods all summer."

Finn's lip twitched and he squinted at me in disgust, but I didn't care. I was determined that we could get past what had happened and all be friends again, but it was not a message Finn wanted to hear.

His mouth curled up at one corner. "Yeah. Lucas has changed so much I hardly *recognize* him," he said, then turned and stomped off.

"What's with Finn?" Tony said, looking after him.

I shrugged. "You know how cranky fishermen can be."

"FAFSA can wait," Elsie said the minute I walked into her office. "I had a brainstorm last night. We're going to do a show of your photographs here, at JSAC, a week from tomorrow!"

"What?" On the walk over I'd been mulling a question about the difference between taxable and nontaxable income, and I couldn't immediately make sense of what Elsie was saying.

"I was trying to think of a way to make your application stand out from all the others so you'd have a better chance to get scholarship money," Elsie explained, "and I realized we could give you a show here! Isn't that a great idea? How many high school students have had a show at an actual gallery? I can tell you: *none.*"

I dropped my stack of papers onto the desk. "But that's impossible. The gallery's booked up a year ahead."

Elsie grinned. "Except there's nothing booked for the next two weeks. I planned it that way so I'd have time to Spackle and repaint the walls and refinish the floors. I thought Cooper and I would do most of it ourselves, but if you can help us—and we'll get Finn too—we can do it in half the time. We can have the opening at the end of next week and the work can stay up for four or five days before we have to get ready for the next scheduled show. I'm sure I can get someone to review it, at least locally, so you'll have a clipping to send with your application. What do you say?" Elsie was practically levitating with glee.

I felt as if all the blood from my brain had puddled in my feet, and I had to hold onto the edge of the desk to keep myself upright. "I don't know *what* to say."

"Say yes, Jacqueline."

I spun around to see Cooper coming through the doorway, grinning, and behind him, Finn, carrying a cardboard box.

"Did you hear this?" I asked them.

"Is Elsie a genius, or what?" Cooper said.

"Genius?" Finn said, scowling. He pushed past Cooper and stacked the ream of copy paper in a corner of the office. "You people throw that word around so much it's lost all meaning. *You paid that bill on time? You're a genius! You found my keys? You're a genius! You got the printer working? You're a genius!* You'd think this place was full of NASA scientists."

I ignored him. "Do you think I have enough stuff for a show?"

"Of course you do," Elsie said. "Although I'd like you to finish one of those horizontal sequences of cloud photos you've been working on. I want to see one of those on the wall."

I squealed. "I can't believe this!"

"Couldn't this backfire?" Finn asked his mother. "I mean, what if you get some reviewer to come and he hates it? Just because you love it—"

And just that quickly, fear crept into the cracks of my happiness. What if Finn was right? What if it turned out to be embarrassing to have my work hanging in public? What if nobody showed up? What if they showed up and *laughed*?

Cooper smacked Finn on the back. "Way to be supportive of your friend, pal."

"I'm not your pal." Finn shrugged away from Cooper and turned to his mother. "I didn't say I wouldn't help you. I will. I'm just asking if you've thought the whole thing through. I know Jackie's pretty good, but she's still a high school kid."

Elsie put a protective arm around me. "For one thing, Jackie's *very* good. And, secondly, I'm not going to ask some idiot to review her. Even if it's not a rave, it'll be a respectful review. I'm not worried."

"Well, I'm happy to help out," Cooper said. "You can count on me." He moved behind me and put his hands on my shoulders which made me shiver a little.

I darted a glance at Finn who seemed to be pissed off at all of us. "I'll bet your old friend Lucas will want to help out too," he said. "He's always there when you need him."

"Right. I forgot Lucas was back," Elsie said, totally misunderstanding the dig. "And maybe your friend Charlotte would help too. Cooper and I can finish packing up Carolyn's show tonight and then we'll all work in the gallery tomorrow and Sunday."

"I'll have to mat things, won't I?" I asked.

"Cooper can help you. Maybe we'll even frame one or two. Bring all your stuff over tomorrow and we'll decide. I'm coming in early, but Finn can give you a ride over mid-morning."

I glanced at him. "Can you?"

He shrugged, then gave a curt nod.

"It's settled then," Elsie said happily. "Team Jackie Silva starts work tomorrow!"

"Team Jacqueline," Cooper said quietly, as if he were speaking only to me.

17.

I floated down Commercial Street in a joyous bubble. My photographs were going to hang in the gallery at the Center, as if I were an actual, legitimate photographer! My imagination was on fire envisioning my pictures hanging on the same walls that showed the work of established artists—people like Carolyn Winter. I dug my camera from my backpack and started clicking away at fences, flowers, chimneys, license plates, streetlights, posters tacked to telephone poles. Every direction I pointed the camera highlighted something I'd never seen before, or, at least, never noticed in quite this way.

"Hey, Jackie! Take *my* picture!" The bleeting voice was immediately recognizable.

I froze in place, but eventually I had to look up from the camera toward the front porch of Old Hat Vintage Clothes. There sat Carla in a rocking chair wearing what seemed to be two or three different outfits from the store, layered one over the other.

"Oh, hi," I said reluctantly. "I didn't see you there."

"You weren't looking. Come on, take my picture. I look good in this dress." She petted the black velvet blouse of her odd costume, then wrapped a green flowered scarf tightly around her neck half a dozen times so it looked as if her head was no longer connected to the gaunt body beneath. "There. Don't I look good?"

"Uh-huh," I mumbled.

"Not as good as I used to," she said, with a sharp laugh. "I should never have had that damn kid. She ruined my whole life. Take my advice, Jackie: Don't ever get yourself knocked up." She hiked her skirt so her knees stuck out, then turned to one side and said, "I like a profile shot, don't you?"

What choice did I have? People on the street were already staring at us—I didn't want to make more of a scene than we already were. I took three or four shots, but just the sight of her through the viewfinder made my hands tremble.

Carla shifted position, sticking her bare feet out in front of her as if showing off the dirty soles. "Now one like this."

I snapped one more, and then made a show of looking at my watch. "Oh, I have to get going. Sorry. I told Mom I'd be home by now." It wasn't much of an excuse, but Carla didn't seem capable of judging.

"Bring me copies of those pictures!" she called after me as I sprinted away down the sidewalk. "Don't forget!"

I ran the length of the block as if Carla were chasing me. I had the awful feeling that I'd never outrun that image of her, her craziness framed forever in my mind. I intended to run all the way home, but suddenly a man came out of the bank and I had to swerve to avoid smacking right into him. In fact, I did clip him on the shoulder and we both whirled in a circle.

"Whoa!" Cooper Thorne grabbed my shoulders before I toppled over. "Where's the fire?"

"Sorry! Oh, it's *you*! I'm sorry!" I stopped to catch my breath and looked back over my shoulder.

"Are you running away from somebody?"

"No, I . . . well, sort of."

Cooper smiled but didn't question me further. I tried to calm down and act like a normal person.

"You on your way home?" he asked.

I nodded. "Weren't you just at the Center?"

"Had to get to the bank before they closed. I'll walk you home, unless you're training for a marathon or something."

Cooper lived in the other direction, across the street from JSAC, and I was flattered that he wanted to walk with me, but I was still kind of freaked out about Carla. My smile felt wobbly.

Cooper narrowed his eyes. "Is something wrong? You look a little strange."

"I *am* a little strange," I said. I was trying to make a joke of it, but it came out sounding like a confession.

"You want to go somewhere and talk?"

The kindness in his voice made me want to lean against him, to follow him anywhere. I looked directly into the abyss of his eyes. "I would. Yes."

He put his hand on my waist, lightly, and led me on a sandy path between two buildings and down to the bay beach. The wind had picked up and we were heading right into it.

"There's this place I like to go sometimes, to be alone and think about things," he said.

Right away I thought of the cabins. Where else could you be alone in this part of town?

"Are you cold?" Cooper asked. "You're shivering."

"A little, I guess." I zipped up my jacket even though I knew it was nerves, not weather, making me quake. The peculiarity of this rollercoaster day was never-ending.

"It'll be good to get in out of the wind." He took my hand gently in his and my panic subsided. Cooper always seemed to show up just when I needed him. Maybe he was just being nice to a silly kid, but I didn't care. My hand felt sheltered in his.

"There are these old cabins down here that get closed up as soon as the season's over," he said. "But it's easy to jimmy the door and get in."

I smiled. "Dugan's Cottages."

"You've been there?"

"I grew up in Provincetown. My friends hung out in Cabin 5 for years."

"What a coincidence. Cabin 5 happens to be the one that's easiest to break into."

We ran the rest of the way. When we got there Cooper took a pocketknife and wedged it into the doorjamb near the rusty lock. The door popped open.

"Wow," I said. "That was fast. We always took the boards off the bedroom window to get in. You obviously have more experience at breaking and entering."

"Oh, yeah, I'm quite the slippery hoodlum," he said, twirling an imaginary mustache. "You have no idea."

He left the door half-open so sunlight could drift into the dank space, but the cabin was still a lot more shadowy than I remembered it. When we were kids it never seemed scary to play here, even though the cabin was dark, but now the place had an eerie, lifeless feeling to it. Thin, watermarked curtains hung crookedly over the boarded-up windows, and one glass waited to be washed in the old stained sink.

"Do you come here a lot?" I asked.

"From time to time. Even in summer the cabins aren't always rented. They're not exactly luxury accommodations."

Cooper opened a closet door and pulled out a blanket to throw over the ancient couch. "If you don't cover it first, the dust asphyxiates you," he said as he sat down.

I wasn't sure if I should sit next to him or not. I didn't want to make any wrong assumptions about what we were doing here. What *were* we doing here? Just talking, right? There was no law against sitting next to the person you were talking to.

He patted the blanket. "Sit down, Jacqueline. Tell me what's going on." His concern wrapped around me and made me feel safe. In a funny way, he reminded me of Lorna—they were both good-looking, of course, but it was the way they radiated confidence that drew people to them. I sat down next to him.

"I just ran into Lorna Trovato's mother," I said.

He shook his head. "I don't know her."

"You're lucky. She's usually drunk and always crazy. For some reason, today she freaked me out even more than usual. I felt like she'd been waiting for me. Like I'd never be able to get her out of my life."

"That's why you were running? I'm so sorry."

"She made me take pictures of her. Look." I pulled my camera from my bag and Cooper leaned over to see. "She had this wild look on her face, can you tell? And she was wearing . . . well, you can see."

He took the camera from me and scrolled through the recent photographs. "Wow, she looks like an older, nuttier version of her daughter, doesn't she?"

Did she? She had last week when she was wearing Lorna's old clothes, but did she look like her even when she wasn't trying to? I scanned the pictures again, even though they gave me the creeps. The highly arched feet that seemed to be running in place, the drama of the decapitating scarf, the fearless you'll-never-take-me-alive look on her face—suddenly I recognized them. There was no doubt Lorna had been Carla's daughter.

"I forgot you knew Lorna," I said.

Cooper shrugged. "Not well. She was always with Finn so I saw her around the Center. You should print some of these photos. They're amazing."

I shook my head. "I don't know."

"At least show them to Elsie."

"Maybe." But I knew I wouldn't. What if Elsie wanted one in the show? No, these were not going to hang on a gallery wall.

Cooper took my chin in his hand so I couldn't look away from him. "You don't have tons of self-confidence, do you, Jacqueline Silva?"

I grinned half-heartedly. "What was your first clue?"

But he didn't smile back this time. "You're full of talent and potential, but you don't seem to believe it. Elsie's giving you a show at JSAC! Do you get what that means?"

"I know, but . . . I guess I'm not used to being the one people notice. That was Lorna—she was always out front. I followed her. I liked following her."

His eyes bored into mine for a long moment. I wanted to look away, but that seemed even more awkward than holding his gaze. Finally he said, "You know, Jacqueline, Lorna didn't put you in second place. You put yourself there."

My tears sprang up out of nowhere, unexpected. "I did?" I asked, blinking in embarrassment.

"Yup, you did." His voice was like a caress. "Oh, *you*," he said, shaking his head. "I knew I should have stayed far away from you." His eyes softened as he leaned over and gently kissed me. *Finally* he kissed me! I felt like I'd been waiting for it forever. He tasted like apples and smelled like Earl Grey tea. I hoped I didn't taste like a salty, weepy baby.

"You probably don't believe you're beautiful either, do you?" he whispered in my ear. "Do you want me to convince you?"

"Yes," I said, wishing I didn't sound like such a little girl.

But when Cooper kissed me again, deeply this time, I didn't feel like a child anymore. I felt like I was being rescued by the one person who could do it. I even felt I *deserved* to be rescued.

"Jacqueline," he whispered and the name had half a dozen syllables, each of them stroking me like a cat's tongue.

In seconds he'd managed to split my brain in half. Cradling my head, he laid me down on the blanketed couch. He kissed my neck as he unzipped my jacket. As his hands slid underneath my T-shirt, my brain shut down and I was all body, all sensation.

Tentacles of joy spread out from every spot Cooper touched and radiated through my whole body. Now I understood it. This was what love felt like: an unbelievable thrill that spread from nerve to nerve until you were, finally, entirely alive.

Cooper lowered his body onto mine, my shield against the world. My back arched to meet him. And then his hand slipped beneath the waistband of my jeans, touching bare skin, sparking wave after wave of excitement.

But as quickly as it began, it was over. His hands stopped moving, his body became as still as stone. He groaned and pushed up onto his knees, then propelled himself to the other end of the couch.

"God, I'm so sorry," he said, his electric fingers pushing the hair out of his eyes. "I didn't mean to take it that far. I just . . . once I kissed you . . . it was hard to stop."

For a minute I was too shocked to respond. It had been so beautiful. Was it really over?

"No," I said finally. "I wanted you to do that."

"Jacqueline, how old are you? Eighteen?"

I pulled myself into a sitting position and straightened my clothes. "Well, not quite."

He groaned again. "I'm *terrible*. We have to forget this ever happened. It can't happen again."

I could feel the delight flowing out of my body like dirty water down the bathtub drain. "I don't want to forget it!"

"I don't know what I was thinking. You make me a little bit crazy, Jacqueline," he said, leaning forward and petting my hair. "But the last thing I want to do is hurt you."

"You aren't hurting me," I said, my breathing still fast and rough. I wanted to say more, to tell him what he'd made me feel, but I didn't know how to say it, I didn't know what words to use, and I didn't have the nerve.

"Sssh." He scooted close to me and held me against his chest, rocking me back and forth until I was lulled into a desperate happiness.

"It's getting late," he said finally. "Look how low the sun is."

We untangled ourselves and stood up, but I felt awkward now. I'd been lying in a dark cabin making out with a thirty-year-old man whom I wanted to fall in love with, if he would only let me. I'd never been in a situation like this before. What should I say?

"I won't tell anyone," I said.

He smiled his softest smile. "No one would believe you anyway. A catch like you with an old guy like me."

"That's not true!"

"Jacqueline, you should go home," he said, a little sadly.

"Okay." In order to postpone walking out the door for one more minute, I grabbed the blanket off the couch and folded it up. Cooper opened the outside door wide to let in the last, horizontal streak of sunlight. I was shoving the blanket onto a shelf in the closet when a sharp beam of light cut across the space and lit up a piece of cloth stuffed into a back corner. It glowed in the sunset. I reached in behind dusty linens to pull it out, but I already knew what it was.

Lorna's white jacket.

18.

I showed the jacket to Lucas and Charlotte the next morning as we stood in front of my house waiting for Finn to pick us up. They were stunned into silence and had barely begun to babble their questions when Finn pulled up and rolled down his window.

"I see the whole entourage is coming," he said, glaring at Lucas.

"They want to help out." I stuffed the jacket into my backpack for the moment.

Charlotte gave Finn a nervous smile, but Lucas kept his eyes on his Bigfoot boots.

"Charlotte can come. *He* can walk."

The bombshells of the day before—from the promise of the show at the Center, to my emotional session with Cooper in Cabin 5, to the shock of finding Lorna's coat stuffed in the closet—seemed to have blown away the cautiousness I'd felt around Finn for months. "Don't be a dumb-ass," I told him. "You can't be mad at Lucas forever."

He looked surprised by my bluntness, but he didn't back down. "Sure I can."

Lucas bent over to look in the window. "Look, man, I'll apologize as many times as I have to. I'm sorry I slept with her. I'm sorry I left without telling you. I'm sorry about everything. I mean that. Isn't there some way we can put it behind us?"

"Not that I can think of," Finn said. He looked like he was barely containing himself from leaping out of the car and pounding Lucas. "Jackie, why are you hanging out with this asshole when you know what he did?"

"He's not an asshole, Finn. He's our friend. I forgave him."

"Well, I guess he didn't sleep with your girlfriend, did he?"

"Oh, for God's sake, he screwed up!" I yelled. "Haven't you ever screwed up, Finn? Lucas has been miserable for months. Isn't that enough punishment? Besides, we have more important things to think about now." I opened the front passenger door and crawled in with my portfolio and backpack.

"Nothing is 'more important' to me." His voice was knife sharp.

"Not even this?" I pulled out the crumpled white jacket with the embroidered black diamonds on the collar and cuffs. "Don't even consider telling me this isn't Lorna's jacket."

Speechless, Finn reached out to touch the grimy, stained coat. Lucas and Charlotte got in the backseat quietly, without further invitation.

"It can't be," he said, as he took the coat out of my hands. He buried his face in it and breathed in the mildew. "Where did you get this?"

"It was hidden in a closet in Cabin 5 at Dugan's."

"At *Dugan's*? What were you doing *there*?"

I felt my face heat up. "What difference does that make? The important thing is I found it."

"But she was *wearing* it . . ." Finn said.

"I know! I mean, I *don't* know. Why do you think it was in the cottage?"

Charlotte leaned forward. "All the reports in the paper mentioned the white jacket," she said. "If somebody found it right away, wouldn't they have turned it in to the police?"

"Maybe somebody found it over the summer," Lucas said. "A tourist who was staying at Dugan's. Somebody who didn't know what happened."

"But why would they stuff it in the corner of the closet?" I asked. "Besides, it's all moldy. It's been in there a while."

"I can't believe it was in Cabin 5," Finn said. "It's too freaking weird. That was *our* cabin."

"So you believe me?" I asked Finn.

"Well, I believe it's her jacket," he said, "but I don't know what else to believe."

Lucas sat forward and spoke to the back of Finn's neck. "I just want to remind you that you said it was 'our cabin.' That includes me, and always will."

"But, sadly, not me," Charlotte said.

Ouch. Charlotte carried a hidden knife too. "See," I said to Finn. "I screwed up too. I was a lousy friend to Charlotte, but she forgave me and now we're friends again."

"Charlotte, did Jackie sleep with your boyfriend?" Finn asked.

"Well, I didn't have a boyfriend in the fourth grade."

"Why is *that* the only unpardonable crime?" I said. "For God's sake, Finn, there are other ways to be shitty to your friends."

Finn chewed his lip. Nobody said a word. Finally I looked at my watch. "It's almost ten o'clock. Elsie and Cooper are waiting for us. We'll talk about the jacket later."

"I can't even think about anything else now," Lucas said.

Finn turned around and glared at his old friend. "You're still in my car."

I sighed. "He's still in your *life*, Finn. Get over it."

Elsie was thrilled to see more willing workers arrive. "With this many people, we should be able to get the painting done by Monday, Tuesday at the latest. I'll book the guy to refinish the floors on Wednesday, and they'll be dry enough for us to start hanging pictures Friday afternoon."

Before she started the Spackling demonstration, Elsie sent me off to look for Cooper. "He's in the print shop. You two can decide what to mat."

I grabbed my portfolio, glad to escape the tense atmosphere in the gallery. Finn was snorting and stomping around like a bull waiting for the rodeo to start, and Lucas was mostly trying to stay out of his way. Of course, I was nervous about seeing Cooper, after yesterday. Were we more than friends now? Were we something other than friends? Were we in some kind of a relationship now, or was I an idiot to think that could happen? Maybe I was blowing the whole thing totally out of proportion. I had no idea, but I knew I wasn't ever going to forget what it felt like to be kissed by Cooper Thorne.

As I approached the print shop, I heard a high-pitched giggle coming from inside. My hand froze on the doorknob and my stomach flipped over. Someone was in there with Cooper. Had the new Fellows arrived already? My imagination conjured up a petite beauty, someone just Cooper's age, with whom he had everything in common.

The giggle burst into a wholehearted laugh. Whoever Cooper was with was certainly enjoying herself. I started to feel ridiculous standing outside eavesdropping, so I grabbed the doorknob and yanked the door open before I could have second thoughts.

Cooper was sitting on a high stool and grinned at my entrance. But Tess, standing beside him, was surprised by the interruption and jumped a little, her laughter cut short. "Oh, Jackie, it's you. God, you scared me," she said, pulling at the raggedy hems of her very short jean shorts.

Immediately I understood what was going on. Tess was flirting with Cooper, and it was kind of adorable. Ever since she'd turned thirteen, all she could talk about was how she wanted a boyfriend, and she was obviously dressed for the hunt today. I could just imagine the argument she'd had with Elsie this morning before she got out of the house wearing those shorts.

"Sorry, Tessie. I didn't know you were down here. Aren't you chilly?" I asked, nodding to her long, bare legs.

She formed her mouth into a pretty pout and shrugged. "A little. It's supposed to warm up later."

"Ah, youth," Cooper said. "She doesn't even feel the cold, do you, Tiddlywink?"

Tess glowered at the use of the nickname her mother had foisted on her years before. "Don't call me that. I hate that name."

Cooper pacified her with his usual radiant smile. "Listen, kiddo, Jacqueline and I have work to do this morning."

She looked confused. "You and *who*?"

I laughed. "He means me. Are you going to help paint the gallery?"

"Who's there besides my mother and brother?"

"My friend Charlotte came. And Lucas."

Tess's eyes widened and she seemed more childlike again. "Ooh, Lucas is here? Finn's so mad at him, and he won't tell me why. This should be good." She banged out the print shop door, eager to see fireworks.

"Hey, you," Cooper said. "How are you doing today?"

"Okay, I guess." I fiddled with a strand of hair and then pushed it behind my ear. If only Cooper had been my age, I'd have known how to handle the situation. Or even if I didn't know exactly, it would be okay, because I'd know that something good was beginning and I could just wait for it to sort itself out. But he wasn't my age. He was a thirty-year-old novelist, an *enfant terrible*, as Carolyn Winter had said. In comparison, I was . . . well, more like a plain old infant.

When Cooper walked me home last night, I was more or less hysterical over finding Lorna's jacket, and he kept his arm around my waist, comforting me without making too big a deal of it. Outside my front door, he didn't even kiss my cheek. Would he never kiss me again? Or was he just afraid my parents might see? Or maybe he'd decided I was just too immature to be kissed. How was I supposed to know? I *was* immature.

"So, let's get to work, huh?" I hoisted my portfolio up onto one of the big tables. We had a job to do—I could stick with that for now. "I brought everything. I couldn't decide."

He stood beside me as I opened the cardboard folder. He was as close as he could be without actually touching me, and I could feel the hair on my arm stand up as if it were reaching out for him.

He flipped through the pages, murmuring kind words. "Always loved this one. Oh, these are new: They complement each other, don't they? Gorgeous, Jacqueline!" I allowed myself to float along on his praise and tried not to think too much further ahead than that.

Cooper started putting the photographs into piles: definitely, maybe, no. I felt sorry for the pictures that went into the "no" stack, but I tried not to be defensive about their rejection. We had to make decisions. Before long I forgot to be nervous, and we began debating the merits of each picture. At the end of an hour we had eighteen Definitelys and a half-dozen others on which Elsie would make the final decision.

"Let's frame this new one with the footprints across it," Cooper said. "It should be the centerpiece of the show. The poem is great too."

"Well, I don't know if it's a poem. It's words."

Cooper read aloud. "*I have kept your shoes/in case I need them./ Do you walk in clouds/without me?* That's a poem, sweetie."

Sweetie. He said it so casually, I knew I shouldn't love the sound of it so much. But I did.

The two of us settled down to measuring and cutting mat board. I'd done it before, but I wanted to make sure these looked as professional as possible, so I watched carefully as Cooper cut his piece. After working silently side by side for twenty minutes, he said, "You can be quiet for a long time, can't you?"

I grinned. "I can. I like silence."

Cooper shook his head. "It makes me nervous. Probably because I grew up in L.A. where there was no such thing as silence. We had a freeway on one side of us and a guy who raised peacocks on the other. Peacocks shriek, although not as loud as my mother."

"You're from L.A.? I didn't know that." I liked imagining Cooper as a little boy with sun-bleached hair, growing up between traffic jams and peacocks.

"Yup. I had the quintessential L.A. childhood. My mother moved there from Nebraska to become a movie star, but poor Noreen was six feet tall and had acne scars, so her career was a non-starter. All she ever landed was a commercial for Pain-Eze. You've probably seen it—it played for years. She's sitting on the edge of a bathtub pretending to have a headache. There's a loud drum booming in the background and red sparks shooting out of her head."

"I have seen it," I said. "That's your mother?"

"Well, she's about twenty-five years older than that now. Only acting job she ever got, but you should hear her; she thinks she's Meryl Streep. Meryl with a migraine. Oh, I shouldn't make you laugh. You'll cut crooked."

I put down the knife. "Tell me more about living in L.A."

"It makes people crazy."

"How?"

"They all want to be famous, one way or the other. It's like a disease." He continued to work as he talked. "When my mother couldn't get any acting jobs herself, she started dragging *me* to auditions, so at least she could be the mother of someone famous. I can't tell you how many hours we wasted sitting in studio waiting rooms full of precocious little brats, all of us practicing our off-key audition songs. *Everyone* had migraines by the time it was over."

I found this glimpse into Cooper's unconventional childhood fascinating. No wonder he was so interesting! "Did you get any acting jobs?"

"No Sugar Pops, no Band-Aids, no Jell-O. My mother decided I wasn't getting chosen because of my name, so she changed it to Cooper."

"Wait, so Cooper isn't your real name?"

"Well, it is now. But I was Howard Thorne, Junior at birth. I'm grateful to her for the name change. It looks better on a book jacket, and besides, who wants to be named after somebody he can't stand?"

"Your dad? Howard Thorne, Senior?"

He grunted. "Believe it or not, the guy sabotaged the only decent acting gig I ever got."

"Tell me."

Cooper handed the knife back to me. "Okay, but keep cutting or we'll never get done here. I landed a role in a TV pilot when I was thirteen. I'd had a small part in a *Law & Order* episode once, but this was the first lead I'd gotten. Noreen was ecstatic."

"What show? Did it get on TV?" I tried to concentrate on my cutting, but it was hard.

"It did. It was a sitcom called 'Master of the House.'"

"I remember that show!"

"Then you probably remember that I wasn't in it. Howard Thorne, Senior didn't want me to do it. He had some stupid excuse about my grades, but I knew he was really just jealous that Noreen liked me better than him, and he damn well wasn't going to sit around and watch me *succeed*. So, he called the director and told him that he'd worked with me before, and he thought the guy should know that I was an unreliable, dope-smoking delinquent."

I put the knife down again. "No! Your *dad* did that?"

"Yes, he did. And, surprise, the director decided I wasn't right for the role after all. Teenage actors are a dime a dozen out there—they don't need to hire the kid who's going to show up late with dilated pupils. I never got offered another gig in Hollywood." Cooper picked up his mat knife and made a long perfect cut. His eyes narrowed as if he were performing surgery, maybe on his father.

"That's terrible!" I wanted to comfort that thirteen-year-old, cheated by someone he trusted.

"Seemed like it at the time, but if I'd been in that stupid TV show I might never have started writing. I'd be some B-list actor living in West Hollywood, hoping somebody recognized me when I strolled down Rodeo Drive."

"Wow, Hollywood. Your childhood sounds kind of amazing."

He shrugged. "Everybody has an amazing childhood, don't they? Life only gets boring when you grow up."

"You think so?"

"Sure. The first time you do something, whatever it is, it's magical. First merry-go-round, first bicycle, first Hollywood audition, first driving lesson, first smoke, first kiss, first sex. Boom! Pow! Socks knocked off! After that it's all downhill."

I made a face. "I hope not."

Cooper gave me a sly smile. "Why? You run through all your firsts already?"

I could feel the blush crawl up my cheeks. Just when I was starting to feel easy with him again too. I picked up the knife and willed my hand steady. "I still have a few experiences to look forward to."

But when Cooper's fingers dug into my shoulders, massaging out the tension, I had to put the tool back on the table. "I'm sorry," he said. "I didn't have a younger sister to tease, so I never got it out of my system."

"Is that how you think of me, like a little sister?" I couldn't believe I'd said that.

Cooper turned me around so I was facing him, then leaned down and gave me a decisive kiss on the lips. "I wish I could think of you that way," he said, moving his mouth to my ear. His breath on my neck once again awakened all my nerves. "Unfortunately, I don't."

I reached up and folded my arms around his neck. It wasn't over—it was just beginning! Just as he leaned in for another kiss, the door banged open and Finn swaggered in.

"I need masking tape. Do you know where—" He stopped talking and stared at us.

Cooper looked up, his arms still around me. "Masking tape? There's a box of it on the desk in my office. You can put the extras in the supply closet."

"Jesus Christ," Finn said as he backed toward the door he'd just come in. "I can't freakin' believe this." He pointed a finger at Cooper while he glared at me. "I'm working my butt off for you, and you're in here making out with *him*?"

I pushed away from Cooper, but Finn was already out the door, slamming it as hard as he could.

"Oops," Cooper said.

I was simultaneously thrilled and horrified by what had happened. At least now Finn knew *somebody* found me attractive. Cooper didn't push me away! But Finn was already mad at me about Lucas—what if this was the final straw that would break us all apart?

Plus, I didn't want Elsie to know about . . . whatever this was. I was pretty sure she wouldn't approve. She might think she should step in and say something embarrassing about our age difference to me or to Cooper or possibly both of us together.

"Do you think he'll tell Elsie?" I asked Cooper.

"Never happen. Teenage boys don't run and tell Mommy. He'll just go off and brood about letting you get away." Cooper grinned. "Meanwhile, caught kissing an older man: another first for you!"

I smiled and lifted my face for seconds.

19.

On Sunday morning I walked to the Center with Charlotte. I didn't bother to call Finn—there was no reason to think he'd show up to help me a second time, not after yesterday.

The dancing policeman at the intersection by the wharf spun in a circle and waved the hordes of people across the busy street.

"Elsie thinks we'll finish a second coat on the walls today," Charlotte said. "We're ahead of schedule."

"I know." I leaned into her. "Thanks for coming today, Char. I didn't expect you to after working the early shift at the café."

"I'm having fun. I like a project."

I nudged her with my elbow. "Is that the only thing you like?"

"What?" Charlotte fought back a grin.

"I saw you and Lucas off in the corner yesterday. You were both working on that one little piece of wall for forty-five minutes!"

"So not true!" Her grin broke through. "He's sweet, though, isn't he?"

"Charlotte likes Lucas," I sung in a quiet, tinny soprano.

"Shut up!"

"I'm happy for you. You make a great couple."

"Yeah, well, we're not there yet, so don't count your chickens. Or my chickens either. And speaking of who-did-what-with-whom, I hear you were caught smooching Cooper yesterday."

I stopped suddenly in the middle of the sidewalk and three people ran into me. "Finn told you?"

Charlotte nodded and pulled me to the curb so the crowd could pass. "I think he was so shocked, he had to tell somebody, and he certainly wasn't going to talk to Lucas about it."

"Did he tell anybody else? Like Elsie?"

"I don't think so. Is it a secret?"

"Sort of. I hope he doesn't tell his mother. Besides, I don't know exactly what we're doing, Cooper and me, and I don't want people to start talking about it. It might not be anything."

"Well, Finn thought it was something, and he's *not* happy about it," she said.

"He thinks Cooper's too old for me. But I'm not a baby."

"I reminded him that the pickings are kind of slim in a small town. Especially one where half the population is gay."

"You told him that?" I laughed.

"Yup. I asked him if he expected you to wait around for him to get over Lorna at age forty."

"You did *not*! Charlotte!"

"Well, it's true, isn't it? If Finn was available, you wouldn't be kissing Cooper."

We jumped the leash of a barking Chihuahua whose preoccupied owner was deep in conversation with a man in a Speedo on a bicycle. I was so discombobulated I almost tripped.

"Oh, my God, I can't believe you said that."

"He couldn't either. It shut him right up."

"Char, I know you mean well, but please don't say stuff like that about me to Finn anymore. It's not going to happen with him. Ever. I don't know why he even cares if I'm with Cooper."

"I don't think he knows why he cares either. But he *does*, believe me."

I shook my head. It was too confusing, and I had too much else to think about.

❧

"Oh good, you're here," Elsie said as we walked in. "I want to tell you all the big news."

To my surprise Lucas and Finn were both there, standing on opposite sides of the gallery, Finn looking as if he'd just had a breakfast of lemons. Rudolph sulked in the background, frowning into a cup of coffee. I assumed Cooper had already heard the "big news"—there was a knowing smile on his face when he came over to stand between Elsie and me.

"There are going to be some changes around here very soon," Elsie said, "and you guys are the first to know. As of Friday, I'm stepping down as Director of the Center and Cooper is taking over the job." She reached out to touch her protégé on the arm as she said his name. He bowed slightly.

A grunt of disbelief escaped Finn's throat. "*That's* the big news I had to come here for?"

Nobody else seemed to know what to say in response to Elsie's announcement. Rudolph, who was obviously already aware of the decision, gave Cooper a disgusted look. Charlotte and Lucas filled the silence with weak applause and, after a few seconds, I realized that I ought to join them.

"Congratulations," Rudolph said to Cooper, sounding completely insincere. "Maybe the next time you give an interview, you'll remember to mention the place you work." Duty done, he stalked out the door and in a moment they heard his car peel out of the parking lot.

I tried not to look stricken. "But why are you leaving?" I asked Elsie. "I mean, Cooper will be great, of course, but you *are* Jasper Street."

"That's exactly why I'm stepping down," Elsie said. "Running the Center has taken over my life. I never meant to be an arts administrator forever. I'm a painter, Jackie. I want to get back to that."

"And it's a great opportunity for me," Cooper said. Did he sound a little miffed?

"Oh, I know," I said. "I'm really happy for you!"

"This just seems like the right moment," Elsie continued. "Cooper's been here so long, he knows the place inside out. There's no one else I'd feel as comfortable turning over Jasper Street to. And," she paused for effect, "I've decided to use the occasion of your opening, Jackie, to formally announce my resignation and Cooper's promotion. All the new Fellows will be here by then and we'll make it a celebration. What do you think?"

I hesitated for just a second, then managed to drum up an enthusiasm I didn't feel. "That'll make it a really special evening," I said. I knew it was selfish of me to mind that my big moment would be eclipsed by Cooper's. After all, he was an adult—this was a big deal for him, whereas my show was just a scheme to bolster my college prospects. It was childish to feel disappointed. Swallow it, I told myself, and act like a big girl.

"That's not fair," Finn said. "Why do you have to combine the two things? The opening should be just for Jackie. Why do you have to stick Cooper in the middle of it?"

"I'm not 'sticking' Cooper anywhere," Elsie said. "We just thought it would make the evening that much more special. Don't you think so, Jackie?"

Finn groaned. "You're putting her on the spot, Mom. What's she going to say?"

Elsie looked sincerely worried. "Am I, Jackie? I thought you'd be pleased."

"I am. It's a great idea," I said, because—Finn was right—what else could I say?

"It's settled then," Elsie said. "Let's get this place painted."

Elsie and Cooper started prying lids off paint cans, but I stood and stared at Finn until I caught his eye. As soon as he looked at me, I mouthed, "Thank you."

❧

I felt like I was in the eye of the storm and didn't know where to run for cover. Standing too close to Cooper or even talking to him in Finn's vicinity seemed like tossing a match into dry grass, so I tried to find places where I could paint by myself.

Lucas and Charlotte were definitely flirting, but they were self-conscious about it and kind of jumpy. Finn wasn't speaking to Lucas, and even though he *was* speaking to Cooper, it was only to complain about his workmanship or chide him for taking too many breaks. When Elsie tried to make a joke about Finn's rotten mood, he bitched at her too. By four o'clock we'd finished painting and I was exhausted, not from the work but from the tension in the room.

"Good job, everybody!" Elsie said, clapping her hands. "Cooper and I will clean up. The rest of you go enjoy what's left of Sunday afternoon."

Cooper tipped his head to me as if silently apologizing for not being able to leave with me. I didn't expect him to. Our relationship, or whatever it was, seemed to bloom only in dark corners and abandoned cabins. I had no expectations of, say, going to a movie or a restaurant or even to the beach with him. Did it matter? I wasn't sure.

The late day sun was warm as we stepped outside and stretched our achy arms and backs.

"I've got my dad's truck," Lucas said. "I can give you guys a lift."

Finn scowled. "I'd rather walk."

"You want a ride, Jackie?"

I glanced at Finn, trying to gauge how much of his anger was directed at me. "I guess I'll walk home with Finn, if it's okay with him."

He shrugged. "I don't care."

Considering his crappy mood, that was practically an invitation. "You walking, Char?" I asked, figuring she'd understand I wanted a few minutes alone with Finn.

Charlotte's eyes crinkled and her round cheeks turned scarlet.

"We're going to the beach," Lucas answered for her.

"Have fun," I said. I was happy that the two of them had connected, but watching them climb into the truck together, I wished for a minute that I had a real boyfriend, an uncomplicated, straightforward I-like-you, you-like-me kind of thing. Someone I could go to the beach with in the middle of the day. Which would probably never be Cooper. Because the age difference *was* a big thing, even if I didn't want it to be. If I was really okay with it, I wouldn't be so afraid of Elsie finding out, or, God forbid, my own parents.

Finn and I walked down to Commercial Street before I finally said, "Are we going to talk about it?"

"What's there to say?"

"I'm sorry you walked in on us."

"Me too. But I guess you're not sorry you're doing whatever it is you're doing with him." He sounded more concerned than angry.

"I know you don't like Cooper, Finn, but he's been really nice to me."

"Yeah, like butting his way into your show. That's *really* nice." When I didn't say anything, Finn continued. "Look, it's not just his age. It's his ego. He's used to getting what he wants, Jackie, and you're used to *giving* people what they want. He'll take advantage of you."

I thought of the afternoon Cooper and I were together in Cabin 5. It wasn't true. Cooper had pulled away before I had. He'd never hurt me.

I shook my head. "He's not who you think he is, Finn."

"Maybe," he conceded. "But he's not who you think he is either."

As usual, Commercial Street had been taken over by bicycles and pedestrians, but we had to move out of the middle when a Winnebago driven by a terrified senior citizen suddenly pulled behind us. The foot and bike traffic gave way just enough for the bus to squeeze through, then flowed back into the street like a river around a rock.

The interruption was a welcome break in a conversation neither of us seemed to want to have.

"This time of the year I can't wait for all the vacationers to pack up and go home," Finn said. "I like it when the weather's cold and the place is deserted."

I laughed. "You're really kind of an old fart, aren't you?"

He reached over and yanked a lock of my hair. "And proud of it, smart-ass." It was such a comfortable gesture, I had to remind myself not to respond in an equally familiar way. Not to smack at his arm, or sass him back flirtatiously. *It's not what he means and it's not what he wants.*

But Finn's mood kept improving as we got closer to the West End, and I felt more at ease with him than I had in ages. As we walked past MacMillan Wharf, Mojo's, the Blue Moon Café, the New Art Cinema, it almost felt like it was *our town* again, the way it used to. Before. We joked with each other, and made fun of the tourists, a pastime locals never got tired of. And when I looked over at him, his face seemed relaxed for the first time in four months.

"I saw Ms. Waller Friday afternoon," he said as we neared his house. "She gave me some brochures."

"*College* brochures?" I tried not to sound as shocked as I was.

He nodded. "Of course, she thinks I should look at Dartmouth, but I assured her that was not happening."

"But you're looking at other colleges? You might apply?"

He smiled. "I might. I'm 'exploring my options,' as Ms. Waller says."

"That's good, Finn. That's really good."

"Yeah, I knew you'd say that. I'm not giving up on boats entirely though. I was thinking maybe I could do something with oceanography, study marine life or something. I don't even know what the possibilities are, but I think I'd like to learn more about the ocean."

"That's a great idea!"

"I'm just thinking about it, so stop grinning at me."

"Okay," I said. But I couldn't stop. And my grin must have been contagious because he gave it right back to me.

20.

Friday night Cooper and Elsie and I hung my photographs in the newly spruced-up gallery. I was amazed by the way the blank walls called attention to the pictures, made them breathe and pulse and become, well, art. My head was buzzing with nervous excitement and I was hardly able to keep from bouncing on the car seat as Cooper drove me home.

When we pulled up in front of my house, he managed to stop my jiggling with a quick, deep kiss. I looked immediately to the window of my parents' bedroom, but the lights were already out.

"An artist is born," he said, scooping his fingers through my hair and pulling it away from my face.

Which was exactly what I was thinking, even if I didn't have the nerve to say it out loud. I had the feeling I'd just glimpsed the path my adulthood would take, and it was wide and long and brighter than I could have imagined. I was having my first show—my life as an artist had begun.

And I was growing up in other respects too. My relationship with Cooper took a leap forward every time we were alone, and I knew, before long, there would be a decision to make. Part of me felt ready to jump into another "first," but I was still nervous too, and tended to pull away a little when Cooper ran his hands over my body, setting off sparks that shocked and thrilled me. As soon as I resisted in the slightest, he stopped and apologized, and then I had to assure him there was nothing to apologize *for*. I was obviously confusing him and I felt bad about it. I wanted to give in entirely, to belong to him, but the decision wasn't quite that simple.

It wasn't that Cooper seemed old to me, but more that I sometimes felt like a child when I was with him. He was, after all, an actual grownup and I was an inexperienced kid. It was what kept us from being a couple in public—we didn't look right. And an insistent little mosquito in my ear kept asking, *Why would he choose you?*

And there was another thing too. Earlier in the week, Cooper and I had gone back to Cabin 5, and while we were lying on the couch together I started to imagine that it was Finn next to me, Finn running his tongue over my lips, Finn making my breath stop. I tried to push the image away, but I was only partly successful. How could I consider sleeping with Cooper if I was still dreaming of Finn? But Finn was *never* going to love me, so why shouldn't I be with someone who actually cared about me? I looked at the question from every angle, but the answer wouldn't come clear. I hoped that maybe one day I'd stop thinking so much and it would just happen.

I let myself into the dark, quiet house and tiptoed to my room. Sleep didn't seem like a possibility, but how else could I fill up the long hours between now and tomorrow night's opening?

The white jacket hung over the back of my desk chair. During the week I'd soaked it in vinegar and hand washed it in detergent to try to get out the stains and smells. I hung it outside in the sun, but the pearly white was still dingy and discolored, and there were splotches of bleach surrounding the spots of mold I couldn't completely wash out.

Quietly, I got the ironing board from the hall closet and set it up in my room. It calmed me down to guide the nose of the iron through the deep wrinkles, even though it didn't do much for the appearance of the jacket. I poked the collar into place and flattened the embroidered diamonds until the cloth was relatively smooth.

I was about to hang it on a hanger, but changed my mind and instead slipped my arms into the sleeves. Heart pounding, I turned to see my reflection in the mirror. I pulled at the tails and straightened the lapels, but the faded jacket did not turn me into Lorna—it wasn't a magic cloak. Still, it fit me as perfectly as it had her, which made me feel . . . stronger. I stood up straight and peered into my own eyes.

Of course I couldn't ever wear it. My best friend *drowned* in this jacket. (Didn't she? But then, how did it turn up in Cabin 5?)

A loose black thread dangled from a sleeve. Absentmindedly, I pulled on it and was horrified to see how quickly one of the embroidered diamonds began to come unraveled. I snipped the thread, but the damage was done.

Reluctantly, I took off the coat and hung it on a hanger on the door of my closet.

After a restless night, I hoped to skip out the back door early the next morning without my mother's usual pleading with me to eat breakfast, but she'd just come back from the bakery with a bag of pastries.

"Got your favorite," she said, holding out an almond croissant.

"My stomach's too shaky to eat. Maybe later," I said, nesting my camera into my backpack.

"You nervous about tonight?" Mom asked as she slathered butter on a roll for herself. "Or is that supposed to be a secret?"

"A secret? What do you mean?"

"Well, you've hardly told me anything about your big show."

"What? I told you all about it."

"Well, you mighta told me, but you didn't invite me, did you?" She sipped from a coffee mug and didn't meet my eyes.

I was stunned. "Do you *want* to go?" It had never occurred to me.

She shrugged. "Well, I *am* your mother. Of course, I guess it'll be all those arty types, like Finn's folks. I wouldn't fit in."

"That's not true," I said. "All kinds of people go to openings. It's a celebration for the artist. You should come if you want to."

She looked skeptical. "You don't want me there."

"Mom, I'd love for you to come." As I said it, I realized it was true. "I didn't think you'd want to come. You've seen all my stuff already." The smell of the croissants was tempting me and I opened the bag to look at them curled together in greasy splendor.

"Well, I've seen 'em here in the house, but it's different when they're hung in a museum, isn't it?"

"It's not a museum, it's a gallery," I explained. "A museum is . . . bigger."

"Well, whatever. I'd never get Marco to go with me anyway. Even if he's home in time, once his butt hits the couch after dinner, he don't move."

"Come with me then."

She grunted. "I don't know. I'll think about it." She grabbed another roll from the bag, and the aroma wore down my resistance.

"Okay, give me half of that," I said, my hand reaching for the crusty, buttery pastry.

"What would I even wear to something like that?" she said, her eyebrows knitted with worry. "I don't have the right kinds of things."

"Sure you do," I said, feeling oddly excited. "I'll help you look in your closet later. We'll find something."

She let out a whoop. "The person who wears jeans and a T-shirt 364 days a year is gonna help me get dressed up? That's rich." But, as the hot coffee fogged her glasses, a rare grin curled up her lips.

It was chilly out that morning. Fall was hurrying toward us. I walked to my usual spots, only this time as I approached the pier where I'd made that disastrous pass at Finn, I thought instead of Cooper, the way he welcomed my arms, my mouth, my body. I'd felt like such a naïve dope when Finn pushed me away—but I didn't feel that way anymore. Cooper appreciated me, told me I was beautiful and talented. Someday he might even love me. Wasn't that where we were headed? I said the word out loud—*love*—to test the feel of it in my mouth. It sounded like a foreign language and I was proud of myself for learning to speak it.

As I approached Dugan's Cottages, I thought of the first time Cooper kissed me, on the dusty old couch where I'd played as a child. It was funny how my life kept circling back here to Cabin 5.

But there was something different about the cottage this morning. At first I couldn't spot the problem, but then, looking closely, I saw that the boards from the rear window were lying in the sand, as if someone had removed them and crawled inside the way we used to years before. Kids, I figured. And I envied them. I wished I could go back to a time when life and death were only games, before I was familiar with the realities of either one.

I walked up to the open window, but I didn't hear any noise. The kids must have left without putting the boards back, which annoyed me. Now the place would be open to the weather unless Mrs. Dugan realized the problem and sent someone to fix it. I decided to take care of it myself. Tomorrow morning I'd come back with one of my dad's hammers and—

Wait. There was a noise. Somebody *was* inside the cabin. I backed away from the window, as if I'd been caught snooping. But then, on second thought, if it was kids, I thought I ought to remind them to put the boards back when they left. And maybe

I should check to be sure that they weren't causing any damage. This was my special place. I was willing to take responsibility for protecting it.

I went around to the front door and tried the handle, but the door was locked from inside. So I knocked, long and loud.

"Is someone in there?" I called.

Slowly, the door began to creak open and then it swung wide. A girl with long red hair falling over her shoulders tilted her head, a wry grin on her lightly freckled face. She leaned one arm against the doorjamb while the other rested across her belly.

"Hi Jackie," Lorna said. "I was hoping it was you."

21.

I didn't scream, but some kind of bewildered yelp came out of my mouth, and for a minute I doubted everything. Was I awake? Dreaming? Hallucinating? Losing my mind? My hands flew up and covered my eyes, just briefly, but when I looked again, she was still there.

Lorna cleared her throat and gave a slightly embarrassed laugh. "Seen a ghost?" Then she took me by the arm and pulled me into the dark cottage.

I couldn't put together words that made the slightest bit of sense, but I gripped Lorna's forearms and held on tight. My body trembled as if some inner earthquake was shaking me to pieces.

"You better sit down," she said, prying my fingers off her arms. She pointed to a kitchen chair and I collapsed onto it. My eyes mapped her body, the same, but different. Her long red hair, always a full mane, hung stringy and lifeless around her face. A scattering of small pimples decorated her forehead on skin that had always been flawless. And she was heavier too, as if she were tied to the earth now, grounded. We stared at each other for a full minute before Lorna broke the connection.

"So, here I am, not dead, not drowned, not even wet." She gave a rusty laugh. "I guess you want to know what happened."

But I couldn't speak, couldn't even imagine what to say.

"First of all, let me just tell you, the water in the bay in the spring is *frigid*. You know I always liked distance swimming, and I'd practiced my swim—from the breakwater, around the point and into the harbor—several times on sunny afternoons, but doing it in the dark, without a wetsuit, in the middle of a storm, was totally different. It was so damn cold that night and the waves were wild. I wasn't even sure I was swimming in the right direction. There was a point where I thought I really *was* going to drown."

Lorna wrapped a blanket around her shoulders and sank onto the couch. It was the same ancient blanket Cooper and I had lain on, side by side, three times now. She continued, "The thing I hadn't counted on was . . . being afraid. I never was before, at least not physically afraid. My body always did what I expected it to do. But when I jumped into that cold water—"

"You *jumped*?" My voice leapt from my throat. "I knew you didn't fall!"

"Of course I didn't fall—you should know me better than that." She smiled easily as if this story were no different than the other reports of her adventures I'd listened to over the years. "But once I hit the water, I thought my heart might stop. I might have even turned around and gone back except the tide was already pulling me out, and that awful wind—there was no choice. I had to swim for my life or be swept out to sea."

I sat there staring at her, frozen. The most amazing, wonderful thing had happened, but I still couldn't quite believe it. For a minute, I almost didn't *want* to believe it, because if it was true, wasn't I a fool for spending the past four months agonizing over my best friend's death? But, no, no. That didn't matter. I shook my head to clear it. Lorna was *back*!

"The tide pulled me as far as the point," she went on. "I expected that. The idea was to let the ocean take me that far and save my energy for the last part, when I had to swim against the tide to get around the point and back into the harbor, to the beach. I could barely catch a breath between the waves, and I knew it was too dark for anyone to see me out there. No one would save me. No one could. The only way to get back to where I left my stuff was to swim like hell."

I thought of Lorna stumbling onto the beach in the dark, half-drowned, chattering with cold. And then one mystery became clear. "You left things here in Cabin 5, didn't you?" I asked.

"A towel, some clothes, my backpack. So they'd stay dry."

The dots were connected. "Which is why I found your white jacket here in the closet."

Lorna beamed. "You found it? That's great! I hated leaving it behind, but I had all these wet, heavy clothes to stuff in my backpack and the jacket was one thing too many. I figured some tourist took it. Do you still have it?"

"Of course I do."

She grinned happily. "Will you bring it to me? I always thought it was lucky. That's why I wore it that night."

"I'll bring it. I tried to clean it up, but I couldn't get all the stains out."

"Thanks, Jackie."

"Do you want your sneakers too?"

The question seemed to puzzle her. "My sneakers? That old rotten pair? Why would you keep those?"

I couldn't answer that. It required more language ability than I had just then.

Lorna sighed. "Anyway, once I dried off, I knew I had to get out of town quickly without anybody seeing me. I wanted to hitchhike up-Cape, but if somebody from town picked me up, my whole plan would be ruined. I walked to the East End on the beach wearing this big slicker I got at Marine Specialties—I figured nobody would be able to recognize me in that, but there was nobody out but me in that weather anyway. I saw these guys loading up their car in front of the Bayside Inn, and I figured they were tourists leaving town, so I asked them if I could have a ride.

They were going to New York City, which was perfect. Even if they eventually heard the news that some girl from Provincetown had drowned, they'd never connect it to me. They took me to Hyannis and from there I got a bus to Boston and then I went on up to Maine to find my dad."

By then I was beginning to trust my voice and my ability to reason. "You did all this so you could run away and find your dad? Couldn't you have just told us where you were going and taken the bus from here?"

She grinned. "What fun would that have been? Anyway, I wanted my mother to think I was dead. She deserved that." She stood up and opened the blanket to reveal her stomach, solid and round under her shirt. "Also, there were certain things I didn't want people to know. At the time, I wasn't planning to come back."

I stared at her body, trying to make sense of all this information, received too quickly. Lorna wasn't just heavier, she was pregnant. Lucas had not lied about that. Still, still, *still*, I couldn't understand. "You were never coming back?"

"That was the plan." She wrapped herself up again and paced around the room. "Don't look so shocked, Jackie. You know I like doing things I'm not supposed to. Just let somebody say, 'You better not' and whatever it is, I'll do it. I can't *wait* to do it. It's like an itch in my brain and the only way to scratch it is to go rogue."

Even though I hadn't really digested what I'd heard so far, I wanted more information. I wanted the whole story. "So, did you find your dad?"

"I had an old address for him, and it turned out he was still in the same place. Even if he'd moved, I'd have found him. He has family around there."

"And that's where you've been? For four months?"

"Pretty much."

"But why? I mean, *why*?" My voice suddenly careened into a wail. My shoulders buckled, and in seconds I was sobbing. "Oh, my God, Lorna, we thought you were *dead*!"

She came over to me and put her arms around my quivering shoulders. Her touch made my nerves jump under my skin, as though I still wasn't convinced she wasn't some supernatural spook. I grabbed onto her arms again and held on tight enough to leave red marks. I thought I might never let go, but Lorna was strong enough to disentangle herself.

"I'm sorry Jackie," she said, backing away. "I had to. I didn't see any other way out."

"I would have helped you! Finn would too!" But even as I volunteered Finn, I wondered what his reaction would be if this baby really was Lucas's. Would that make him stop loving Lorna, or would nothing, no betrayal of any kind, halt his devotion?

I sucked up my tears. "Whose baby is it? Lucas says you told him—"

"That was an idea I had at the time, but . . ." She shook her head.

"So, Lucas is *not* the father?"

She frowned, maybe annoyed by the question. "I'm not 100 percent sure at the moment."

"But you think that Finn is . . . ?" Was that a better option? Better for whom?

"I'm so thirsty these days," she said, grabbing a bottle of water from the kitchen counter. She took a long drink and then announced, "The baby's a girl, by the way. Due middle of January."

"Oh." I had no idea how to react. What I felt like saying was, "What difference does that make? That's the least important piece of information you've given me." Instead, I just said, "A girl. That's nice."

"I want to name her Lucy. That's a good name, isn't it?" When I didn't answer, she said, "You want to know who the father is, but I can't tell you right now. It *could* be Finn."

"You don't *know*?"

She tipped her head to the side like a puppy who knows he'll be forgiven. "Could be somebody else altogether."

"Somebody *else*? *Who*?"

"I can't tell you right now." She smiled at me. "I'm sorry. Am I shocking you?"

I stood up, holding on to the lip of the table. It felt as if my eyes were bouncing out of my head like those joke glasses with plastic eyeballs on metal springs. "Are you kidding me? I'm so far beyond shocked, there's not even a word for it! You didn't drown. You jumped in the water on purpose. You're pregnant. And the baby's father is either your boyfriend or some unnamed stranger. I feel like I've wandered into an alternate universe!"

I almost never got angry at anyone, and here I was yelling at Lorna who was not, after all, dead, but standing right in front of me. I knew I should be so relieved that I didn't care about any of the rest of it. But apparently I did care.

"I thought you'd be happy to see me," Lorna said, pouting a little. She flopped back onto the couch, her knees pulled up to her chin, the blanket anchored tightly by her stocking feet.

I massaged my forehead, as if I could knead Lorna's revelations into my brain. "I *am* happy to see you. Of course I am. But I thought you were *dead*! We all did! Do you get that? There was a memorial service. We cried for days! For weeks! We still do!"

She looked surprised. "Really? There was a memorial service? Whose idea was that? I'm guessing not Carla's."

"Ms. Waller organized it, but your mom was there."

Lorna suddenly sat forward. "Did she cry? My mom. Did she?"

"I . . . I'm not sure. I mean, I couldn't see her very well."
I thought of Carla, sitting in the front row in her black pajamas,
rustling through her purse, looking distracted.

Lorna gave a snort. "I bet she didn't. I'm surprised she even
showed up. Do you know that crazy bitch didn't even get in touch
with my dad? She thought I was dead and she didn't even tell
my father! Of course, I figured she wouldn't—they haven't spoken
since he left us. If she'd contacted him, the cat would have been
out of the bag right away. So, who else came to the memorial?"

"A lot of people. Kids, parents, teachers. The auditorium was full."

"Really?" Her cheeks glowed.

"Of course!"

"Are you glad I'm not dead, Jackie?" There was no self-pity in
the question. She really wasn't sure.

I sank down onto the couch next to her and grabbed her
hands. "Of course I am. Are you kidding? I just can't quite believe
it yet—it's like a dream come true."

She nodded. "Thanks."

"Tell me the rest of the story," I said. "You went to Maine and
found your father, and then what?"

She rolled her eyes. "My dad lives in East Snowshovel. He's
a carpenter, handyman, whatever, but also kind of a hermit. He
doesn't even have a phone. Can you believe that? Communication
is not his thing. Which I liked at first—just the two of us alone.
It was so quiet and peaceful. I sat around and read library books
for two months. Dad was kind of flipped out that I was there, so
I kept a low profile. I told him I'd run away because Mom had
gotten even crazier, and, of course, that part was true and easy
for him to believe. I thought he might want me to finish up the
school year, but it didn't seem to occur to him. He's not really
normal either. Big surprise."

"It sounds kind of nice, though," I said.

"It was, at first. I didn't tell him I was pregnant, but after a few months it became kind of obvious. He warned me right away he couldn't stand crying babies. Never could. And since I'm the only crying baby he's ever been around, I guess he really meant he couldn't stand me. Anyway, I could tell it wasn't going to work out. I had this fantasy that he'd be happy to see me again, and he'd get all excited about being a grandpa, but that wasn't going to happen. He likes being alone. I figured once the baby was born, there was a good chance he'd just leave us. That's his pattern. Which would make me *my* mother, poor and alone, with nobody to take it out on but my kid. No thanks."

"So you came back here," I said.

"Not right away. I've been in Boston for the last few weeks. I stayed at a women's shelter for a while. That's where I went to a clinic and found out I was having a girl. I thought maybe in the city I'd meet somebody who'd help me out."

I was confused. "Like who?"

She shrugged, and then grinned. "A guy, maybe. Men always like me."

"What do you mean, 'a guy'?"

She sighed. "Jackie, you're so *perfect*, you don't know what it's like for somebody like me."

"Are you kidding? I know you better than anybody does."

"You think you do." Her eyes sparkled like glass. "I needed money, Jackie. I thought about hooking. Thought about it *seriously*."

My shock was only tempered by the realization that Lorna was enjoying shocking me.

She gave a short laugh. "I didn't *do* it. I mean, I'm pregnant. I have to take care of myself for the kid's sake."

"Well, I'm glad *something* stopped you!" I didn't want to sound like a judgmental prude, but I couldn't help it. This latest revelation was too much, even for Lorna. Although, it had never crossed my mind that she'd faked her death either, so maybe I had no idea what was too much for Lorna.

She hugged her knees. "I have this crazy idea that I can be a better mother to my daughter than Carla was to me. That shouldn't be too hard, right? She set the bar pretty low."

That was an understatement. As soon as I thought of Carla's mothering skills, I had to forgive Lorna for everything. I thought again of that awful day on the beach when Carla gleefully untied the bow on Lorna's bikini. Escaping from her mother was so necessary for Lorna, I didn't blame her for doing whatever she had to do to get away.

"Of *course* you'll be a better mother than she was," I said. "No contest."

She picked at the knobs of fuzz on the old blanket. "I guess we'll see. Anyway, by the time I got to Boston, I needed money. The people at the shelter tried to help me get a job, but it turns out I can't even *apply* for a job."

"Why not?"

"Because I'm dead, Jackie. Lorna Trovato's dead. And if I'm not her, who am I? I'm nobody, and you can't get a job if you're nobody. So I had to come back. I had to bring Lorna Trovato back from the dead."

I laid my head against her shoulder. "I'm glad she's back. I'll help you. Whatever you need, I'll help you."

Lorna smiled a lazy smile. "Thanks, Jackie. Knew I could count on you."

"You should have come to me sooner. Before you came up with this whole terrible scheme. Did you think I'd be mad at you because of the baby? I would have stuck by you, Lorna. I would have helped you."

"Yeah, well, there was this other problem too."

The cabin suddenly felt claustrophobic. Dark, airless, full of secrets.

"You mean, a problem with the person who's not Finn or Lucas? The guy you think could be the father?"

"Yeah."

"*Is* he the father?"

She shrugged. "Probably."

My head was spinning, but I had to know all of it now. "Does *he* think you're dead too?" Lorna nodded and I sucked in a lungful of amazement.

"I know, I know," she said. "I'm going to see him. Soon. But you have to keep this a secret until I do. Please! I need to talk to him before anybody else knows I'm here."

"Even Finn?"

"Especially Finn. Promise me."

"But—"

"Jackie, please!"

"Okay, I promise, but Finn needs to know you're alive, Lorna. You can't imagine how upset he's been. He still loves you so much."

Her mouth turned down at the corners. "Oh, Finn."

"You still love him, don't you?"

She stared into the distance and wrinkled her forehead as if she was trying to frame her answer correctly. "I always *liked* Finn, Jackie, but not as much as you did." She stuck her legs out in front of her and caressed her belly. "I've only ever loved one person."

One person who was not Finn, I thought. *And not me either.*

22.

I stumbled through the A&P in a fog, picking up a box of Saltines, a jar of peanut butter, a bag of Chips Ahoy! cookies, Lorna's favorite foods. I bought strawberries, melons, a wedge of Jarlsberg cheese, yogurt with honey, apple cider, Cherry Garcia ice cream, thick salsa, and chips dusted with lime—I wanted to overwhelm her with food, with concern, with gratitude for coming back. I spent all the cash I had on me, but managed to keep myself away from the ATM for fear I'd empty out everything I'd saved for college and hand over every bit of it to Lorna. Just because she wasn't dead.

I was headed out through the automatic door when I heard somebody call my name, but my reaction time was slow, and by the time I turned around, Lucas had passed me on his way in. Which gave me ten seconds to think of what to say to him while he entered the store, then came back out through the exit.

"You look like you're sleepwalking," he said. "I called you three times before you heard me."

I tried to smile like a normal person would. "Sorry. Daydreaming."

"Worried about tonight, I guess."

Tonight? I gave him a blank look as I struggled to remember what was happening tonight.

"Your show? At the Center? Jeez, Jackie. Are you okay?" He put a hand on my arm as if to steady me.

Lorna's reappearance had so completely overshadowed everything else that I'd forgotten what was supposed to be the most important day of my life so far. Lucas was looking at me as if I'd lost my mind. If I couldn't keep the secret from him, what chance did I have of deceiving Finn?

It took all my energy to haul up a chuckle from deep inside. "Oh, the *show*. Yeah, sorry, I'm a little distracted. My mom isn't feeling well and I'm in kind of a hurry to get this stuff home to her."

Lucas peeked in the top of my bag. "Strawberries and ice cream? That's what your mom wants when she's sick?"

I tried to keep the phony laugh bubbling. "Well, she's not *really* sick. You know. She's just . . ." Just *what?* "Cramps. You know."

I couldn't believe I'd fallen back on such a stupid excuse, as if my mother really sat around eating ice cream when she got her period. If Lucas had had a mother or a sister, he wouldn't have bought it, but, lucky for me, his family was all men. He just blushed and shut up.

"I'll see you tonight, huh?" I tried to sound excited, happy, just a little rushed, as I scurried away down the sidewalk.

"If you want to wait, I'll give you a ride," he called after me.

"I'm good."

"Okay." He waved and disappeared into the store.

By the time I got back to Cabin 5 I was sweaty and just a little sick to my stomach.

"Okay, I got you a few things at the store. And I stopped for coffee."

Lorna grabbed for the hot cup as I took the food from the plastic bag. "I can bring you more stuff from home tomorrow if you want, but, I mean, you aren't going to be hiding out here much longer, are you? It's getting cold at night. You're going to tell people soon, right?" It had to be soon. Already I couldn't stand the pressure of knowing this enormous secret and not being able to tell the people who needed to know it.

"A day or two. That's all. I just need to talk to . . . somebody. Then I can be alive again, which, believe me, nobody wants more than I do." Lorna dipped a cracker into the peanut butter jar.

I still had hours before I needed to dress for the opening, but I was afraid if I stayed any longer, I'd find out more secrets I didn't want to know and certainly didn't want to keep to myself. I didn't know how I'd keep *this* one. "Listen, I have to get going. I almost forgot that my pictures are hanging in the gallery at JSAC tonight. An opening. It was Elsie's idea." For some reason I didn't want to go into the whole thing with Lorna, didn't want to seem proud of myself in front of her.

"Your photographs? Really? You're having a show?" Peanut butter dripped onto the Formica table.

"Yeah, it's not a big deal." Of course it was a big deal! "Elsie's trying to help me get into college. Art school. You know."

Lorna dipped another cracker. "She's, like, in *love* with you." She made it sound shameful. Or unfair.

"Not really. We like each other."

"She's Finn's *mother*."

"So?"

She shrugged. "It's weird that you're such good buddies."

"I don't think so. Anyway, I have to go."

"Go, then." She sounded a little put out.

"I'll be back in the morning. Okay? Early."

"Don't forget to bring my jacket."

"I won't."

I half expected to be seen leaving the cabin, but the beach at Dugan's was as deserted as always. I guess there was a part of me that wanted to be caught. To be forced to tell someone the incredible news.

When I got up to Commercial Street, tides of people washed past me again. I wondered if any of them could tell by looking at me that my life had changed dramatically in the past few hours. Lucas had known something was going on—he was probably still mulling over my idiotic excuses. What if he had more questions for me tonight? What if Finn did? Everything about going to the gallery tonight and being the center of attention was terrifying. People would expect me to have conversations about my work, they'd expect me to make sense. How was I going to be able to do that when all I could think about was Lorna, sitting half a mile away in a dark cottage eating peanut butter? *Alive!*

It wasn't fair that I was the only one who knew this—it was too big a secret. Lorna had said specifically that Finn shouldn't find out, so not even a hint could be leaked to any of his friends or family either. But, couldn't I tell *someone*? Someone who didn't even know Lorna that well, someone who was trustworthy enough to keep a big secret, someone who could help me make sense of it all. Of course there was only one person who fit that description. If I couldn't at least tell Charlotte I would explode.

"What is *wrong* with her?" Charlotte screamed. We were walking in front of the Meat Rack, the crowded benches that line the sidewalk in front of Town Hall, and dozens of eyes turned toward us.

"Charlotte! Keep it down!" I hissed. "I told you, nobody can know about this."

"I'm sorry, but I can't help it! This is the craziest thing I've ever heard!" Charlotte pulled one of her tight curls straight out to the side and then let it boing back to her head.

"Okay, down to the beach," I said. We didn't say another word until I'd maneuvered her a block and a half and we were alone, looking out into the harbor.

"You can't keep this from Finn," Char said.

"I promised I would. And you promised me *you* would. It's only for a few days."

She shook her head disgustedly. "God, Lorna magically reappears and within hours you're already lying for her."

"I'm not lying. I'm just . . . respecting her wishes."

Charlotte snorted. "Right. Because she deserves that."

"You don't understand how hard this is for her, Char. She's got no money and no job. She's pregnant and she's alone. I have to help her."

"Oh, please. Lorna's never alone." Charlotte's voice sounded like acid dripping on metal. "As soon as it gets out that she's alive, everybody will be flocking to help her. Just like you."

I was stunned. "You sound like you're mad she's alive."

"I'm mad that she can hurt—no, *ruin*—her best friends' lives, and then when she shows up again, you're not even mad at her. All is forgiven. Did she even apologize? She plays the most horrible trick ever and it's all okay with you. The queen is back on her throne!"

I stared at her, open-mouthed. "I thought you'd help me, Char. I need you to help me make sense of this."

"There's no sense to make of it. I'm sorry, Jackie, but this is the most screwed-up thing I've ever heard. I know you think that having a crazy mother gives Lorna the right to do whatever she pleases, but she made up an elaborate scheme to fool the entire town and it's not right. She pretended to be dead rather than fess up and tell people she was pregnant by some mystery guy. What the hell? And now you're all 'poor Lorna.' I can just see what's coming. Any minute now Finn will ride in on his white horse, and probably . . ." She pinched the bridge of her nose and stared at her shoes. "And probably Lucas will too."

I had to admit, it was a scene I'd been imagining: the four of us back together again, stitching up our wounds, putting everything back the way it used to be. And it was true Charlotte wasn't in that picture. Could she be?

"When it comes to Lorna, you're still ten years old," Char said, her face tight and twisted. "You'd do *anything* for her, wouldn't you?"

I should have realized Lorna's return would stir up Charlotte's old jealousies. She was right that Lorna's disappearance had been terrible for Finn and Lucas and me, and I *didn't* entirely understand why she'd had to do it that way. But she was back now, and I couldn't turn away from her. Is that what Charlotte expected me to do?

"Char," I said, pleading, "she's my best friend."

Charlotte threw back her head and looked up into the sky. "I was waiting for you to say that. You haven't changed at all." She walked away then, her backward glance freezing me to the bone. The shrieks of hungry gulls echoed her accusation.

23.

As the gallery began to fill up, I was grabbed and hugged by people I'd known my whole life and by people I hardly knew at all. It was so overwhelming I was almost able to push Lorna to the back of my mind. Almost.

"I did not know you were such an ar*teest*," my mother's friend, Sal, said, smacking me lightly on the hand. A whole herd of Mom's friends had shown up with her, women I'd known forever, all of them dressed in oversized flowery shirts as if they'd decided together this was the only outfit that would do. Had my mother asked them to come? Begged them? They seemed a little lost wandering through the two rooms, nodding their heads at the strange cut-up images of the town they'd lived in all their lives.

Al Anthony, one of my father's fisherman friends, stalked around the gallery, his six-and-a-half-foot frame allowing him to see the pictures over everyone else's heads. Finally he came up and shot a finger gun at me. "I told your dad you were somethin' else. I told him."

And, oh no, Mr. Carver was here, too. The high school art teacher from whom I'd purposely never taken a class grinned at me over his three chins as if I were a side of barbecued ribs. "I'm so proud of you," he said, and I could tell he was taking a certain amount of undeserved credit for my success.

By six-thirty the place was so full I couldn't see my photographs at all anymore, and I'd completely lost track of my mother. All the newly arrived Fellows had shown up, looking a bit lost, and a sampling of local artists, some celebrated, some self-proclaimed, sipped wine from plastic glasses while scanning the walls with their laser vision. It would have been unnerving even under ordinary circumstances, and today had been anything but ordinary.

I wondered if Charlotte would come and was glad to see her arrive with Lucas and his dads. Fortunately, Simon and Billy were chatty enough that no one but me noticed how quiet Charlotte was.

"I've been looking forward to this all week," Simon said, kissing my cheek. "You are on the move, kiddo, and we knew you *when*."

I tried not to look at Charlotte as Billy complimented the dull outfit I threw on in desperation at the last minute. My mother, in her Lane Bryant tunic, looked more fashionable than I did in gray pants and a dark blue cardigan sweater. (I'd stuffed the bright pink scarf from Elsie into my backpack, but now that I was here, I wasn't sure I wanted to stand out any more than I already did.) If Charlotte had helped me get ready, I might have put together something a little quirkier, more daring, but after our argument at the beach, I couldn't ask her.

Not that I thought her anger was fair. I *liked* Charlotte—Lorna coming back wouldn't change that. After all, I wasn't a child anymore. But my relationship with Lorna was deep and wide—it felt *ancient*. Lorna came first. Period. If Charlotte couldn't accept that, well then, maybe our friendship *was* over. I was pretty sure anyone seeing the two of us this evening would assume we were barely even acquaintances.

As I was pulled from person to person, I somehow managed to skirt the wine and cheese table where Finn was busy uncorking bottles. I was afraid my face alone would give away the secret I couldn't tell. If I opened my mouth to say anything at all to him, everything I knew might spill right out.

"This is so awesome! Aren't you psyched?" Tess asked. She danced around me enthusiastically, and then bounced off across the room in sparkly ballerina flats. Just a few years ago Tessie would have been padding around the gallery in her stocking feet or even flannel pajamas, everyone's favorite mascot. I kind of missed that little girl. Anyone seeing her now, wearing a tight JSAC T-shirt, her eyes thick with black liner and metallic dust, would think she was much older than thirteen. Suddenly I was blinking back tears, appalled at how close to the surface my emotions were. Like the days just after . . . *Don't think about that! Just concentrate on here, now.*

Finally there was a moment I wasn't being pulled at by anyone, and I found myself looking around the room, studying all the young men, wondering who might be the one Lorna loved. Could it be Kip Michaels, the young reporter from the local paper who didn't seem to own a pair of shoes that weren't Birkenstocks? Or that painter who stayed on after his fellowship ended last year, the one who called himself "Jag"? Or maybe it was someone from out of town. Wellfleet or Orleans. But how did she meet him? Did I know him? Was he a summer person? A tourist? My imagination touched down on every guy in the room, which gave me a headache. I couldn't imagine Lorna with anyone but Finn.

I'd been too agitated to eat anything since that half a croissant early this morning, and now my stomach was growling so loudly the couple next to me turned and stared. No doubt it was cowardly to want to escape the people that came to see your work, but I needed a break, so I ducked into the office. There, in the shadowy light of a desk lamp, Elsie and Cooper sat huddled together.

Elsie jumped up from her chair, her wine-red skirt grazing her ankles, long, silver earrings peeking out from beneath her hair. "There you are!" She gave me an excited hug. "Isn't this fabulous! What a crowd!"

I couldn't keep myself from sneaking a glance at Cooper who was leaning back as far as the office chair would allow, his legs sticking straight out in front of him. His smile was full and confident, and just for me. I was so grateful there was at least one person—one important person—for whom Lorna's return wouldn't have any particular significance.

"We were just talking about you," Cooper said with a lazy sweetness. I could feel the blush creep up my cheeks all the way to my hairline, and I was thankful for the dim lighting.

"I'm getting ready to give my little speech," Elsie said. "And I need you. You're the star of the evening!"

I leaned back against the wall. Why did anyone ever want the spotlight to shine on them? It was much too bright. "Oh, Elsie, I don't think I have enough twinkle left to be a star. I'm not used to everybody looking at me. It makes me nervous."

"Well, *get* used to it, Jacqueline." Cooper narrowed his eyes at me. "Ninety percent of stardom is *acting* like a star."

I groaned. "But I hate being the center of attention. They all want to talk to me and I don't know what to say to them."

Elsie thought for a moment. "Did you bring your camera?"

"It's in my backpack, in the closet." I almost hadn't brought it, but it didn't feel right to leave it home. After all, I wouldn't be having the show without it.

"Get it," Elsie said. "It's your shield. If you're taking pictures, no one will bother you."

I got the camera and hung it around my neck. "I don't usually take pictures of people though."

Cooper stood behind Elsie and gave me a secret smile. "First time for everything. Remember?"

I froze where I stood. Cooper was flirting with me right in front of Elsie! What if she picked up on it? But she grabbed my hand, oblivious, and led us back into the gallery where someone had set up a small platform with a microphone in one corner. Elsie stepped up to the mike, dragging me behind her.

"Can I have your attention, please?" she said in her melodious, but commanding, voice. The talking subsided and people turned toward her. "I want to introduce you all to my talented young friend whose work is on display here tonight."

Elsie put an arm around my waist. "She's a local girl—born and raised right here in Provincetown. Tonight you lucky folks are the first to see her remarkable photographs hanging in a gallery. This is her first show, but I predict there will be many more to come. Ladies and gentlemen, Jackie Silva."

Elsie started clapping and so did the entire audience. I was stunned to be standing up in front of a roomful of adults, all of whom were staring at me and applauding. What was I supposed to do now? Did I have to make a speech? Why didn't I ask Elsie before we got up here? As the applause died down, I could feel myself starting to panic, and I scanned the room, searching for help. When my eyes collided with my mother's, way in the back of the room, I realized that she was mouthing something to me. She was saying . . . *thank you.*

Of course. I stepped to the microphone and took a deep breath. "Thank you so much," I said. "I'm so grateful to Elsie and to the Jasper Street Art Center for the opportunity to show my work, and to all of you for coming to see it. I'm just . . . flabbergasted." The audience tittered kindly. I looked at my mother and repeated her words. "Thank you, again."

I stepped back to another brief round of applause, and then, before the crowd could return to their interrupted conversations, Elsie grabbed the mike again. "The other order of business this evening is an announcement. I'm sure you all know how much the Jasper Street Art Center has meant to me since Rudolph and I opened these doors twenty years ago. However, as of this evening I will be stepping down from my administrative position here in order to concentrate on my painting."

There were a few gasps of surprise, but Elsie kept on going. "I'd like you to welcome the new director of the Jasper Street Art Center, a man who has helped us grow for the past eight years, and who has himself grown from a youthful Fellow into a well-respected writer—our own Cooper Thorne."

This time the applause was enthusiastic, accompanied by a few whistles. I couldn't help but feel proud that someone so well-liked and respected liked *me*. Cooper jumped up onto the platform, bowed deeply, and laughed his sweet laugh. He gave an overview, with jokes, of his years at the Center, and within minutes, he owned the room. People smiled and laughed, and when he finally wrapped up his talk, they cheered appreciatively. I couldn't help feeling embarrassed by the difference between our two speeches. It was obvious how much younger and less sophisticated I was than Cooper. Did that bother him?

We stepped off the platform and Cooper unplugged the mike while people came up to congratulate him on his promotion. Thank God for Elsie's suggestion that I hide behind my camera. That would help me get through the rest of the evening with less anxiety.

As I passed through the crowd, I snapped randomly, sometimes framing the shot, sometimes not. It was a different way of working for me, but it was kind of exciting. The pictures might be composed of a chin, two hands and a pair of wine glasses, or a window with a blond ponytail swinging in front of it. No one interrupted me as long as the camera was up to my face. I was surprised at how much I enjoyed juxtaposing unrelated elements: elbows, eyebrows, shoes. I imagined the ways I might use the images in my collages.

As the crowd thinned out, I saw my mother putting on her jacket in the doorway and hurried over.

"Are you leaving?"

"Yeah, I'm tired. I figured you'd want to go out celebrating with Charlotte or Finn or somebody. You can get a ride home with one of them, can't you?" She patted my shoulder awkwardly and turned to go.

Cooper, I thought. Maybe I'd celebrate with him and he'd drive me home. Still, I wasn't going to let my mother slip away so easily. She had to say *something* about the show. "Did you enjoy yourself?" I asked.

"Oh, Jackie, I don't know beans about art," Mom said, but she stopped trying to hustle out the door. "I'm a fisherman's daughter and a fisherman's wife. I've never even been to an art show before. I didn't know what to expect."

"Really? Never?" It was hard to believe that someone who grew up in Provincetown, a place with at least two dozen galleries and a small, well-respected museum, had never been inside any of them.

"Wasn't the kind of thing we did, your dad and me. I always figured I wouldn't know what I was looking at," she said. "But I can see why people like looking at pictures. It's fun and kind of exciting. Or maybe I just feel that way because these are my daughter's pictures." She gave me a hesitant smile. "Maybe when the show's over, you might want to hang a few of them in our house."

"In *our* house?"

"If you want to," Mom said. "That way I can look at them some more."

Nothing anyone had said to me all night meant more than that. "I'd love to, Mom."

"Good." She zipped her jacket, but hesitated at the door. "Being here tonight, seeing all this," she said, waving her hand around the room, "I had a feeling maybe I *could* see your future after all." Before I could think of a response, she gave me a speedy hug and was gone.

The opening was over and I didn't know whether to feel grateful or sorry.

Elsie and Cooper corked the leftover wine bottles while Finn put the remaining fruit and cheese into plastic containers. Rudy grabbed a chunk of watermelon from a plate and said, "I'm taking you all out for dinner." He gestured grandly to those who were left, which seemed to include Charlotte and Lucas, whispering in a corner.

"Oh, Rudolph, I'm not sure I can," I said, trying to pull a viable excuse out of my mushy brain. I knew it would be too much, that my façade couldn't hold up through an entire meal.

"Nonsense! You probably haven't eaten a thing all day, have you?" he bellowed.

I laughed nervously.

"Me too?" Cooper asked.

"You too, Thorne. I'm a forgiving man, and we're celebrating. Elsie's escape from office work, and Jackie's escape from, well, I guess from Provincetown. At least, eventually, when she gets into some fabulous art school. How's that sound, Jackie?"

Escape? Is that what I'd be doing? No. Provincetown wasn't just the place I lived—it was who I *was*. My identity. In the excitement of applying to RISD, I'd forgotten that in order to go, I'd have to leave P'town behind.

At the moment, however, the thing I was most afraid of was spending the next two hours sitting at a table filled with people to whom I couldn't tell the truth. Elsie didn't know about Cooper. Finn didn't know about Lorna. Well, *no one* knew about Lorna, except Charlotte, and she was silently furious about it. Each bite of food I put in my mouth would be seasoned with deception.

But what could I do? I pulled out a smile from the place I apparently kept all my other lies. "Well, then, thank you Rudolph. Dinner sounds great!"

24.

I couldn't believe the way Finn muscled Cooper out of the way so he could sit next to me in the restaurant. Why tonight of all nights, when I wanted to stay far away from him? The whole dysfunctional bunch of us were stuffed into a corner table in Ciro's candlelit basement, me sandwiched between Finn and Rudy, Cooper across the table between Elsie and Tess. Charlotte was there too, huddled next to Lucas at the far end of the table, looking as if she'd rather be just about anyplace else. I wasn't going to be able to swallow a bite.

Rudolph threw both arms up into the air. "Champagne for everyone!"

"Rudy, there are only three of us at the table old enough to drink champagne," Elsie said, shaking her head at her indulgent husband.

"Oh, come on. Who'll know?"

"They won't serve the kids. Especially Tessie."

Tess grabbed at her napkin and the silverware on top of it clanged to the floor. "Why do you always have to say stuff like that, Mom? Like I'm such a baby!"

"Because you *are*—"

Rudolph interrupted his wife. "Now, now. No fighting. This is a celebration. If we can't have champagne, we'll all have filet mignon or something."

"Very Lord-of-the-Manor of you, Rudy," Cooper said.

My eyes fell to half-mast and I let my head drop into the palm of one hand. If only I'd sneaked out with my mother and gone home to bed. I wouldn't have been able to sleep, of course, but at least I wouldn't be sitting here next to Finn, Lorna's for-God's-sake *boyfriend*, holding onto a secret that would change his life.

"Are you okay?" Finn leaned over and put a hand on my leg, which jerked involuntarily at his touch. I'm sure he felt it.

"I have a headache," I said, wishing he'd lift his hand.

"Hard being a star, huh?" he mocked me gently.

"I'm not a *star*."

"Oh, excuse me. I should have said, 'Diva.'" He removed his hand and I immediately missed it.

"Sorry," I said, giving him a sideways glance. "I'm tired. I probably should have gone home with my mother."

Rudolph overheard me. "What? And go against an age-old tradition? When an artist has an opening, he or she is required to go out and get smashed afterward!"

"Rudy!" Elsie shook her head.

"You know what I mean. Celebrate! Enjoy the moment! Successes don't come around all that often."

"Oh, I don't know. You've had your share," Cooper said, perusing the menu.

"My *share*?" A shadow crossed Rudolph's face. "What's that supposed to mean? You think I've had too many? I'm not allowed any more?"

"That isn't what he meant," Elsie said.

"How do you know what he meant?" Rudy huffed. "Are you his interpreter? He can speak for himself."

"All I meant was you've had many successes," Cooper said, calmly. "No offense intended, Rudy. I don't know why you insist on thinking I'm defaming you."

Rudolph held his menu in front of his face. "Well, perhaps because that seems to be your favorite pastime lately."

Finn leaned over and whispered to me, "This should be worth the price of admission. Rudy's been itching to lay into Thorne ever since that radio interview." His breath on my ear, his mouth against my hair, made me dizzy. I closed my eyes and leaned back in my chair.

"Forgetting to mention your name on NPR is not 'defaming you,'" Cooper said, rolling his eyes.

Rudolph slapped the menu on the table. "Of course it is! Everyone knows you've been my protégé for the past eight years. For you not to mention me—"

"*Everyone?*" Cooper gave a scornful laugh. "I don't think most people give a damn about either one of us."

Rudolph's face turned crimson and the volume of his voice increased. "It was a slap in the face and you know it. You *meant* it to be. You were interviewed for half an hour, and in all that time you didn't once mention either me or Jasper Street!"

"Oh, good Lord, Rudy. I'm sorry. I've apologized six times. It was an oversight. What do you want me to do?"

Rudolph jabbed his finger into Cooper's face. "It was rude and embarrassing, and I'd be happy to tell you *exactly* what to do—"

"Daddy!" Tess interrupted him. "People are staring at you."

"Rudy!" Elsie reached across the table to smack his arm. "The waiter's here."

Rudolph looked up at the boy with the notepad and said, grumpily, "I'll need another moment."

The waiter turned to the other side of the table where Cooper was grinning widely. "I'll have a martini, please, and then the filet mignon."

I kept spinning the spaghetti around and around on my fork, unable to lift it to my mouth. This evening was endless.

Finn pointed to my plate. "On this planet, we actually eat the food."

I gave him a half-hearted smile. "I'm not that hungry." I couldn't believe how nice Finn was being to me tonight. If only I could fall against his shoulder and rest there a few minutes. I wished he'd allow it. I wished I deserved it.

"Try some of my chicken Marsala," Lucas said. "If you like it better than yours, I'll switch with you."

Finn glowered at him. "Or you can have my Alfredo if you want."

Charlotte didn't offer food or sympathy. I couldn't even look at her for fear her eyes would scald me. What if she decided to blurt out the truth? What would I do? Better to keep my eyes on my plate.

"No thanks, really," I said. "The pesto's good. I'm just tired from, you know, everything." I managed to force a tiny bite of pasta between my teeth and gulp it down.

Finn leaned close again. "Something's wrong, Jackie. I can tell you're upset. Did something happen tonight?"

Oh, Finn, if only I could tell you! "Tonight? No, no. I'm just—"

"Stop saying you're tired. That's not it." He sounded worried. Would he be angry with me when he found out the truth? Probably. Probably he'd be furious.

I tried to keep my eyes hooded so he couldn't look into them and see the lies balanced on the lower lids, threatening to leap off in a fountain of tears. But they didn't seem to be under my control. They drifted up until Finn caught them. We stared at each other, eye to naked eye, and I could feel myself drowning.

Rudolph and Cooper had been chugging down martinis for forty-five minutes and were both the worse for it.

"You know, Rudy," Cooper said, stretching across the table and tapping his index finger against the side of Rudy's plate, "Sometimes you remind me of my father."

Rudolph cut another piece of his steak and swirled it through the mashed potatoes. "Am I supposed to be flattered by that?"

"Not at all. He was a jealous old bastard."

"Cooper!" Elsie's mouth fell open.

Rudolph drained his glass and said, "Thorne, are you trying to make me clock you? Is that your plan? Are you hoping someone will write it up in the *New Yorker* and you'll get a little more free publicity at my expense?"

Cooper smirked. "Oh, Rudy, you do think you're Ernest Hemingway, don't you?"

"Stop it, both of you," Elsie said. "You're ruining the evening."

"I feel sorry for your poor father," Rudy continued as if she hadn't spoken. "If I had a son who turned out to be an ungrateful parasite like you, I'd shoot myself."

"Funny, that's just what he did," Cooper said. "To no one's regret."

The table went completely silent until Tess started to cry. Cooper and Rudolph stared at each other as if they were arm wrestling, and no one else knew where to look.

My head had started to swirl like the inside of a tornado. I pulled my gaze away from Finn and stared at the wormy pasta on my plate, trying to bring it into focus. When I felt Finn slip his hand into mine, I jumped to my feet and launched myself back from the table, the screech of my chair against the wood floor ripping through the thick silence.

"I should go," I said, holding on to the table edge as the room spun around me. "I'm not feeling—"

I think it was Charlotte who shouted, "Jackie!"

And it might have been Finn who put his arms around me as I fell. But there was no time to appreciate it before I lost consciousness.

25.

"You said you were coming *early*." Lorna left the door ajar so a little light could penetrate the dank room.

"Sorry. I came as soon as I could. Here's your jacket," I said, tossing it to her. She hugged it to her chest.

"Oh, I missed this!" She held the coat at arm's length so she could study it. "It's kind of a mess now, isn't it?"

"I tried to get the stains out, but I guess they were in too long."

She slipped her arms into the sleeves and tugged the jacket on, but it gaped wide over her belly. "Damn," she said as she yanked on the lapels. "Reality check."

"You're lucky I got here at all," I said, as I unloaded the food I'd sneaked out of my mother's kitchen, mostly day-old bread and pastry from the Portuguese Bakery. "My mom wanted me to stay in bed all day."

Lorna removed the jacket and threw it in a heap on the couch. "Why? Are you sick?"

"I fainted last night. At a restaurant. In front of Finn and his parents and pretty much everybody I know."

She snorted. "Oh, my God. Because you were so nervous about the opening?"

"That was part of it. I hadn't eaten anything all day." I put a bag of rolls on the table and a container of cream cheese. "I hope my mom doesn't miss this stuff."

Lorna grabbed a roll from the bag. "I'm starving. I could eat three of these."

I found a bowl in a cupboard and arranged an apple, a banana, and an orange in it. I got a knife from a drawer and laid it on the table in front of her.

"The thing is . . . " I said, then stopped. Did I really want to get into this?

"What? The thing is what?" She smeared a thick layer of cream cheese on a roll and closed her eyes as she took a bite. "Oh, this is good." She reached for the apple.

If only I could've opened a window, let in the morning sun. The cabin felt like a cave; the walls pulsed around me. The air, damp and musty, pressed against my chest and pushed out the words I'd been holding in.

"It wasn't just nerves about the opening," I said. "It was you too. I mean, it was *mostly* you. God, Lorna, you blew my freaking mind showing up here yesterday! I couldn't think about anything else. And I couldn't talk to anybody about it, and I felt like I had this huge secret that I couldn't tell the people who'd most want to know it. I felt like I was lying to them!" I fell into a kitchen chair across from her. "You wrecked me."

She crunched into the apple. "I appreciate it, Jackie, I really do. You know that."

"I don't know how much longer I can keep this a secret. What are you waiting for, Lorna? How much longer are you planning to hide out?" It made me shiver to imagine curling up on a damp mattress in this lonely place.

"Not much longer. I couldn't . . . do what I needed to do last night. But I will tonight. And then I'll come out of hiding. I promise. You can deal with it one more day, can't you?"

I wasn't actually sure I could, but I didn't say that. "I guess you're afraid to see Carla too. That'll be hard."

Lorna made a face like she'd just found a worm in her apple. "I'm not afraid of anything, Jackie, especially not my mother. You should know that."

"Well, maybe not afraid, but it'll be hard, won't it?"

"Everything to do with my mother is hard."

"I saw her a few days ago out in front of Old Hat," I said, remembering how that green scarf disconnected her head from her body.

"They still let her work there?"

"I don't think she does much work. She's . . . bad."

"Some things never change."

"No, I mean *really* bad. Like, crazy."

Lorna put the half-eaten apple on the table and stared at it. "That's not *new*, Jackie. She just used to hide it better. I'll probably end up like that too, eventually. One of the town crackpots. Like mother, like daughter." She rubbed a circle on her belly, like she was apologizing to the baby.

I didn't remember ever hearing Lorna admit to a weakness before, especially one as awful as that. I reached across the table and grabbed her hand. "No you won't. Don't say that!"

She pulled her hand away. "Crazy's not the worst thing. Not for the crazy person, anyway. Of course, eventually the rest of you will get totally sick of my bullshit. You'll wish I *had* drowned."

"Stop it! You're nothing like your mother."

She shrugged. "I guess we'll see."

"You aren't. When Carla sees you're alive, maybe she'll straighten out a little bit too."

A low growl rattled in Lorna's throat as though she thought I'd said an incredibly stupid thing. "You don't really believe that, do you?" She squared her jaw and I could see her fierce confidence return. In fact, she seemed tougher than ever—unbreakable. "I'd be happy if Carla never found out I was alive, but I suppose she has to. God, people are going to act like it's such a *big deal*, aren't they? Coming back from the dead is going to be a giant pain in the ass."

There was a long silence while I tried to beat back the anger that flared in my chest. It was going to *irritate* Lorna to deal with everyone's happiness over her return? There was a taste in my mouth as if I'd been chewing on tin cans. I felt like my emotions had been squeezed into a spongy ball that Lorna kept lobbing into a wall with a tennis racket.

Finally I couldn't hold in the explosion any longer. "It *was* a big deal! How do you not get that? *You died!* And everybody who knew you was horrified and destroyed, including your mother. The entire town has been obsessed with your drowning." My voice was getting louder and louder. "You can't just show up all of a sudden and expect people to pretend it didn't happen. 'Oh, look, Lorna's back. Isn't that nice?' No. They *mourned* you. They'll be shocked, and some of them will be damn mad that you made fools of them!"

Lorna raised her eyebrows. "You sound like you're one of the damn mad ones."

"Well, maybe I am, a little bit. How could you do this to us?"

Lorna kept her face blank as she closed up the cream cheese and cinched the plastic bag of rolls with a twist tie. "How could my father leave me when I was eight years old and never get in touch with me again? How could my mother be a drunken bitch who hates me? How could my baby's father want me to—" She looked up at me. "Shit happens, Jackie. I'm sorry if I made you *cry* or whatever, but I had to do it this way."

I got up from the table and walked across the room, trying to calm down. "If that was an apology, it was a really crappy one."

Only somebody looking at her as closely as I was would have seen Lorna's shoulders sag. "Is that what you want? An apology? You know me, Jackie, I'm not good at apologies."

"Try."

She took a deep breath and focused on a spot just over my head. "I'm sorry, okay? I know I probably should have told you or something, but I couldn't. You can barely keep my secret for a day—how would you have kept it for four months?"

"I could have helped you find another way—"

Lorna waved me off. "Okay, okay, whatever. Maybe I was wrong. And I apologize, but it's over now. And I need you to help me come back home."

She'd finally said the right thing. She *needed* me. I couldn't let her down. "Okay. God, I can't believe you're back and we're *fighting* with each other. I don't want to argue with you."

I would have gone to her and given her a hug then, but she walked away to stash the food in a cupboard. "Neither do I," she said. "You can tell people soon. I promise. Maybe tomorrow."

"After you talk to him? The . . . father?"

Her head bobbed, the briefest nod. "Then you can tell everybody. Announce it on the radio, put it in the newspaper. You can even tell my mother if you want to. Just don't expect me to go over there and give her a big kiss."

"Okay. I'm sorry I got mad."

"You're allowed to." She smiled crookedly, then looked away. "So, give me some news. Tell me what went on while I was gone," she said.

"What do you want to know?"

"Are you dating anybody? Are you madly in love by now?"

Was I? "Sort of," I said. "It's still kind of a secret, but I really like him."

Lorna smirked. "Oh, so you're keeping secrets too? It's Finn, isn't it? You can tell me. I knew once I got out of the way the two of you would get together. You were always crazy about him."

What? I couldn't stop shaking my head. "No! Not Finn! No! I wouldn't . . ." *Oh, yes you would.* "I mean, he wouldn't . . ."

"Oh, come on, Jackie. He cried on your shoulder and you loved it, didn't you? I don't blame you. You thought I was dead."

I put my hands over my face. The shame of that afternoon under the pier crawled back under my skin. The moment I'd made a fool of myself *and* betrayed my best friend. "I, I did kiss him. Once. But he didn't kiss me back. It was terrible. It was stupid. I'm so sorry, Lorna!"

But when I looked up, she was smiling. "I don't know why you're apologizing. You saw an opportunity and you took it. I would have done the same thing."

"No, you wouldn't."

"Of course I would! And if I were Finn, I would have kissed you back."

"He didn't though. He pushed me away." I wanted to be sure Lorna believed me. Finn was blameless.

"Well, Finn doesn't always make the right choices," she said. "He may live to regret that one."

26.

"I can't believe you slipped out while I was on the telephone," Mom yelled the minute I walked in. She'd obviously been standing in the kitchen, waiting. "You fainted last night, Jackie! You shouldn't even be out of bed!"

"Mom, I'm fine. I told you, it was just because I forgot to eat yesterday."

My mother's fists seemed to be planted permanently into her waistline, her elbows pointing in opposite directions. "Nobody 'forgets to eat.' That's ridiculous. If you could have seen how pale you looked when Finn brought you home last night. Poor kid was so scared, I thought *he* was gonna pass out."

"I was only unconscious for a few seconds." I didn't want to dwell on the memory of Finn's arm around my waist, my heavy head resting against his shoulder. Even at the time I'd tried to pretend it wasn't happening.

"More like a minute is what he told me. He was so worried. He said you stood up and just fell over!"

"I know, Mom, but I'm fine now. Really."

"What was so important you had to go out this morning, anyway?"

"I didn't *have to* go out. I wanted to take a walk. Get some fresh air."

She smacked a cast-iron skillet on top of the stove. "Well, now I want you to go up to your room and get in bed and rest. Get some old, stale air. I'm making you lunch. Some *protein*." Under her breath, she mumbled. "Forgot to eat, I never heard such a thing."

I piled a few pillows against the headboard of my bed and climbed in under the covers. It was kind of nice to have Mom making a fuss over me today. I *was* tired, tired of thinking about what would happen next, who would be ecstatic and whose heart would be broken. I deserved some special care, if only for a few minutes. Once the truth came out and all hell broke loose, rest might be hard to come by for a while.

As I waited to hear Mom's footsteps on the stairs, my eyes fell on the small shrine in the corner of my room, the bookshelf where Lorna's old sneakers had waited for four months. But what had they been waiting for? Lorna didn't want the shoes she used to strut down the street in, the shoes she twirled and jumped and danced in. *I have kept your shoes/in case I need them.* When I wrote that line across the photograph, I wasn't sure what I meant by it. I still didn't know. Did I think the shoes, like the jacket, would turn me into Lorna? Maybe I just needed the shoes as a reminder of my amazing childhood that got lost in outrageous grief.

Mom came in with a tray and saw me looking at the sneakers.

"I wish you'd throw those smelly things away," she said as she cleared a space on my bedside table. "Here. I made you a grilled cheese sandwich. And I want you to drink this whole glass of milk too."

"Thanks, Mom." The gooey, delicious sandwich was just what I needed.

She straightened up and glared at the shoes.

"Can't I just get rid of those?"

"No! If you want me to eat, don't touch those shoes."

She sighed. "They're not magic, you know. They won't bring her back."

Something did. "Maybe I'll wear them someday," I said.

"Don't be silly. They're not even your size. Your feet are much bigger than hers."

It was true. Everything about Lorna was small and tight and measured. She didn't have accidents. She didn't faint or fall. She didn't have large, clumsy feet that didn't know where they were going or what to do when they got there.

Mom wandered over to the bookcase and picked up the photograph that stood guard over the shoes. "This is a good picture. You caught the real Lorna. She's looking at you, but at the same time, you can tell she wants to get away."

"Let me see that."

She brought the picture to my bedside and handed it over. "It's like she wants to walk out of the frame or something."

I'd never been satisfied with that photograph. I didn't think I'd managed to capture Lorna, to frame her wildness, to nail down her rebellious spirit, but now I could see what my mother saw. This was why Lorna hadn't liked being photographed. Photos tried to contain the uncontainable, which Lorna couldn't bear. I would need to take a hundred pictures, a thousand to tell a story as complicated as hers. But my mother was right—this *was* the real Lorna, always on the move, always hidden, always trying to escape. The picture I'd wanted to take was of the person I wanted Lorna to be. The Lorna who would stop moving and wait for me.

"Jackie! Did you hear me?" Mom yelled from the bottom of the stairs.

"What?" There was drool on the pillow. I must have dozed off.

"Finn's here. He wants to see how you're doing."

I swung out of bed fast. "Tell him I'll be there in a minute."

I tried to calm down as I washed my face, brushed my teeth, and pulled my hair back into a ponytail. In a few more hours he'd know, I told myself, and then things would be the way they were before. Or at least, whatever way they were going to be from now on out. I decided not to brush any color onto my cheeks or change my shirt. Because it didn't matter whether I looked good or not. It didn't make any difference now.

Finn stood just inside the kitchen screen door, playing with the hook and eye, locking and unlocking it.

"Supper's in an hour," Mom said, standing in her usual spot at the stove. "If you want to stick around, Finn, you're welcome to some fish stew."

I was surprised Mom was being so nice to Finn. Because he escorted her feeble daughter home last night? Or because she went to the Center and saw for herself that the Rosenbergs were not pretentious snobs? Whatever it was, I was pleased about it. I couldn't, however, believe I'd passed up the chance to eat chicken pesto pasta at Ciro's last night when the only food that ever seemed to land on my own dinner table was fish.

"I can't stay, Mrs. Silva, but thanks. I just wanted to see if Jackie was well enough to take a short walk."

Mom frowned at me. "She already went out once today when I thought she should stay in bed."

"I'm fine," I said. "I took a nap."

"Don't worry, I'll have her back soon," Finn said. He gave Teresa his knight-in-shining-armor smile.

My camera was lying on the kitchen counter and I picked it up before I went out the screen door. Not because I thought I'd be taking pictures on the walk, necessarily. I just felt more comfortable with it hanging around my neck. Like Elsie said, it was my protection.

"You sure you're feeling okay?" Finn asked as we started toward the bay beach.

"Yes. I don't know why everybody's making such a big deal out of this. You'd think I was the only person who ever fainted."

"Easy for you to say—you didn't see it happen. You scared the crap out of me."

I grimaced. "I can't believe I passed out in front of a whole restaurant full of people."

"Well, they might not have noticed if they hadn't already been staring at Rudy and Cooper's pissing match."

"That's right. I forgot Rudy and Cooper were arguing."

"Yeah, it was quite a scene. The two of them kept tossing back martinis and poking each other with sticks. I was surprised Cooper did it in front of Mom. She got to see his dark side for a change."

Obviously Finn was pointing it out to me too in case I'd been too sickly to notice. "I wasn't paying much attention," I said, hoping to avoid an argument about Cooper. Was it really his fault? Rudy was pretty belligerent too.

"Of course, Cooper won with that line about his father shooting himself," Finn said.

"Oh, my God, I forgot that!"

"It shut Rudy up, but later he said he didn't think it was even true. Apparently that's what happens in Cooper's book."

All of a sudden I realized we were headed straight for Dugan's Cottages, and I stopped in my tracks. "Could we sit down a minute? I guess I'm not feeling as great as I thought I was." Understatement. Just a glimpse of the cabin had made my stomach roll over.

"Sure." Finn cleared away the seaweed from a sunny patch of sand and we sat down. I hugged my knees to my chest and rested my head on them. Could Lorna see us here if she looked out the bedroom window? I'd have to tell Finn I was tired so he'd walk me back home. There was no way I could sit here with Finn, practically in Lorna's shadow, and keep this enormous secret. I was afraid to tell him and I was afraid not to tell him.

Meanwhile, Finn was concentrating on making a highway in the sand between us, or maybe he was digging a trench. He seemed nervous. "I have to tell you something, Jackie. The thing is . . . I haven't been fair to you the past few months, and I feel stupid about it now. It's been hard for me to face . . . the truth. In fact, I'm just starting to realize what the truth is."

Oh, God, was this going to be a serious talk? I didn't think I could stand it if he started being all *honest* with me, especially sitting right here, fifty yards away from the *real* truth.

"Do you remember that day we were walking on the beach under the pier and you, you know, kissed me?"

He wasn't really bringing *that* up, was he? I could feel him looking at me, but I didn't meet his eyes. My legs felt shaky, and I wondered if I could get to my feet if I wanted to, if I could get up and run.

"The thing is, Jackie . . ." He scooted across the homemade gully between us and leaned his leg against mine, put a hand on my arm. "The thing is, I couldn't deal with it then. It was too soon . . ."

"Absolutely. I totally get it." I moved my leg, but his hand still grasped my arm. "I don't know why I did that. I was just so sad, I guess."

"It wasn't only sadness. We were so close then, Jackie. It scared me how close we'd gotten. I'd just lost Lorna, and I was afraid to feel that way about somebody else."

Finn tried to look into my eyes, but I closed them. What the hell was happening?

"I think about that day all the time and I wish I could do it over." Finn's voice massaged me and I felt my spine loosen.

"I think about *you* all the time, Jackie, even though I try not to. I was so confused after Lorna died, but I'm starting to see things differently now. I'm starting to see them the way they really are. And I think I want to be with *you*."

And then he pulled me into his arms and kissed me, sweetly, lovingly. For a moment my heart broke open and let him in. I couldn't help it. This was what I'd wished for so long. I think it was the camera, caught between us and digging into my chest that reminded me where I was and who was waiting in a cabin just down the beach.

I broke away. "Finn, we can't do this."

"Sure we can, Jackie. You're the one who said it to me. We have to live our lives."

"I know, but I haven't been honest with you either." I pushed away from him and got unsteadily to my feet.

He jumped up. "You mean you don't feel that way about me anymore?"

"No, that's not what I mean." I held out my hand and he took it. "I might as well just say it. I've loved you for a long time, Finn, but it doesn't matter now."

A smile broke over his face. "Of course it matters!"

I shook my head. "There's something you don't know. Something . . . big." I started walking down the beach, pulling him with me.

"Is this about Cooper?" His voice dropped to a lower register.

"No." *Cooper. Did I love him too? Maybe, but not like this. Not like Finn.*

"What then?" He tried to pull me close, to keep me from walking, but I was on a mission.

"You'll see. It's not far."

By the time we got to Cabin 5, my legs felt almost too weak to hold me up. From this moment on, everything would change, but what choice did I have? I banged on the door, eager to get it over with.

Finn was confused. "Why are we here? The cabin's closed up."

"Not entirely," I said.

The door swung open, first just a little, then all the way. Lorna, wearing the stained white jacket that no longer fit her, gave me a tight smile. "Way to keep a secret, Jackie."

Slowly she turned her gaze to Finn and I could see it in the way her lip trembled, the way the muscle in her cheek jumped. *Lorna was scared.* Without really thinking about it, I raised the camera and I caught it.

27.

Finn stared at Lorna as the late-day sun illuminated her flaming hair. His eyes blinked rapidly and he didn't seem to be able to move or speak. When Lorna backed up, I led him into the cottage by the arm.

"You promised you'd wait, Jackie," Lorna said.

"I couldn't. Not another minute."

When Finn looked at me, I could feel his shock. I'd known this and I hadn't told him.

He kept looking back and forth between the two of us until finally he realized that what seemed to be true *was* true. "Lorna!" His voice was raspy and her name was a prayer on his lips. "Oh, my God, Lorna! How . . . ? How . . . ?"

Lorna seemed resigned, but once again in control. She held out her arms, and Finn rushed into them, crushing her to his chest.

"Sit down, Finn," she whispered to him. "Sit with me and I'll tell you."

They huddled close together on the old couch, their hands clasped, as Lorna began the story of how she didn't die, but swam against the tide and was swept up on the bay beach like a goosefish, only not quite dead.

I turned away from them and walked to the door of the small bedroom. I didn't want to hear the saga again, but I couldn't get far enough away in the small cabin. The story washed over me again, an unstoppable wave. There were a few slight inconsistencies between this version and the one Lorna had told me. I wished I wasn't looking for them.

"I'm sorry, Finn," Lorna said, tipping her head sideways. "I know I hurt you. I didn't want to."

But it wasn't Lorna Finn seemed to blame. He looked at me the way I was afraid he would, as if I'd betrayed him. "You *knew?*"

"Only since yesterday morning. I found her here."

He turned an ear toward me as if that might help him to better discern whether I was telling him the truth now or spouting more lies. "But you knew all day. You knew at the opening, and at dinner, and just now, on the beach—and you didn't tell me." The voice that had soothed me moments ago snapped at me now. I wasn't surprised. I could have written this scene myself.

"I asked her not to," Lorna said, drawing Finn's attention back to her. "Don't blame Jackie."

"But I don't see why . . . ?"

"I knew it would be a big shock for you, Finn," Lorna continued, "and I wanted to tell you myself, but I needed to do a few things first. Carla doesn't even know."

"Well, let's go tell her! Let's tell everybody!" Finn jumped up and tried to pull Lorna toward the door, but she stood firm.

"We will soon, Finn. Tomorrow." She beamed at him and I could see his body vibrate as the smile hit its target. "I've missed you."

"You've missed *me?*" His laughter was pure effervescence bubbling up from a deep well. "I just . . . I can't . . . this is the happiest day of my life!" He embraced her again, this time kissing her, hard, wild, crazy.

I couldn't stand it. Could. Not. Stand. It. Minutes ago Finn had been kissing *me*, but obviously those budding emotions were easily washed away by Hurricane Lorna. I expected that, didn't I? Why was I getting so upset about it? I tried to think about

Cooper and how *he* made me feel. I wasn't *his* second choice. But even thinking of Cooper didn't make up for having to witness the joyous reunion in Cabin 5.

"Aren't you going to ask her why she did it?" I lost control of my thick, furious voice. "She made us think she was dead! And I guess you're just going to ignore the fact that she's pregnant!"

Finn looked down at Lorna's stomach, his face registering surprise, but also . . . what? Eagerness? Delight?

"You're amazing," he said, as though getting pregnant was a difficult accomplishment for a teenage girl. As though he'd been *hoping* to find his presumed-dead girlfriend merely knocked up instead. I realized then that nothing else mattered to him. For Finn, the only important thing was that Lorna was back. His fingers wove through her hair. "I can't believe I can see you and touch you. It's a miracle."

"And a virgin birth too, I guess." My voice was flat and accusing. I hated myself for being mean, but I couldn't seem to stem the flow of nastiness.

"Jackie's right," Lorna said, leaning into Finn's shoulder. "I owe you an explanation, Finn. The thing is, I was desperate. When I found out I was pregnant, I knew Carla would freak out and want me to have an abortion or something. I wasn't thinking straight. I knew I had to get away from her."

Finn nodded, his arm still tightly around her waist. "I'm not mad at you. I just wish you'd come to me for help. Why didn't you?"

It was a question Lorna hadn't yet answered to my satisfaction either. Why hadn't she let us help her? Why did she have to pretend to be *dead*, for God's sake?

"I know," Lorna said, her head bowed. "It seems crazy now, but I had this idea that I'd go live with my dad in Maine and start all over. I was desperate to get away from Carla—I wasn't going to let her ruin another person."

"You aren't ruined." Finn hugged her close. "You're perfect. And the baby won't be ruined either. I won't let that happen. But tell me, the baby, it's not Lucas's, is it?"

Lorna hesitated only a second and then raised her eyes to stare into Finn's. "No. It's not."

Finn's head bobbed back in relief as she continued, "I did sleep with him though, and I don't even know why. I'm so sorry, Finn. I screwed up." She pulled away from him. "That's another reason I left. I was so embarrassed."

But Finn didn't let go of her hand. "So, that means . . . ? We were always so careful about it, but—"

Lorna shrugged, then grinned. "Accidents happen."

Not to Lorna, they didn't. Lorna didn't have accidents.

Finn whooped and picked her up off the floor. "That's my kid in there? Oh, my God, this is *totally* the best day of my life! I'm gonna be such an awesome father!"

She laughed. "I know you will, Finn. You've always taken good care of me."

Anguish flickered across Finn's face. "But I didn't try to save you when I should have," he said. "By the time I realized . . . I didn't think . . ."

"Sssh. You're saving me now." She whispered the words right into his mouth.

I slammed the cabin door behind me as I ran out, unable to listen to one more inexact truth, one more seductive lie. Lorna was afraid of her mother? Never. She was embarrassed about sleeping with Lucas? Not likely. But the worst deception of all was that Finn was the father of that baby. Whoever *was* the father, Lorna had chosen him very deliberately. It was no "accident." But I knew Finn wouldn't believe me, not me, the girl who dared to kiss him under the pier. Even if he found out the truth, what difference would it make?

Finn would never love me now.

28.

Why did I feel so stabbed and left for dead? I had no claim on Finn. One kiss on the beach, which I didn't even see coming, was the beginning and the end. But the ache I couldn't seem to outrun as I rushed away from the cabin was not only about losing Finn. It seemed as if I'd also lost my perfect friend, the heroine of my childhood. *That* Lorna was dead. More dead now than when I thought she'd been pulled beneath the waves by the ocean. It had taken me a long time to notice the imperfections in Lorna's powerful personality, but now that I'd seen them, I couldn't see anything else.

She'd needed us, but she hadn't loved us. She'd made up the games and we'd followed along. Was it Lorna's fault we adored her? No. Did she see our love as a weakness she could take advantage of? Maybe. How conscious was she of leading us where she wanted us to go?

As I headed for home, I forced myself to think about the future. College, photography, making art. I thought about Cooper. Thank *God* for Cooper, who was smart and sensible. Cooper, who I could count on. Who had beautiful eyes and a sexy smile that made my insides tremble. Cooper, who I knew now would be my first lover. In fact, maybe that should happen sooner rather than later. Maybe it should happen tonight.

I went home first to satisfy my mother that I wasn't a wilting flower anymore. I sat at the table between my father and her and slugged down a bowl of fish stew, then slathered butter on a piece of bakery bread and forced that down too. Fortunately, they were, as usual, too tired by dinnertime to make much conversation. Dad grunted about how the weather had turned warm again as he scarfed down half a loaf of bread by himself. Mom said the color had come back to my cheeks—the walk in the sun had been a good idea.

"That Finn's a good kid," she said, a remarkable statement coming from the woman who previously believed the Rosenbergs were washashores who should all be sent back to whatever useless place they came from.

Despite my mother's belief that the afternoon walk did me good, I was sure she wouldn't want me to go out again after dinner. I didn't want her waiting up for me to get home either, so I waited to sneak out until they'd fallen into bed at their usual early hour.

There was still a leftover orange glow in the sky over the bay as I walked down Commercial Street. I thought of calling ahead to make sure Cooper was home, but I'd never actually called him before, and the idea of talking to him on the phone seemed strange. I figured I'd know what to say when I looked into his eyes, but I couldn't imagine finding the right words to say into that hunk of plastic. Was he my boyfriend if it seemed weird to phone him? Whatever. After tonight we'd be together and, for better or for worse, everybody would find out about it. Even Elsie.

I didn't want to take the chance of bumping into anyone I knew, especially Finn, so I turned off the main street onto a darker, more secluded one and worked my way over to Jasper Street by a zigzag route. At some point I noticed someone walking about a block ahead of me, making all the same turns I intended to. A small man, I thought at first. He had a hooded sweatshirt pulled up over his hair, and he kept his eyes locked on the ground. But as I pulled a little closer, I changed my mind. It was a woman, for sure. A woman who walked quickly, lightly, barely touching the ground.

By the time I got to Bradford Street, the woman was passing beneath a streetlight. Even with her head low and her hair covered, I was sure it was Lorna. Where was she sneaking off to? Her mother's house was in the opposite direction. I dropped back into the shadows, not sure if I was actually following Lorna or just walking the same way.

She turned onto Jasper Street and passed the Art Center, keeping her face turned in toward the hedges. Wait. What? This made no sense. Lorna seemed to be heading the same place I was: Cooper's house.

I watched her pad down the sidewalk to the back door of the small clapboard cottage. Stomach churning, I ducked behind the neighbor's fence to watch her. The hood fell back off her face as she stood peering into Cooper's open kitchen window. From my hiding place I could see him too, sitting at his kitchen table, tapping on the computer. Writing something brilliant, no doubt, unaware that Lorna was hiding in the shadows outside his door like some creepy stalker. Should I do something? Call her name?

But then I saw her take a deep breath and knock on Cooper's door, at first hesitantly, then hard, loud.

"Door's open," Cooper called out as he continued typing. Lorna hesitated for just a moment and then shoved the door open.

The moment she disappeared inside, I raced around the fence and down Cooper's sidewalk. I folded myself onto the ground beneath the open window where I couldn't be seen from the street. I didn't dare peek inside, but I could still hear Cooper drumming on the keyboard so I figured he hadn't turned around yet to see his visitor. The smell of curry and garlic wafted out through the window.

Finally the typing stopped and there was a pause before I heard a startled intake of breath. "Jesus Christ!" Well, Lorna must be happy with that response. Another person thoroughly shocked.

"Surprise! Apparently, I'm not dead." Her voice was playful, almost flirtatious.

"I see that."

A chair squeaked across the floor. Cooper must have stood up. "I can't believe you're here! Wow! I'm speechless." Neither of them spoke for a moment and I wondered what looks were passing between them. And why. Then Cooper spoke again. "I'm sure there's some long, crazy explanation for this, Lorna, but I don't really have time for it right now. I have to finish this chapter tonight. I have a deadline—"

"That's all you have to say when you find out I'm not dead? You have a *chapter to finish*?" Lorna sounded exceedingly pissed off.

I was surprised, too, by Cooper's indifference, but it proved he didn't really know her that well, didn't it? Did Lorna think everybody ought to fall to their knees over her sudden reappearance?

"I'm sorry," Cooper said, although it didn't sound as if he meant it. "I'm glad to see you've somehow cheated death, but you really can't be here. You know that." He sighed heavily. "Does anybody else know you're here? Does Finn know? Elsie?"

"Know I'm *alive*, you mean? A few people know, most don't. I was waiting to talk to you before I made my big comeback." I could almost hear the smile in her voice.

Wait, no. That couldn't be why she came here. I tried my best to ignore the mounting evidence.

"I don't see why you need to talk to *me*," Cooper said.

I didn't know either. I wanted to shout, *Leave him alone!*

Lorna's voice soared. "Because you're the father, you asshat. Why do you think?"

My head fell backward and cracked into the wooden siding. It hit so hard it hurt, and I wanted to smack it again and again and again. I wanted to knock all the stupidity out of my brain.

To cause pain to the idiot who had adored these two people, who believed in the mythology of Lorna and the tall tales of Cooper. Instead I let the tears slide silently down my cheeks and kept listening. I wanted to hear it all now, even if it smashed my mushy heart to pieces. I wanted to hear who'd been telling what lies for how long.

"I did it to protect you, Cooper," Lorna said, a whimper in her voice now. Was she really such an excellent actress or was she telling the truth? How could I not know? "Your book was coming out and you didn't want bad publicity. You said Elsie would fire you if she found out. I disappeared so you wouldn't be hurt."

Something heavy banged onto a countertop. A book? A fist?

"You expect me to believe that? You left to punish me, Lorna! You figured I'd be so miserable thinking you'd killed yourself that when you suddenly showed up again I'd proclaim my undying love. That was the plan, wasn't it? You thought I'd marry you and we'd raise our little brat together."

This was a different Cooper than the person I thought I knew, as hateful as "my" Cooper had been kind. They were silent. I wished I could see the looks on their lying faces. Finally, Lorna said, "I thought if you had time to think it over—"

"I'd change my mind? Jesus, Lorna, grow up."

"So, you didn't miss me at all?" Lorna's voice hardened, then splintered into sharp pieces, which cut even me, sitting outside, hating her. "Were you glad I was dead?"

He sighed. "Of course I wasn't *glad*. But, Lorna, you expect something from me that I can't give you. You should have taken my original suggestion. Then we could have continued the way we were."

"Abortion was not an option for me."

Fish stew swirled unhappily in my gut. I didn't know these people *at all*.

"Why not?" Cooper said. "You aren't even religious. Nobody would have found out. We could have gone to Boston and—"

"Cooper, I have no family. At least none that's worth anything. I wasn't going to give up this chance!"

Cooper yelled so loud, the windows rattled. "You're seventeen years old, for God's sake! This isn't your last chance to reproduce. Jesus, Lorna, I thought you were like me, that we were two loners who didn't need a lot of bullshit *family*, who'd learned the hard way to only rely on ourselves."

"Just because I don't *have* a decent family doesn't mean I don't *want* one."

He lowered his voice and I had the feeling he was standing close to Lorna now. I imagined him looking down at her with those dazzling eyes, breathing his spicy breath right in her face. "I'm going to tell you one more time. *I don't love anybody and I don't want to love anybody*. Are you listening to me, Lorna? If you tell anyone that baby is mine, I'll deny it. I'll make you look like a damn fool."

I'd kissed this man. I thought I was *in love* with him. But he was as selfish and shameless as Lorna. Worse! At least she was trying to protect her child—he only wanted to protect himself. *I* was the damn fool in this story. I'd come over here thinking Cooper could save me. I was going to sleep with him!

I managed to stumble back down the sidewalk and into the street before my stomach revolted. Leaning into the neighbors' bushes, I vomited up fish stew and four months' worth of lies.

29.

I lay in bed staring at the ceiling for hours. Sometime in the middle of the night my anger dissolved into self-pity, and the crying wore me out enough that I fell into a half-asleep stupor. When the phone rang at six-thirty, I incorporated it into the dream I was having in which Lorna, in the white jacket, could not stop laughing at me.

"Jackie! Finn's on the phone," Mom yelled.

Memories of the day before smacked me in the face. The last thing I wanted to do was talk to Finn.

"Tell him I'm sick," I called downstairs. *Sick and tired.*

"Get up and talk to him. You don't even know if you're sick until you get up."

I dragged myself out into the hall to the phone. "'Lo," was all I could manage.

"I need to talk to you, Jackie. This morning. Before school."

"Why?"

"You know why. I'll pick you up in half an hour. We can drive out to Herring Cove. I'll get coffee." He hung up before I could argue with him.

My hair was still damp as I climbed reluctantly into Finn's car. I'd stayed in the shower so long there wasn't time to dry it, but twenty minutes of hot water beating on my face had not made confronting the day any more appealing.

Finn had picked up coffee and bagels from The Coffee Pot and I took a big gulp from my cup immediately.

"Careful! It's hot," Finn said, but it was too late. My tongue was already scorched, the back of my throat seared. I moaned and fanned my mouth, but in truth, I was glad for the pain. It reminded me that the day ahead would hurt, but I could stand it.

We didn't say anything else until Finn pulled the car into a parking space at Herring Cove Beach where we had front-row seats for the everyday miracle of sparkling waves breaking onto miles of sand. There were a few fishermen farther down the strand, but nobody else was here at this hour of the morning.

Finn took a sip of his coffee and launched into what he had to say. "First of all, I want you to know I'm not mad at you."

It wasn't the opening shot I'd expected, but then, nothing had been predictable the past few days. "Okay. Thanks, I guess." I blew on my coffee, hesitant to try another sip.

"I get why you didn't tell me right away. I'm sure you were as confused by the whole thing as I am."

Oh, I'm much more confused, I thought. Still, I intended to wait to hear what Finn had to say before deciding how much, if anything, to tell him.

He turned to me. "But the main thing I need to say is that . . . what I told you on the beach, right before . . ."

I sighed. "Look, I get it. If you'd known Lorna was alive, you never would have said anything. You wouldn't have kissed me. I know you're still in love with her. I'll forget the whole thing. In fact, I have already." That last part was an exaggeration, but I wanted Finn to see that he didn't have to worry about me, I wasn't going to faint again, or weep uncontrollably, or crumble into pathetic pieces all over his car seat.

"That's not what I was going to say, Jackie. I *do* love Lorna—of course I do—but now I think I love you too. I can't help it."

I felt like someone had pumped helium into my head and it was suddenly going to take off and float away from my body.

Finn could *not* have said what I thought I heard. My hands were trembling when he reached across and took one of them in his. He rubbed his thumb gently across the palm of my hand, and I could feel tears start to gather. Was this the last time I'd feel his touch?

"I'm so mixed up about this, Jackie. I want you to know the choice wasn't easy."

But you've made a choice, haven't you?

"Lorna's pregnant. I can't abandon her," he said. "I promised myself, I promised God, if she came back, I'd watch over her, I'd keep her safe. And now here she is: Lorna's *alive*, and she's pregnant with my child!"

I remembered promising that too four months ago, when I thought things couldn't get any worse. My tears dried up and I tried to pull my hand away from his, but he held on tight. "It doesn't change the way I feel about you, though, Jackie," he said. "It doesn't. You believe me, don't you?"

I believed him, but what difference did it make? He didn't love me *enough*. "Thank you for telling me," I said, finally. "It might be hard for you now, but as time goes on, you'll forget about—"

"I won't." He shook his head earnestly.

"Of course you will, Finn. You have to if you're going to be with her. She's not going to *share* you. Lorna *wins*. She always wins."

Our hands pulled apart in slow motion, as if they were slightly sticky, and we stared quietly out the windshield for some time. A flock of gulls came in for a landing in front of us. They foraged in the strewn seaweed, coming up with mussel shells and the occasional clam. Gulls are the pigeons of Cape Cod, ever present, taken for granted, but if you look at them closely, gliding on air currents, wing and tail feathers spread wide, they're just as beautiful as the shearwaters or cormorants the birders spend their days searching for. I wished I had my camera.

"Lorna's going to be staying with us," Finn said, almost whispering. "She went to see Carla last night, and they had a terrible fight—no surprise. Carla won't let her come home."

Was that *before* she went to see Cooper? No, it must have been after. I was sure if he'd welcomed her, Lorna wouldn't have gone to see her mother at all. And she wouldn't be staying with the Rosenbergs either.

"Not that Carla's place was ever much of a home," Finn continued. "It's probably just as well Carla wouldn't let her stay there. You can imagine the response she got when she showed up at our house. Mom and Tess took her in like she was a wounded bird."

Of course they did. "And Rudy?" I asked.

Finn shook his head. "You know Rudy. The minute he saw she was pregnant, he started huffing and puffing. He took me aside to ask me if I was sure it was my baby. Which really pissed me off."

God. "He's just looking out for you, Finn." Shouldn't I be looking out for him too? After all, Finn had been the only person to warn me about Cooper, not that I'd believed him. What were my choices here? Finn wanted this baby to be his—it would hurt him so much to find out it wasn't. That, of all things, it was Cooper's child. Should I tell him anyway? If Lorna denied it, which she would, Finn would hate me forever.

Besides, didn't the baby—Lucy, she already had a name—deserve a father like Finn? A family like the Rosenbergs? What good would it do anyone to know that Cooper was her father? Of course, the thing I hated about that scenario was that Cooper got away scot-free. He got to continue his life of irresponsible selfishness without anyone else knowing. The unfairness made me furious and I twitched in my seat.

"Dad keeps asking me if I know what a huge responsibility it is to be a father. I *do* know, or at least, I can imagine. I know I'm not ready for it, but I don't have a choice. If I turned my back on them, I'd feel guilty forever." His eyes latched onto mine. "I'm doing the right thing, aren't I, Jackie?"

The truth pounded away in my chest. "Oh, Finn. You can't ask me."

He nodded. "I know. I'm sorry." He smacked the palm of his hand against the steering wheel. "It's going to be weird between us now, isn't it? I mean, you've been my friend for so long. *More* than a friend. Is that over?"

I took a bite of my bagel so Finn couldn't see my chin quiver. "I think it is. I think it probably is."

At lunch I sat alone at a table in the back of the cafeteria. The story of Lorna's reappearance was spreading through the high school like an oil spill—a jangle of excited voices rang through the room. Finn was surrounded by his basketball buddies who were bombarding him with questions. Charlotte and Lucas sat at a table with her Drama Club friends and everybody there was in a manic frenzy too. Lucas looked like he'd been hit in the head with a board, his eyes a little loose in their sockets. Had Char told him, or had he heard it from Finn?

A few kids said things to me too, things like, "Pretty amazing about Lorna, huh?" in answer to which I just smiled and said, "I know." I knew, all right. I knew more than I ever wanted to know. If only I could *un*-know it. If only I could go back in time to Friday and have it all turn out differently. If only Charlotte was still my new best friend, Finn was still an impossible dream, and Lorna . . . Lorna was still dead.

Obviously, I was the queen of the jackasses for thinking I'd be off better if Lorna had stayed dead. I didn't really want her dead, just *gone*. Why couldn't she have stayed in Maine or Boston?

Why did she have to come back here and ruin everything? Now I'd have to live without her even though she was *right here*. And it looked like I'd lost Finn and Charlotte and maybe even Lucas in the bargain. Maybe I'd even lost Elsie, now that she had that broken bird to care for right in her own house, not to mention a granddaughter on the way.

I tried not to think about Cooper at all, though I couldn't help wondering if I'd ever be able to trust my instincts about anyone again. Every time the scene between Cooper and Lorna replayed in my mind—and it was on an endless loop—I felt nauseated all over again. He was the *one* person Lorna loved, but he didn't love anybody. Which, of course, included me. The only thing that made me feel a little less like an idiot was that he'd fooled Lorna too, and that wasn't easy to do.

Finally the school day was over. I passed Finn in the hallway and he gave me a quick, sad smile. No doubt that would be the new normal for us.

Then, just as I was turning away from my locker, Lucas appeared beside me, a scowl on his face. "What the hell, Jackie? Why didn't you tell me? You told Charlotte before you told me! I was *there*, Jackie! On the breakwater. I deserved to know!"

I opened my mouth to defend myself, but I had no words left. He was right. Every decision I'd made lately had been a mistake. A groan started from somewhere so deep inside me that I felt it before I heard it, and then the tears gushed down my face, right there in the hall where every gossipy snoop could see.

Lucas's eyes went wide with panic. "Hey! Come on, Jackie. I'm sorry. I didn't mean to make you . . ."

I couldn't seem to stop sobbing so he took me by the arm and pulled me into an empty classroom. I fell into a desk chair while Lucas dug through his pockets and came up with a handkerchief.

"Here. It's clean."

Still crying, I looked up at him and said, "You, you, have a han, a handkerchief?" For some reason it suddenly struck me as hilarious that Lucas, the backwoods hiker, should be carrying around such a thing as a clean, white, *pressed* handkerchief, and that was enough to turn my sobs into gulping giggles. Halfway between crying and laughing, my emotional upheaval quickly turned into a monumental case of the hiccups.

"Simon always makes me carry one," Lucas said. "I mean, he doesn't check to make sure or anything, but he always put one in my pocket when I was a kid and I just got used to it."

"I love Simon," I said, as I dried my face with the cloth.

"Jackie, look, I'm sorry I yelled at you."

"It's okay," I said, hiccupping. "I deserved it. I'm just having a bad day."

"A bad day? I thought you'd be ecstatic. Lorna's back!"

I nodded and a few more hiccups escaped. "Yeah, well, things are weird. I'm sorry I didn't tell you right away. She didn't want me to. She wanted to do it herself. You heard she's pregnant?"

"Yeah. Finn told Charlotte the baby's his. Which is a huge relief. I mean, I sure don't want to be somebody's daddy at eighteen!"

"Even if the baby is Lorna's?"

Lucas looked surprised. "Are you kidding?"

"You said she was your miracle."

"Yeah, she was my fantasy, but I could never deal with the reality of her. I mean, she made us all think she'd died! It was just an elaborate joke to her, like the bear running off with her father's leg. Don't get me wrong—I'm glad she's alive. Hell, I'm thrilled. But I don't know what to think of her anymore. Bottom line, I'd much rather have a real girl like Charlotte than some daydream about Lorna."

It was the first hopeful thing I'd heard all day. "I'm glad you and Char are together, Lucas. She's great, isn't she?"

"I think so."

"I miss her."

"Well, God, Jackie, why were you so mean to her? She thinks you abandoned her all over again, just like the first time Lorna showed up. She's unbelievably mad at you."

"I know. I screwed up. When I found Lorna again, I just wanted everything to go back to the way it was before, with just the four of us. I wanted it all to be perfect again."

Lucas shook his head. "It was never perfect, Jackie. It was always the two of us following the two of them. And I was getting tired of that, weren't you? Anyway, things change. There's no going back."

I took a deep breath and folded the wet handkerchief into a droopy square. "Will you tell Charlotte I'm sorry? I know it's not enough, but I just want her to know."

Lucas smiled and took the limp hanky from my hand. "I'll show her your tears."

30.

I managed to convince my mother I was sick enough to stay home from school the next two days. It wasn't that hard. By then she'd heard the news of Lorna's return and assumed that my "illness" had to do with that. She didn't ask for details and I didn't supply any, but it didn't stop her from denouncing Lorna.

"Of course it makes you sick. It makes me sick too, the way she fooled all of you like that. Fooled the whole town, really. I never trusted that girl—she's just like her mother," Mom said as she slapped a huge bowl of oatmeal on the table in front of me.

"She's not nearly as bad as her mother," I said. "Carla's the reason she ran away." Or, one of the reasons, anyway.

"Don't stick up for her! She ran away because she was pregnant and she was ashamed of it!"

Not quite true, but I didn't feel like arguing about it. I'd asked for the oatmeal sitting in front of me, but now I didn't think I could get it down.

Mom took the chair across from me. "And to think that she's going to ruin poor Finn's life too. Saddling him with a baby when he's not even out of high school yet. His parents must be out of their minds."

Sympathy for the Rosenbergs? This was definitive proof that people could change.

"They're dealing with it." I dotted the cereal with raisins and sprinkled more brown sugar over the top.

"I bet she planned the whole thing, pregnancy and all. I wouldn't put it past her. I wouldn't be surprised if that baby isn't even Finn's."

My spoon stood up straight in the thick cereal. "Why do you suddenly hate Lorna so much?"

"Why are you still defending her, is what I want to know? She lied to all of you! She was always a schemer, always trying to get the rest of you in trouble. Oh, she was a lot of fun, I could see that. She had that wild energy. I always figured as long as Finn and Lucas were along you wouldn't get into *too* much trouble, but I never trusted that girl. I never did."

"Hindsight is 20/20, Mom."

"Well, I hope your eyesight is good enough now to see her for what she really is. So you don't get taken in again."

"She's not the devil. There are worse people." *Worse people?* That was all I could come up with in defense of my best friend?

"Well, none, I hope, that *you* get involved with!"

Thank God she didn't know how close I'd come to getting involved with someone *much* worse. The sugar and raisins couldn't completely disguise the porridge I suspected Goldilocks would turn down, but I ate half a bowl anyway. My mother was watching.

On Thursday I went back to school. The excitement around Lorna's return was somewhat back-burnered by then because of a traffic accident the night before involving several students. Updates on their conditions varied depending on the source, and rumors ran wild. It was only broken bones, not tragic enough to take my mind off my own problems, but I was glad that the student body was no longer focused primarily on Lorna.

I kept to myself, which wasn't hard. Charlotte still wasn't speaking to me, and when Lucas was with her, which was always, he stuck to the most minimal of greetings. If I saw Finn in the hall or the cafeteria, I kept my eyes on the floor.

I told myself it was time to start thinking about my own future. I'd been so preoccupied with Lorna since she came back, my photography had taken a backseat, but I needed to get a portfolio together soon if I was going to apply early decision to RISD. The third Thursday of the month was always the JSAC Trustees Meeting, which Cooper, as the new director, had to attend, so this afternoon seemed like a perfect time to use Elsie's photo program without running into him. I couldn't imagine what I'd say to Cooper when I saw him again. It was bound to happen sometime, but the longer I could put it off, the better.

I wandered through the gallery before settling down at the desk. My pictures were already off the walls, stacked by the door waiting for me to take them home. Tomorrow morning Cooper would hang a new exhibit and my brief moment of modest fame would be forgotten. The opening had been less than a week ago, but it seemed as if an eternity had passed during these six days— the best and the worst of my life—and I wondered if my emotions would ever recover.

The afternoon turned out to be rainy and windy, which kept most of the Fellows inside their studios, so I was alone in the office. I was relieved to feel my excitement return as I looked for the first time at the photos I'd taken at my opening. Some of them lent themselves to collage, but some were better as standalone shots. Once again, I was thankful to Elsie. Now I'd be able to show the college admissions committee that I could photograph people as well as landscapes.

I cropped and printed a shot of Finn and Rudy bent head to head over the cheese platter, looking solemn but united, and another one of local painter Selena Foster backing Billy into a corner, her fingernail pointed right at his eyeball. Both photographs thrilled me. They were dynamic and moving and told stories. Of course my cloud pictures told stories too, but maybe it was time for me to look away from the sky for a while, to take a closer look at the people standing right next to me.

There were also a number of very dark pictures that I took from inside the gallery looking out toward the parking lot. The resolution wasn't good, but the outdoor lights threw shadows on people's faces, which the program allowed me to manipulate in interesting ways. The more comfortable I became with the software, the more I appreciated it. I wasn't so much manipulating the reality of the photographs as it was finding deeper truths that weren't immediately obvious to either my eye or the camera's.

At first I didn't think the dark pictures would be usable. The program could lighten and sharpen them, but, even cropped, I didn't like the composition of most of them. I kept tinkering with the lighting just because it was fun to use the program, and all of a sudden I recognized one of the faces that had been highlighted by an outdoor lamp. It was Cooper, and he was leaning over a much smaller woman, her face in shadow. I went back to look at the other pictures in that series and I realized Cooper was in a lot of them, but I couldn't make out the woman. It looked like she was wearing a lavender JSAC T-shirt. Was it one of the new Fellows?

Had Cooper been hitting on somebody else right in the middle of my opening? Would I ever stop being astounded and appalled by his nerve? I brought up the clearest shot of him with the woman and zoomed in, adjusting the brightness and contrast as much as possible until I could clearly see his cocked head and luminous smile. And then, finally, the pixels arranged themselves so the face of the second person emerged too. For a minute, I couldn't breathe. Cooper Thorne was leaning down to kiss Tess Rosenberg.

It's possible I sat there for ten minutes without moving, paralyzed by the extent to which I didn't want this to be true. If I'd fallen under his spell at seventeen, why should it surprise me that Tess, at thirteen, had also been spellbound by his insidious charm? And Cooper, unbelievably, had taken full advantage of it. Finally, I roused myself, printed out the evidence, and stuck it in my backpack along with the other photos.

Then I started to move fast. It was still raining steadily, but I hardly noticed as I ran down Commercial Street, dodging pedestrians. By the time I got to the Rosenbergs' house, I was soaked.

Lorna answered the door, barefooted. Her hair, clean now and shining once again, was caught in a high clip at the back of her head, and she was wearing a pale pink cardigan sweater I recognized as Elsie's. We stared at each other a moment and then she took a step back and said, "Come in," as if it were her right to issue the invitation.

A puddle immediately formed at my feet as I stood in the marble-floored foyer. Even on such a cloudy day, the Rosenberg house with its white walls and windows on the bay was bright and cheerful.

"Did you want to talk to Finn?" Lorna asked. "He went out to—"

"No, I want to talk to Tess. Is she here?"

"Tess? Yeah, I think she's up in her room."

I kicked off my soaked shoes and shrugged out of my dripping raincoat, leaving them in a pile by the door.

"Why do you want to talk to Tess?"

I looked right into those bright eyes that thought they had everything figured out. "She's next in line for Cooper. After you and me."

For a few seconds Lorna's face didn't move at all, not the tiniest muscle. Then slowly it began to fill with outrage. I'd shocked her for a change, but I wasn't taking much pleasure in it.

She tried to pull herself together. "I'm not sure what you mean by that."

"You know exactly what I mean. You can stop lying—I know everything. I know Finn is not Lucy's father, and I know it was Cooper, not Carla, who wanted you to have an abortion."

Lorna grabbed my arm and looked around frantically. "Jackie, *please*! Rudy's in his office down the hall."

"I didn't come here to give away your secrets. Although maybe I should—I don't know."

The hard outer layers of her face seemed to have been peeled back to reveal the unblemished girl who lived beneath. I remembered that child. When Finn and Lucas and I hid from her behind the trees, it was that girl who thought she'd been abandoned. I'd felt guilty then.

Lorna took my hand and led me into a small alcove off the entryway where we couldn't be heard. "I can't believe Cooper told you. Have you . . . been with him?"

"Sort of. It was just starting. I never slept with him. And now I have proof that he's been coming on to Tess too."

She winced. "I thought I was special to Cooper. He denied it but I didn't want to believe him."

"He didn't tell me. I went to his house last night and heard you talking. I was outside the window."

Her eyes blinked wide. "Eavesdropping?"

"Kind of a minor crime, don't you think? Considering."

"You heard everything?"

"Enough. I know Cooper's the father. He's the one you love, isn't he?"

She looked down at her belly and pulled the pink cardigan tightly over her breasts. "He's the only one. Ever. I didn't even know what Finn was talking about when he used to say he loved me—I didn't know what the word meant until Cooper. I wish

I still didn't know." She looked so powerless I couldn't bear it. I had the urge to shake her, to hug her, to remind her who she was. If Lorna could be defeated, what chance did I have?

"I'm sorry," I said. "I get it. I thought I loved him too." But I was only playing with the idea, wasn't I? I never felt for Cooper what I did for Finn.

A corner of her lip turned up in an almost-smile. "Cooper's the male version of me. Kinda crazy, a little bit mean, totally dangerous."

"Lorna, did you get pregnant on purpose?" By now I was pretty sure I knew the answer.

She shrugged. "Maybe. I wanted a way to hold on to him, to make sure he didn't leave me. I should have known a baby would do just the opposite. I mean, look at my own father."

"And you ran away because he wanted you to get an abortion."

She nodded. "I kept thinking, what if Carla had had an abortion? If she'd listened to my dad, I wouldn't even be here. I mean, she's a crazy bitch, but at least she didn't scrape me out of her uterus. I couldn't do it. But I had to protect Cooper— I didn't want him to lose his job because of me. That's why I slept with Lucas—he was my backup. I knew people would assume it was Finn's kid, but if for some reason that didn't work out, if Finn didn't believe it or something, well, Lucas was in love with me too, and I figured maybe he'd step up to the plate. He was my insurance. The more people it could have been, the less chance anyone would suspect Cooper. But then, the more I thought about it, I decided if Cooper wasn't going to be Lucy's father, I didn't want anybody else—I'd just go away and do the whole thing by myself."

There was pride in her voice as she spelled out her complicated plan.

My spine stiffened. "But now that you realize it's too hard to do it by yourself, you've decided it's okay to make Finn think he's the father of a child that's not really his? You didn't want to hurt Cooper, but it's okay to hurt Finn and Lucas?"

Her face was once again guarded, her eyes shuttered. "Look, I'm sorry about Lucas, but he'll get over it. I heard he's got another girlfriend already. And Finn will be more hurt if he finds out he *isn't* the father. You know it's true, Jackie. He's all excited about it. He'll probably want to get married now too."

"You just said you don't even love Finn!" I wanted to slap her, to slap the self-assurance off her face. Slap her, just once, because it felt like maybe she'd been smacking me around for years and I hadn't even known it.

Lorna rolled her eyes. "Do you really think everybody who gets married is in love, Jackie? Guess again."

I backed away from her. "You're right. I'm naïve. All these years I actually thought you were my friend."

Her grin faltered, but she didn't contradict me. I turned and walked up the stairs.

Tess's door was open, but I knocked anyway.

"Jackie! Hi. What are you doing here?" She jumped up from the upholstered chair where she'd been reading and gave me a hug. "Are you looking for Mom or Finn or . . ."

"Looking for you, actually. We need to talk."

She looked surprised, but pleased. "Okay. I'm so bored with this rain. Sit down."

She gestured to the other pretty chair, covered in pink-striped fabric. I'd always loved this room with its four-poster bed and brightly flowered quilt. It clearly belonged to the well-loved child of well-heeled parents. Of course, it hadn't kept Tess any safer than the ancient wallpaper and hand-me-down bedspread in my room.

"Did you talk to Lorna?" Tess asked. "It's a miracle she's back, isn't it?"

"Yeah, I guess so."

She looked expectant, but she obviously wasn't anticipating what was coming. I wished I didn't have to be the one to wallop her with the ugly truth, but I didn't have a choice. "I know you like Cooper Thorne, Tessie. I know he kissed you."

Her smile morphed into a frightened pout. "Who told you that? It's not true."

I opened my backpack and took out the photograph. "That's not you?"

She grabbed the picture with shaking hands. "Were you spying on us? God, Jackie, you're jealous, aren't you?"

"Tessie, you can't be with Cooper."

"Well, that's not true, is it? Here's proof that I can!" She stood up, ripped the picture into pieces and threw them in a wastebasket. "You want him for yourself, but he picked me!"

She'd rather believe that *I* was hurting her, not Cooper. How did he do this to us? "I can print another one, you know. If I need to."

"Why are you doing this to me, Jackie? I *love* him!" Her stance was defiant, her small chest pushed forward.

"No, you don't, Tess. You can't love Cooper Thorne."

"Why not? Just because he's a little bit older than me?"

"He's more than twice your age!"

"So what? He's a lot older than you too and I saw you making out with him! How do you think that made *me* feel?" Her brave façade collapsed and she was suddenly in tears. "He's the first boy who ever liked me!"

She fell onto her bed and I sat down next to her. "Cooper isn't a *boy*, Tessie. He's a man. And he shouldn't be kissing you, and . . . he shouldn't have been kissing me either. And he won't be, not anymore. You haven't done anything *more* than kiss him, have you?"

She shook her head. "I've only kissed him a few times, but Jackie, he said he really likes me. I'm sorry that you thought he liked you. I never meant to hurt you, but Cooper told me he didn't love you, so I thought—"

"I'm not mad at you, Tess, but you have to listen to me. Cooper doesn't love anybody."

"How do you know that? It *feels* like love."

"Because I heard him say it when he didn't think I was listening. He said, '*I don't love anybody, and I don't want to love anybody.*'"

I stayed with her until she wore herself out crying. I tucked her in bed under the pink quilt and slipped downstairs, unseen. My wet shoes felt like a punishment as I slogged the rest of the way home.

31.

I leaned against Charlotte's locker, waiting. She spotted me from thirty yards off and didn't look pleased, but I was determined to do this.

"What do *you* want?" she said.

"Char, I'm sorry. I was wrong about Lorna. She's not who I thought she was."

Charlotte nudged me out of the way and poked through her locker. "Really? Did she club a baby seal to death in front of you? I can't imagine what else would have changed your mind."

"It turns out she's been lying to everybody about pretty much everything."

"Is that all? I didn't think that bothered you. I thought Lorna the Magnificent could get away with things ordinary mortals couldn't." She grabbed a few books and slammed the locker door louder than necessary.

"I don't blame you for being mad at me. I know I've been a jerk lately. Or maybe I've been a jerk since the fourth grade."

"You got that right." She started to turn away, but I put a hand on her arm.

"Look, I'm really sorry, Charlotte. I want us to be friends again. I'll do anything. What do you want me to do?"

Her reply was immediate. "I want you to *see* me, Jackie. *Me.* The whole, quirky, interesting person. I'm not just some second-rate replacement for Lorna."

"I know that. I never thought that. I just got confused when Lorna was suddenly *not dead*. I'm *so* sorry. I miss you, Char!"

She stared at the floor. "I don't know, Jackie. I don't know if I trust you anymore. I can't be your friend if you're still *her* friend. And even if you say you aren't, what's to keep you from changing your mind again?"

I plunged my hands into my jeans pockets, searching for an answer that was both true and reassuring. "I don't know. I can't *make* you trust me. And I can't promise you that Lorna's completely out of my life either—I don't hate her, even now. She's screwed up, and if she ever needed my help, I'd probably give it to her. It's possible my life will always be a little tied up with hers—I don't know. But she's not special to me anymore, she's not extraordinary. And she's not my friend—that I *can* promise you."

Charlotte stared into my eyes as if she might be able to see beneath their surface. "You really hurt me, Jackie. Twice."

"I know. And I want to make it up to you. *Please* be my friend again."

"I want to, but—"

"Yes!" I grabbed her hands. "You *want* to. That's all I need to know. After school I'm taking you to Scoops. This is the last week they're open for the season. Hot fudge sundaes—on me."

"Literally?" Char smiled crookedly. "Because I wouldn't mind seeing chocolate sauce dripping from your hair onto that nice blue T-shirt."

"Whatever it takes. And while we're stuffing ourselves I'll tell you the latest twist to the story."

"Do I really want to hear it?"

"I think you will. It involves Cooper Thorne."

❧

Charlotte practically choked. "*Tess Rosenberg?*"

The two of us were hiding in the back corner of the almost-empty ice cream shop, but I put a finger to my lips anyway, then handed Char her glass of water.

"She's a baby!" Char said when she could speak again. "Isn't she, like, twelve?"

"Thirteen. But still."

"And he's the father of Lorna's baby?" she whispered.

I nodded. "I'm telling you all this to prove how much I trust you. I'm not telling anybody else."

"But shouldn't Finn know? It's not right that he thinks the baby is his."

"I don't know. I keep changing my mind. It would kill him if he found out Lorna was with Cooper all that time. He adores her. If she's having a baby, he wants to be the father." I stirred my ice cream into a chilly soup.

Charlotte spooned up a thick mix of chocolate and whipped cream. "Are you sure? It seems like he should have the choice."

"I'm not sure about anything. But I'm afraid if I tell Finn he'll hate me forever."

"Should *I* tell him?"

"No!" I yelled. "Promise me you won't. And you can't tell Lucas either."

"Okay, okay. It's none of my business anyway." She licked a drip of ice cream from her lip. "But it doesn't seem fair that we know and he doesn't."

"You're right, but nothing about this is fair. I keep thinking about Lucy too and what's best for her."

"Who's Lucy?"

"The baby. Isn't it better for her to have Finn for a father than Cooper, who doesn't even want her? Is it fair that crazy Carla is the poor kid's only relative? At least the Rosenbergs will give her a real family. She doesn't deserve to pay the price for this mess. It's not her fault."

"But Finn doesn't deserve to pay the price either."

"He's getting something in return. He's getting what he always wanted: Lorna."

Charlotte dredged up the last glob of chocolate sauce from the bottom of the glass. "I know what you're thinking."

"What am I thinking?"

"That Lorna didn't deserve the mess she was born into either."

I pushed away my melted, half-eaten sundae. "I wonder sometimes what she would have been like with normal parents."

Charlotte's spoon clanged in her empty glass and she licked her lips. "You know you have to tell Elsie about Cooper and Tess. You can't keep that a secret."

I looked out the window toward the wharf. The sun was going down earlier and earlier—already it was dusting the rooftops gold. "I know. I just haven't been able to make myself do it. She likes Cooper so much."

"All the more reason. The guy's evil. I mean, what if he'd gotten *Tess* pregnant?"

Char was right. I didn't have a choice.

"Where would Elsie be this time of day?" she asked. "Her studio?"

"Probably."

Charlotte pushed back her chair. "Let's go. I'll walk you over."

"I hate to bother you," I said when Elsie opened the door. "Do you have a minute?"

"For you, always," she said. Which made me feel like the devil coming to stick a pitchfork in her heart. "I'm just cleaning up for the day anyway. Come in and look at my new piece."

A huge canvas hung on the back wall of the large, sunny studio. I recognized Elsie's signature colors, the blues and greens of Cape Cod. But the composition was much freer than the small, restrained designs she'd become known for. The lines raced across the canvas like giant waves, out of control.

I approached the painting reverently. "This is so . . . powerful."

"That's how I've felt making it," she said. "Which scares me a little bit. It's as if I'm starting over, becoming a new person. Or maybe finding the person I used to be." She smiled and shook her head. "I sound ridiculous. Having so much time all of a sudden is making me giddy."

Time. Elsie had time to paint because Cooper had taken over responsibility for the Center. Cooper, who she trusted and admired. I was about to spoil all that.

She took her brushes to the sink in the corner and ran cold water over them. "I've been meaning to tell you—I've gotten the best feedback on your show. You should expect a great review in the *Banner* next week. I wish we could keep it up longer."

"Uh-huh." My eyes roamed the studio restlessly. I was twitchy with nerves and didn't know how I was going to begin.

Elsie noticed. "Is something wrong?"

I nodded. "I have to tell you something."

"Well, just spit it out. It can't be that bad."

I opened my backpack and took out a second copy of the photograph Tess had ripped up. "Remember the night of my opening you told me to take pictures?"

"Right. You were nervous about having to talk to so many people and I thought the camera would shield you a little." She dried her hands on her jeans so she could take the photograph from me, but I kept holding it just out of her reach. I wanted her to be prepared.

"Yeah. I didn't get around to looking at them until yesterday afternoon. Some were really dark because I took them looking out through the doorway, and I was curious to see who the people in them were so I zoomed in and played around with the lighting and . . ."

"Well, let me see," Elsie said, and grabbed for the picture.

I couldn't think of anything to say that would soften the blow. "I'm sorry," I said, handing her the evidence.

At first she seemed puzzled by the photo, but I could tell the exact moment that the portrait came clear to her. Her breathing seemed to stop and her hand flew to her mouth.

"No, no, no. What is he doing with—" Her hands trembled as she soaked in the image.

"I know you and Cooper are good friends, which makes this so much worse. And I need to tell you that I've been, sort of, seeing him too. Not for that long, and I know now that it was a bad idea, but—"

"*You've* been seeing Cooper," Elsie repeated, as if trying to understand a difficult concept. "And *Tessie* . . . ? Oh, dear God." She looked around for a place to sit down and nearly fell onto a nearby stool. "I can't believe this."

"I went to your house yesterday to talk to Tess as soon as I saw this," I said. "She was pretty upset, but she said she hadn't actually done much with Cooper, a little kissing is all. And I think she understands now."

"That's why she was so quiet at dinner last night. I knew something was wrong." The photograph fluttered to the floor as Elsie's head dropped into her hands. "How could I be so blind? I am an *idiot*!"

"Elsie, it's not your fault. You can't know every single thing that goes on around here. I saw Tess flirting with him once, but it never occurred to me that it was more than that."

For a long minute, Elsie said nothing. Her body seemed to collapse in on itself. As the bearer of the bad news, I felt terrible. What if she found out about Lorna and Cooper too? She'd be almost as upset as Finn would be if he knew.

I put a hand on her shoulder. "It'll be okay. Tess will get over him—I already have." There had been so many other shocks to absorb lately, losing Cooper had been little more than a gentle slap.

Elsie looked up. "Thank you, Jackie. Thank you for telling me." She bent and picked up the picture from the floor. "Do you mind if I keep this?"

"No, but, do you really want to?"

"For a day or two. Then I'll cut it up with scissors and burn it in the fireplace."

She seemed even more upset than I'd expected her to be. But then, Tess *was* only thirteen. Elsie stood and grabbed her sweater from a hook, the photo still clutched in her hand.

"Would you do me a favor, Jackie? If you could just clean out those brushes for me and lock up the studio—"

"Of course."

"I need to get home and talk to Rudy. You know where to leave the key."

"No problem. Go ahead."

As Elsie stormed out the door, I heard her mumble, "That jackass will not get away with this."

32.

An emergency meeting of the Jasper Street Art Center Board of Trustees was held at eight o'clock that night, and a decision was made to fire Cooper Thorne immediately. The *Provincetown Banner* article only said that there had been a disagreement between Cooper and the Board over "administrative issues," but Elsie told me what had happened. She'd given Cooper an ultimatum: Leave town within twenty-four hours or she would make sure every artist and writer she knew (and she knew lots of them) would find out that he was, in her words, "a sexual predator." Taking it a step further, Rudy promised to do his best to damage Cooper's reputation even if Cooper disappeared on the spot. And under no circumstances would he be taking a recommendation from the Jasper Street Art Center with him.

I didn't see any reason to speak to Cooper again, but on my way to the Center I saw him packing up his car. I hardly recognized him at first, his posture was so slumped. But when he saw me, he straightened up and glared at me, the usual sparkle in his eyes replaced by glittery anger, then stomped back into his apartment and slammed the door. It hadn't occurred to me that I would have to carry the weight of Cooper thinking I'd betrayed him.

Of course, Cooper was the bad guy here, the one who'd lied to just about everybody, but that wasn't all he was. He was also the person who gave me confidence in myself as an artist, who made me feel my goals weren't impossible achievements for a girl from a family of fishermen, who made me believe I never had to accept second place. He *saw* me—at least I thought he did—and even though it confused me to have a kind thought about the guy now, I had to admit I was a little bit grateful to him.

A week passed. Elsie returned to work as the Center's director, subdued and unhappy. When I came by after school to see what I could do to help, Rudy was sometimes there too, grumbling a little, but filing papers and stacking boxes, doing what he could. One afternoon he sent Elsie to her studio and sat at the computer himself, trying to make sense of the spreadsheet that kept track of all the applications that came in. Until now, I'd never seen him do much more than pass quickly through the office, or show up at openings to eat the hors d'oeuvres, but these days he was working too. I was glad to see him step up when Elsie needed him. Or, possibly, he just didn't want to stay home alone with Lorna.

I tried to pretend life was getting back to normal, but it still felt as if the earth had tilted on its axis and any of us could fall off at any minute. An unseasonably cold spell hit the first week of October and suddenly the stores were empty and you could drive a car down Commercial Street again. But instead of feeling relieved that the hectic summer was over, I had the feeling I was letting go of Provincetown, one month at a time. September was gone. Would I ever see another one here? Where would I be a year from now?

One Saturday afternoon I was at the town library picking up books for a history paper on the Cold War when I saw Finn sitting alone at a table in the front reading room. Automatically, I started toward him, then stopped, remembering that times had changed and we were not exactly friends anymore. Although not exactly *not* friends either. Still, what did we have to say to each other?

"Jackie!" he called.

Oh, well. I manufactured a smile when he motioned me over. I had to learn how to handle a situation like this. It was a small town, especially in the off-season, and running into Finn was not going to be an uncommon event.

"Good to see you," he said.

"You too." Rather than make eye contact, I flipped over the cover of the book in front of him to see what it was. *How to Prepare for the GED Test.*

"What's this for?" I asked, as if there was more than one reason to be looking at a book with that title.

"I talked to Ms. Waller yesterday. She says I shouldn't have any trouble passing the GED, but I want to make sure what's on it. Study up a little. Rudy and Elsie are having fits about me not going to college, so I thought I'd read the book here instead of rubbing their noses in it."

"You're dropping out of school? It's your senior year! What about oceanography?" Suddenly I was so angry—Lorna was ruining *everything*. And then I thought, *I could tell him. It's not too late.*

"I'll have time for that college stuff later," he said. "The baby's due in January. I have to get a job to support my family."

My family. The words exploded in my ears, deafening me for a moment, but I didn't flinch. It was already too late. "Your parents will help you, won't they?"

"I don't want them to. It's my responsibility."

And then our eyes met, and I saw nothing but determination in Finn's. I wondered if he could read my emotions too. Was the sorrow of losing him etched in my eyes?

"What are Elsie and Rudolph saying?" I wanted to hear their objections, which surely carried more weight than mine.

He shrugged. "You know Rudy. He says I'm 'reckless and foolhardy' and that leaving school is 'out of the question.' But I'm eighteen—he can't stop me."

"And your mom?"

Finn hesitated and looked down at his book. "She started crying when I told her, which made me feel terrible. But I'm not sure she was even crying about me. She's been a wreck ever since that whole thing with Cooper Thorne blew up. Have you seen her lately? She's mad at everybody all the time—you can't look at her sideways without getting barked at. And she looks like hell. I mean, normally she wears makeup and earrings just to go to work in her studio, but yesterday she went to the grocery store in *sweatpants*. I didn't even know she *owned* sweatpants."

"She's disappointed about having to be the director of the Center again," I said. "And, you know, she liked Cooper. She didn't see this coming."

"You didn't see it coming either, did you?" Finn said, gently. When I didn't answer, he said, "I should have gone over there and beaten the crap out of him before he left."

I was so surprised, I laughed. "My hero," I said, which made him snicker too. The laughter made me feel more at ease, as though we'd recaptured something between us that was almost lost. I sat down in the chair next to him.

"So what kind of job do you think you can get with your mad basketball skills and all?"

"I've already got a part-time job on the wharf, helping unload the boats," he said proudly. "I'm hoping when I get to know some of the fishermen better, I'll get hired on to go out with them. Fishing."

I rested my head in the palm of my hand. "You're really serious about this fishing thing?"

"I want to at least try it. See if I can do it. It would make me a real part of Provincetown—like you are—not just some washashore artists' kid."

I'd never understood why this was so important to Finn, but I knew it was. "I'll talk to my dad. Maybe he knows somebody who's looking to take on a know-nothing rookie."

He smiled. "Thanks. I appreciate it."

A shadow fell over the two of us. Lorna had crept up without making a sound. Her expanding belly pushed against Finn's shoulder. "What do you appreciate? Besides me?"

Finn stood up immediately and gave her a hug. "Hey, there you are. Jackie's going to talk to her dad about helping me get a job on a boat."

Lorna turned her fluorescent smile on me. "Great! Thank you, Jackie." As though the favor was for her too, which I suppose it was.

I stood up. "Anyway, I have to get going—"

"Did Finn tell you about this?" Lorna presented her left hand to me as though she were royalty and expected a kiss. A diamond ring glittered like rays of sun peeking over the horizon.

I was speechless, but I took Lorna's hand in both of my own. Had I ever doubted that she would get what she wanted?

"It was my grandmother's," Finn said, as if that explained what it was doing on Lorna's finger.

"So this means . . . ?" I couldn't make myself say the word.

Lorna supplied it. "Engaged. We'll wait until after the baby comes to get married though. Maybe we'll even wait until Lucy's old enough to be our flower girl. I'd like her to be part of it."

"It's your wedding," Finn said. "You can do whatever you want."

"One thing's for sure," Lorna said. "I'm going to wear a stunningly beautiful dress and do a handstand on the beach!"

Finn's look was a shower of admiration. "You're going to do a handstand in your beautiful dress?"

"Of course I am! Do you think I won't?"

"Oh, I'm sure you will." They looked into each other's eyes as if I were not there.

Please, I prayed to the gods of college admission, *please let me be gone by the time they get married.*

33.

The early admission deadline for the Rhode Island School of Design was November 1. Getting my portfolio together—twenty examples of my work, two additional assigned drawings, and several writing samples—would consume most of the fall, but it would be a welcome distraction from the rest of my life.

Sorting through my work, I decided I didn't want to send only the photographs and the collages. I wanted to send some drawings too, to show a larger range of my abilities. The problem was, I didn't have many current drawings and my older ones didn't satisfy me. I went out to the dunes a few times, but the usual subject matter, clouds, dune grass, the shacks, felt a little stale to me. I think I knew what I wanted to draw. It just took some time to admit it to myself and get down to work.

I printed out the photo I'd taken of Lorna the afternoon she opened the door of Cabin 5 to Finn and me, the one in which she looked so vulnerable and human and scared. That picture and the other, earlier one I'd taken that sat on my bookcase, I moved to my bedside table so I could study them before I went to sleep and as soon as I woke up. Then one Saturday I started to draw her, over and over.

I spent weeks drawing Lorna, some quick sketches, some more complete drawings, in charcoal, in pencil, in pastels. Lorna in motion, not smiling, never stopping. Lorna walking toward me, one foot raised in the air, the other balancing her, holding her to the earth. Then Lorna suddenly quiet, heavier, older, frightened. Over and over I drew her, one Lorna and then the other. I never tired of the subject—it seemed as if I could draw her for years and still not get to the bottom of the mysteries. What was she thinking? Where was she going? Why couldn't I come along?

The drawings were good. Some of them were *very* good. I didn't need to have Elsie or Cooper or some newspaper reviewer tell me this was the best work I'd ever done. I didn't show the drawings to anyone. I suppose I might have shown Elsie under other circumstances, but she was overwhelmed by her own life just then, and I didn't want to bother her. Besides, I didn't need Elsie to convince me. I looked at the drawings and I knew. For the first time, I really *knew*. I was an artist.

After that day at the library, I managed to avoid running into Finn or Lorna for a while, but I continued to re-examine the Big Question. Was I really going to let Lorna get away with deceiving Finn like this? Did the benefits outweigh the consequences? Of course, Lorna had been screwed over by Cooper and that wasn't fair either. But was it right that the Rosenbergs were being duped into caring for a child that had no relation to them? What was right for baby Lucy? And for whose sake was I keeping this secret, anyway—for Lorna, for Lucy, or because I feared that Finn would take his disappointment and anger out on me? I couldn't pull the strands apart. Maybe there was no right answer.

In late October Elsie insisted on taking me to visit the RISD campus. Somehow she even convinced my parents to allow her to pay for our overnight stay in Providence. Marco just rolled his eyes and said, "*Art school*," as if the words were synonymous with "waste of time." But Mom, I could tell, was a little hurt.

"That Elsie acts like *she's* your mother," Mom said. We were cleaning up the kitchen after dinner, and I scrubbed away at the stovetop as though it took all of my concentration. "I know she's helped you a lot, but it still worries me, Jackie. She's giving you hopes that might not pan out."

"I know that, Mom. I do. But I still have to try, don't I? You said yourself, you think I'm good."

"I know what I said." She continued to knock plates around in the soapy sink. "That school will probably look like heaven to you. You're going to want to go there so much, and we don't have extra money, Jackie. How could this work?"

"I don't know. I'm not thinking too far ahead. I just want to see if there's any chance."

She nodded. "I know she means well, that Elsie. I just worry."

"I know you do, Mom, but try not to. If I can't go to RISD, I'll figure out something else. It won't be the end of my dreams. I'll find another way."

"Maybe I should thank her," she said. "I never thought a child of mine would be an artist. Sometimes I'm shocked at how good you are!"

She looked up from the sink with a look of amazement on her face, and I had to give her a hug, the first one my tough mother had allowed in a long time.

As Elsie's car crossed the Sagamore Bridge onto the mainland I could almost feel myself becoming a different person. It seemed as if the whole huge country was opening out in front of me, as if I was leaving behind all the fears and secrets and heartaches of my life on the Cape. I'd only been off Cape Cod two or three times in my whole life, and the idea that I might actually live somewhere else, in another state altogether, was beyond exciting. Later, as Elsie and I walked around the campus, peeking into dorm rooms and art studios, watching rooms full of students standing at easels and bending over pottery wheels, I felt as if I were a million miles from home, but exactly where I was supposed to be. I could start over here. I could learn from the best teachers. I could make art. I could—maybe—put Finn and Lorna and Cooper behind me.

Before we left the campus, Elsie insisted on buying me a RISD T-shirt, but I told her I wouldn't wear it unless I was accepted to the school. It seemed like tempting fate to announce my desire too soon. After dinner, in the hotel, I put it on just long enough to look at myself in the bathroom mirror. It fit me perfectly.

Elsie had been animated during the drive out and while we toured the campus, remembering stories about her own years at the school. It was the first time I'd seen her happy since Cooper left. But on the drive home, she got quiet again, and when we crossed the bridge onto the Cape, her shoulders sagged and she seemed to shrink behind the wheel.

"Are you okay?" I asked her.

She sighed. "Oh, you know. Sure. I'm just tired."

"But you had a good time this weekend, right?"

She smiled at me. "An excellent time. It was great to be back on campus and feel all the excitement of young people just starting out on their careers. Thanks for letting me come with you."

"*Letting* you? I wouldn't have gone without you!"

"Well, someday you will. You'll go to RISD or the Museum School in Boston or some art school somewhere. And I'll stay in Provincetown." I guess she realized how grim she sounded and she tried to laugh at herself. "Good Lord, I'm making Provincetown sound like a jail sentence! Don't pay any attention to me."

"You'll hire someone else, right? You'll be able to get back to your painting soon."

She concentrated on the road. "I guess so. We'll do a search for a new director. I haven't had the energy since, you know." I did know. She never mentioned Cooper's name anymore, and I wasn't going to if she didn't.

Elsie fixed a bright look on her face. "Anyway, I have Lucy to look forward to now. How wonderful will that be?"

"I know!" I said, equally bright and shiny. "You must be so excited!"

Elsie's happiness looked as false as mine felt, but it was clear neither of us was going to speak the truth on this subject either. For the next hour we sat quietly as the Cape unspooled behind us and we headed for its farthest, wildest edge. Home.

The Saturday after I sent in all the RISD application materials, I met Lucas and Char for breakfast at the Blue Moon. Charlotte was working, but the crowds were slim on a chilly, overcast November morning, and she had plenty of time to hang out with us in the booth by the window.

"You're lucky you're done with it already," Char said. "I haven't even started on my essay."

"I'm only done if I get into RISD," I said. "And I can't count on that. I have to at least start on the other applications."

"When do you hear about early decision?" Lucas asked.

"Mid-December. So it's either a great Christmas present or it ruins my whole vacation."

"It's so weird that next year at this time, we'll all be somewhere else," Charlotte said, ripping a paper napkin into strings. "I miss you guys already."

Lucas put his arm around her shoulder and she leaned against him. "Maybe we'll both be in Vermont. Let's think positively."

Happy as I was for Char and Lucas, it was sometimes hard to be around a couple riding the waves of their first love, and I could only stand it for so long. "Gotta go study," I said. "Spanish test Monday."

They pretended to wish I could stay longer, but I knew they were both busy with senior year projects too, and the opportunity to spend a day alone, staring into each other's eyes, was a treat. I hugged them and wandered off down the street. I didn't intend to go right home. The Spanish test wouldn't be difficult, and after the stress of getting the RISD application in on time, I wanted a little break from obligations.

I'd been giving Old Hat Vintage Clothes a wide berth ever since the day, months ago, when Carla sat out front and made me take her picture. But Carla wasn't likely to be sitting outside on a chilly November day so I figured it was safe to walk by. I was just approaching the store when the door banged open with a jangle of bells and I heard Lorna shout, "What do you want from me, Mom? *What do you want?*"

I stopped in my tracks. It had been a month since I last ran into Lorna, and I was hoping the streak would last. But there she was, her back to the doorway, hands spread wide, pleading with her crazy mother.

Carla's voice carried out the door and a young couple walking by looked around to see where it was coming from. "I want you to undo the last seven months of your life!" she screamed. "Of *my* life! You let me think you were dead! I'm your mother, for godsakes!"

"How many times do we have to do this?" Lorna yelled back.

"For the rest of your goddamn life, Lorna, because I'll never get over it!"

"You'll get over it. Just pour yourself another vodka martini." Lorna turned and stalked onto the porch, then down the stairs. A high-heeled shoe came flying out of the doorway, narrowly missing her head. Carla stood in the threshold, a red satin bow tied around her neck as if she were wrapped for Christmas, a second shoe in her hand.

"Sure is great to be home. Just like old times, huh, Mom?" Which is when Lorna noticed me, frozen in place, watching.

"Enjoying the show?" she asked. Her face was flushed as if she were overheated, even though her beloved white jacket, now more ragged-looking than ever, gapped wide over her belly.

Carla was still raving. "You think you're hot shit marrying that Rosenberg kid, but you're dumber than I was. At least I wasn't seventeen when I got knocked up."

"I may be dumber," Lorna said, coolly, "but I'm not half as crazy."

Carla let the other shoe fly, but this time Lorna caught it. "Get outa here and don't come back!" Carla screamed.

"With pleasure." Lorna dropped the shoe to the sidewalk, stomped on it and kicked it back toward the store. The door banged shut.

Lorna stood with her eyes closed for a few seconds and when she finally opened them, I noticed they were ringed with dark circles. She turned to me with an artificial grin plastered on her face. "Well," she said, "that was enough fun for one day. You walking home?"

"More or less. Just killing some time."

"I'll kill it with you," she said, not waiting for an invitation. "I need to talk to a normal person for a change."

"I'm normal? Is that a compliment?" I fell in beside Lorna so naturally, as if our friendship had not been kicked around and stomped on like that old shoe.

"By 'normal' I mean more like me. From a family that's not so damn perfect. It's exhausting living with Saint Elsie and the Royal Rosenbergs. Obviously, they're easier to get along with than my insane mother, but still. I don't fit in with Finn's family. I'm not like them."

"I don't think they expect you to be like them, do they? I'm not like them either, but Elsie's always been great to me."

Lorna shook her head. "It's not the same. Elsie talks to you about art, which you want to know about. With me it's a lecture on how to roast a chicken or what kind of soap to wash baby clothes in. Like she's teaching me how to be a wife and mother. Like she's some kind of freaking role model."

"You could have a worse one."

"I *did* have a worse one, but that doesn't mean I want to be Elsie's clone. I'm not like her and I never will be."

"Have you talked to Finn about it?"

She puffed out a scornful sigh. "Finn. He's never even home. And when he is, he stinks of fish, even after he showers. Sleeping with him is like curling up with a flounder."

It took every bit of self-control I had not to yell at her. *This is what you wanted! He smells like fish because he's taking care of you and that baby that isn't even his!* But what good would that do? Lorna would just think I was jealous, and she wouldn't be completely wrong. Besides, I had to admit, I took a certain satisfaction from knowing that her life was not working out quite the way she'd imagined it.

As we walked along silently, I couldn't help noticing the way people stared at her, often disapprovingly, their eyes traveling a rude path from her face down to her stomach. The story of her epic swim had made the rounds of all the locals and a lot of people were indignant at having been fooled. Those who knew Carla liked to say how apples fell close to their trees. By the time Lorna spoke again, I was starting to feel sorry for her, which she would have hated to know.

"You don't like me the way you used to," she said. It wasn't a question. "You used to . . . look up to me."

"I used to idolize you. I used to trust you too."

"I guess I miss that."

"Sometimes I do too," I admitted. "But it wasn't a good thing for me, following you around like that."

"You needed a leader," she said, tracing the black embroidery at her wrist with a fingernail.

"And you needed followers. Not just followers—spectators. People to watch and applaud."

She pouted. "That's kind of mean."

"*I'm* mean?" I laughed, but the tamped-down anger rose into my throat. "God, Lorna, you still don't know what you did to us."

"I apologized, didn't I? You're just like my mother—you want me to apologize forever."

"No, I don't. I just want you to understand what it was like for us. Those of us who watched you *die.* Did you know that Lucas jumped in after you that night?"

She shrugged. "I read the newspaper article."

"*He* could have died if the waves hadn't pushed him back against the breakwater."

"You're not blaming me for that, are you? I mean, what the hell was he thinking? He's not even a good swimmer."

"He was thinking you were pregnant with his kid."

She adjusted the elastic on her pregnancy jeans. "Look, I get it. I did a shitty thing, and Lucas risked his life, and now you're all mad at me. Forever, apparently."

"All except Finn," I said. "He thinks he failed you because he *didn't* jump in and risk his life. He's thrilled he's getting a second chance to save you."

"Which makes you mad, doesn't it? You think he's risking his life now. You think he's throwing it away on me."

I turned to meet her eyes. "I hope he isn't, but I think he might be."

"You could always tell him," she said, her gaze unwavering.

"Not a day goes by that I don't think about doing that."

We were almost to the Rosenbergs' house by then and Lorna stopped walking. "Jackie, do you *hate* me?"

I'd never seen that look on her face before. It was not unlike the way Finn and I looked those first weeks when we were crushed and broken, our lives upended. But it gave me no pleasure to see Lorna grieving too. It was just another reminder that we would never again be who we once were.

"I don't hate you. Of course I don't. But you can't expect me to trust you again."

"Or to be my friend?"

I nodded. "Right. You still amaze me, though. I mean, you might not have made the best decisions, but you made them by yourself. I was always in awe of that."

She gazed down at her big belly. "I miss you," she said quietly.

I decided not to say I missed her too. Instead I said, "You and Cooper are kind of alike."

She gave a half-smile. "I told you we were. Selfish, but a hell of a lot of fun."

"You both came from tough backgrounds, too. He had that pushy Hollywood mother and a father who shot himself. That's a lot to deal with, but he survived it and even wrote a book about it."

Lorna's face lit up and a chuckle escaped her throat. "That's what happened in the book, Jackie, but it didn't happen to *him*. Cooper's mother is a kindergarten teacher and his father's an insurance salesman. They live in Nebraska, where Cooper grew up. He told me they were both fat and boring as hell."

"What?"

She laughed. "Did he try to sell you that story about his mother being in that Pain-Eze commercial when he was a kid? He said Elsie believed that too."

He lied to me about everything.

I just stood there staring at Lorna as her laughter ballooned into a howl. "The look on your face, Jackie! He totally got you, didn't he? You're so gullible!"

As I walked away, she called after me, "Thanks, Jackie. This is the first good laugh I've had since I got back!"

I was pretty sure I'd never forget the look of glee on her face. Lorna thought she'd reversed things, put herself back in the top spot. But she was wrong. I was never going to stand behind her again.

My mother was in the kitchen putting away groceries when I flew through the back door. "What are you—?"

I put up a hand. "Wait a minute. I have to do something." I ran up the stairs into my room, grabbed the sacred blue sneakers from their shrine, and hurried back down to the kitchen. I opened the lid of the metal trashcan that stood near the sink and plunged the shoes deep down into the can, then banged the lid shut.

Mom smiled. "Well, it's about time."

34.

I told my parents first, as soon as the letter arrived. They tried to be happy for me, but I could tell they were mostly worried, uncertain about what it would mean for all of us. Dad picked nervously at a scab on his arm. Mom patted me on the back, but said little.

I knew my news would be more properly appreciated at Jasper Street, so I pulled on a coat and boots to trudge through the skim coating of early-season snow. As soon as I turned onto Commercial Street I saw the square white sign, always a harbinger of change, and it took my breath away. At the head of the path that led down to Dugan's Cottages, the sign read: FOR SALE, COTTAGE COLONY, Bay Front Realty.

Anyone who'd grown up here would know what that meant. The cabins were in terrible shape and they took up a lot of prime beachfront property. Whoever bought the place would certainly tear down the cottages and probably put up fancy condominiums they could sell to summer people for ridiculous amounts of money.

I walked down to look at Cabin 5. The door was padlocked now, and it occurred to me I'd probably never go inside again. The old mattress would be hauled to the dump along with the dented pots, the mildewed blanket, and the sagging couch on which I'd lain with Cooper. And where, it just occurred to me, Lorna had too. I leaned against a boarded-up window and inhaled the damp wood, scrub pine, and seaweed smells that were a memorial to my childhood, which already seemed irretrievably lost.

When I got to JSAC, Elsie was at the desk in the office, sorting through piles of applications for the director job, as she'd been doing for weeks.

The minute I came through the door, I unbuttoned my coat and held it open to show her the bright red RISD T-shirt. "I got my miracle," I said.

It took Elsie a minute to stop what she was doing and look up, but then she screamed. "You got in!"

"Full scholarship!"

She leapt up and grabbed me in a hug, tears sliding down her cheeks. "You did it! You're going to RISD! *Full scholarship?*"

"All paid for," I assured her. "Well, tuition, anyway. I'll have to get a job to pay the room and board. This wouldn't have happened without your help, Elsie. Thank you so much. The show, the review, your recommendation—"

She batted away the thanks. "You deserve this, Jackie. I just made sure they knew it. I've never been happier for anyone." She took the letter from my hand to read the details for herself. I couldn't help but notice a brief flash of disappointment flicker across her face, but she beat it back. I knew she must be thinking of Finn, who wouldn't be going to college, at least not anytime soon.

"What's all the yelling in here? Good news, I hope." Finn stood in the doorway, hands on hips. I hadn't seen him in weeks and he looked different to me, more like Rudolph somehow. More . . . satisfied.

"Tell him," Elsie said.

"I got a full scholarship from the Rhode Island School of Design."

A smile crept over his face. "That's great, Jackie. Congratulations." He took a few tentative steps toward me and gave me a quick hug. I tried to feel it only on the outside, on my skin, no deeper. "I guess it's a good thing you didn't listen to me," he said.

"You mean the part where you told me being an artist was not an appropriate choice for a fisherman's daughter?" I said it with a grin, but he grimaced.

"What?" Elsie put down the letter. "You said that?"

"Well, Mom, it's not like Jackie's parents can help her out if she can't make a living with art. I didn't want her to be a starving artist."

"Jackie will not starve," Elsie said. "She's a smart girl who'll do what she has to do to pay the rent." She turned to me. "And if you need help, you'll ask me. Okay? Promise me."

I put up two fingers. "Scout's honor."

"I take it all back, Jackie," Finn said, grinning. "Congratulations on pulling yourself up out of the muck of everyday life."

I was as surprised by his memory as I was by his vote of confidence, and I'm pretty sure I blushed.

"We'll have a real celebration very soon," Elsie said. "Unfortunately, I have to keep plowing through these applications this afternoon."

"Come down to the Common Room," Finn said. "I'm building bookshelves, and one of the Fellows brought over a plate of chocolate chip cookies for me. Since we're celebrating, I'm willing to share."

I followed him down the corridor to the Common Room, trying not to notice the muscles in his arms, which had taken on a life of their own since he'd been hauling around crates of fish on the wharf. "So you're working here at the Center too?" I asked.

"When there's something for me to do. Dock work is sporadic at the moment. I don't know if fishing will work out for me after all. I'm thinking maybe I should apprentice with a carpenter or something."

"Really? I thought you were in love with the romance of fishing?" *Oceanography,* I would have said, but I didn't want to remind him of what he'd given up.

He laughed half-heartedly. "Yeah. But it turns out Lorna's not in love with the *aroma* of fishing."

And just that fast, Lorna stood between us, wearing the coat she drowned in, reminding me who Finn would always belong to. And it wasn't only Lorna in the room with us either. The shadow of Cooper Thorne was there too, his bare feet up on the coffee table, charming as ever. Lorna and Cooper. Between them they'd managed to screw up the lives of everyone I cared about. It bit into my joy knowing Finn was stuck here, working two low-wage jobs to provide for his make-believe family. He deserved a bigger life. Could I give it to him?

We sat at either end of the couch and Finn handed me the plate of cookies. "So I guess your future is all planned out now," he said.

"For four years anyway. Who knows what comes after that?" I took a bite of the cookie, but it seemed to be more wheat germ than chocolate chip. One of those good-for-you sweets that turn to dust in your mouth. I laid it aside.

"What are Lucas and Charlotte doing next year?" he asked. I was glad he wanted to know about Lucas. I hoped someday they'd be able to inch toward friendship again.

"Char's hoping to get into the New England Culinary Institute in Vermont, which she probably will, and Lucas has applied to the University of Vermont. They'd be about an hour away from each other."

"So they're more or less a couple now?"

"Definitely more," I said. "They're good together. They're nice to each other."

He nodded. For now that was all the Lucas-news he wanted.

"Oh, my God, did you see that Dugan's is for sale?" I asked, sitting forward.

His face softened. "Yeah. Hard to believe. Another part of old Provincetown gone."

Another part of *us* gone is how it felt to me. "I can't bear the idea that those cabins won't be there anymore."

Finn grabbed another dusty cookie. "Everything changes, Jackie. You may as well get used to it."

It sounded like something an older person would say. But then, Finn did seem older. He was thinner, stringy, except for those muscly arms. As if he'd lost a pound for every one Lorna had gained.

Looking around the room, I began to mourn Jasper Street too. This place had meant so much to me. The idea that there would still be openings here every few weeks, that Elsie would hire a new director I'd never met, that Finn would build shelves and eat cookies the Fellows made, that life would go on as always even though I was far away, was suddenly terrifying. Who would I be if I wasn't here? What if leaving was a huge mistake? What if I was closing a door I could never open again?

And what if I was closing a door for Finn too? A door he didn't even know he *could* open? How could I leave Provincetown without telling him what I knew? Even if he hated me for it. Even if it changed everything—again.

Once the decision was made, I was calm. "I have to tell you something, Finn, something you probably don't want to hear." *Say it.* "About Lorna. About the baby."

"Jackie, you don't need to."

"I do. I should have told you—"

Gently, he put a hand over my mouth. "No, you don't. Really. Don't say it out loud. Neither of us is ever going to say it out loud."

He took his hand away and we stared at each other for a long time, my mouth frozen open. Finally I whispered, "You *know*? She *told* you?"

He shook his head. "I figured it out. I didn't want to see it at first, but the pieces just didn't fit together any other way."

"And you know *who* . . . ?"

He looked away. "I have a pretty good idea."

"Not Lucas."

"I know."

"But then why are you—?"

He took my hand in his and stared down at the two of them, intertwined. "Lorna doesn't know I know, Jackie. And I'm not going to tell her."

"But Finn, you don't have to do this. You don't have to give up your life!"

"I'm not giving it up. This *is* my life, at least for now. This is the way it has to be."

I was stunned. "But if you *know* . . ."

He shrugged. "Jackie, we all make choices. I'm finally jumping off the breakwater."

For half a second I wondered what I would do if someone had given me the choice between going to Rhode Island for art school or staying in Provincetown, marrying Finn, and having a child. I was surprised to find it was an easy decision. I loved Finn, but I wasn't even eighteen. My life was all out in front of me. I was so grateful to have dodged the bullet that took down Lorna, but I was deeply sorry that Finn had been caught in the crossfire.

And yet, not surprised. "You *are* a hero," I said.

A lazy smile picked up the corners of his mouth. "Some people would say I'm a fool."

"Maybe you can be both things at once." I picked up my coat. "I should get going."

He nodded. "Okay. We'll see you before you leave. You've got a while yet."

"Sure," I said, even though I felt like I'd said my goodbyes already.

"And you'll come see the baby when she's born, won't you?"

"Sure. I'll come see Lucy."

He walked me to the door, his hand grasping my arm. "You won't leave P'town for good. You'll come back, right? I mean, you're not going to go off to college and forget all about us, are you?"

"How could I forget Provincetown?" I said. *Or Lorna. Or Lucas. Or Cooper. Or Elsie. Or Charlotte. Or you, Finn Rosenberg.* And then I had a vision of what it would be like, sitting in a dorm room in Providence, Rhode Island, meeting people from other cities, other countries, and telling them about the beautiful place where I'd grown up and my amazing friends. And hearing their stories too, of faraway places I'd never been, of the people they'd loved and left behind. Suddenly I couldn't wait, even though I knew it meant I'd have to jump off the breakwater too.

When I hit the water, I'd swim for my life.

Author's Note

Although I've reconfigured the land near the breakwater and reopened the shuttered high school to suit my story, for the most part this is the Provincetown, Massachusetts, I've known and loved for almost forty years. A unique and beautiful splinter of land surrounded on three sides by water, P'town feels like both the last place on earth and the destination of your dreams. This tiny town has nurtured artists and writers for a century (Eugene O'Neill, Tennessee Williams, and Robert Motherwell, to name only a few) and sheltered LGBTQ people for almost as long. It's also been home to generations of mostly Portuguese fishing families whose fortunes have nose-dived with that industry. It's a town where the sad, the sick, and the lost have often washed ashore and felt themselves at home at last.

I've used the real names for some of the iconic spots in town like Herring Cove Beach, Mojo's, and the Portuguese Bakery, and made up others like the Blue Moon Café. The Jasper Street Art Center bears some similarity to the Fine Arts Work Center. Another of my inventions here is Dugan's Cottages. No place that rundown has existed on the pricey bay beachfront for decades, but there are many longtime locals like the imaginary Mrs. Dugan who, if they'd owned such cottages, would have held out against the developers as long as they could. And, in fact, having a bunch of old cabins just down the beach from the Rosenberg mansion seems to me to describe the flavor of Provincetown perfectly. It is a three-mile-long hodgepodge of a town where variety is the spice and diversity is the norm. There is no place like it.